ODETTE

ODETTE

JESSICA DUCHEN

For Richard and Simone,
with all best wishes,

Jessica Duchen

This edition first published in 2018

Unbound

6th Floor Mutual House, 70 Conduit Street, London W1S 2GF

www.unbound.com

ISBN (eBook): 978-1-78965-001-3
ISBN (Paperback): 978-1-78965-000-6

Design by Mecob

Printed and bound in Great Britain by Clays Ltd, Elcograf S.p.A.

For my dear friends, who make life magical.

Super Patrons

Rebecca Saire and Roger Allam
Judith Barnard
Janice Barnett
John Batten
Monica Bohm-Duchen
Hannah Bohm-Duchen
Debra Boraston
Richard Bratby
Sidney Buckland
David Cairns
Trevor Campbell Davis
Dennis Chang
Keith & Edna Clarke
Marie-anne Cody
Alexandra Coghlan
Clare Colvin
Tamsen Courtenay
Hilary Craig
Ellen Dahrendorf
Margaret Dane
Dr Marc Desautels
Cathy Desmond
Emmanuel Despax
Emma Diamond
James Dixon
Peter Donohoe
Michael Duchen
Lily Dunn
Pip Eastop
Brian Elias
Tara Erraught
Katie Fforde

Paul Fincham —

Margaret Fingerhut

Jo Forrest

Oli Foster

Marjolaine Fournier

Sophie Fuller

Charlotte Gardner

Florence Garel

Sarah Goulding

William Griffin

William Griffin

Thomas Guthrie

Tina Halperin

Marc-André Hamelin

Jane Hanson

Rustem Hayroudinoff

Christine Holliday

Guy Holloway

Jennifer Holloway

William Howard

Tristan Jakob-Hoff

Kerensa Jennings

Rebecca Johns

Richard Johnson

Galen Johnson

Marjan & Jane Kiepura

Dan Kieran

Patrick Kincaid

Shona Kinsella

Kristian Rahbek Knudsen

Piers Lane

Anna Lapwood

Mookie Lee-Menuhin

David Leibowitz

Ann Liebeck

Tasmin Little

Gergely Madaras
Charlotte Martin
Anthony Marwood
Hugh Mather
H Mathieson
Eva Mayer
Christine McGuinness
Viv McLean
John McMurray
Alice McVeigh
John Mitchinson
Andrew Morris
Nina Kaye and Timothy Nathan
Nicolas Nebout
Richard Norris
Francis Norton
Ilona Oltuski
Rebeca Omordia
Roxanna Panufnik
Birgit Pappers
Lev Parikian
Tara Persaud
Joanna Pieters
Justin Pollard
Caroline Potter
Sophie Ransby
Stephen Richards
Seb Scotney
Helen Sherrah-Davies
Sue Shorter
Mary Sigmond
Clare Slator
Jane Spencer-Davis
Nicholas Spindler
Eleanor Stanier
Henriette B. Stavis

Elli Stern
Gillian Stern
Clare Stevens
Katherine Sunderland
Candida Thompson
Christopher Tin
Liubov Ulybysheva
Angelo Villani
Jo W
Ricki Wagner
Duncan Ward
Shirley Whiteside
Lorraine Womack-Banning
Katherine Youn
Alan Yu

With profound thanks to my brother, Michael Duchen, who has believed in me and in this book through thick and thin.

OVERTURE

The swan was high above the coast when the storm broke. Soon after sunrise she had flown up from the lake, skimming the tips of the birches that sheltered her refuge. Balancing on currents of air, she swooped over the island's rocky shore, then left it far behind. Nature was her homeland, the embrace of light and the open joy of the heavens.

The gusts were blowing more fiercely around her and the swan sensed their threat, but when she tried to turn back the wind was against her. Swelling banks of cloud blotted out the breaking day. Raindrops pelted her eyes and the gale seized her and tossed her left and right, until she was too numb and frightened to know where she was or which way she was going. She mustered her strength, set her wings and focused on riding the currents, telling herself that soon she must and would land.

Flailing, tired out, after how long she had no idea, the swan was still over water – but it was endless water, rough and wild, and she could smell the salt in it as she dodged a wave that rose into the sky, then hammered down, voracious, around her. She dared not guess the extent of this ocean. Her wings weighed like gravestones on her shoulders. Dreading that night would fall before she reached sanctuary, she spurred herself on. She tried to harness the storm's violent momentum, letting it carry her. She knew that if she could not land by sundown, she would die.

At last, a curving coastline: low cliffs, agricultural fields, then haphazard villages and towns – tame and crowded compared to her home – all of them silvery with rainwater. She was too exhausted to fight the force that was driving her down among the buildings: narrow lanes, steeples, towers of carved stone and, in the middle, a river, studded with tidy bridges. Fighting on, she aimed for the water. She lost altitude and tried to land, but still the wind would not release her.

The swan fixed on a final hope. By the river ran a street, lined on the other side with a terrace of houses. Her gaze lighted upon an upper window partly sheltered by a chestnut tree. The branches might break the gale and let her gain control. She turned towards it, stretched her neck forward, poised to strike, wings locked back – and dived. Her beak met glass and shattered it with a crash. Pain sliced across her shoulder as the sharp edges cut. A surface thudded up under her belly; lying still at last, she lost consciousness.

1

Mitzi Fairweather, half asleep, could hear an owl calling in the distance. Odd. Owls didn't usually haunt Richardson Road. Exhaustion clogged her eyes. She thought she heard the hoot again, through the rumbling undertow of rush-hour traffic – and in discomfiting counterpoint, the high-bassoon snores of the man asleep beside her.

There'd been a party. Lara, the only one of Mitzi's college friends who still lived in Cygnford, had turned thirty and mixed her birthday with pre-Christmas celebrations. Earlier, Mitzi had been catching up on flat-cleaning and laundry; she missed dinner, slung on a short dress and cycled to Lara's place, where she drank three glasses of home-made punch, containing something green and astringent, on an empty stomach.

'Absinthe from Prague,' he'd said, coming to her aid. He found her a chair, gave her a mug of good, clear, pure water and fetched her a ham sandwich.

'I'm vegetarian,' Mitzi said. Laughing, he insisted that meat was good for you. She returned her strongest words about additives, hormones and antibiotics, and just had time to wonder exactly what ingredients were in the absinthe before the room swung upside down and she found herself staring straight into woollen knots of blue carpet. Her new friend, who admitted to being in financial services, bundled her into his Saab and civilly dropped her at her front door.

Two days later, he coaxed her out for a dinner date. She was stressed after work, so they'd consumed a good meal of comfort food at Brown's under the tinsel garlands (he had a burger, she didn't), polished off two bottles of red wine – and he stayed over. Never mind having nobody to love – why did she keep ending up in bed with men she didn't even like?

'Hullo, sweetie. Still asleep?'

Before he could pounce on her again, she swung herself upright. 'Coffee?' Smile. Bright smile.

'Milk, two sugars.' He looked boyish against the bed's heavy, carved wooden headboard, sleepy gaze fixed on the arc of her hip under her dressing gown. He was all right, really. Just not someone she wanted to wake up next to, ever again.

In the front room a bay window magnified the morning sunlight, which cast pale slanting rays onto the ceiling-high wooden bookcases. Her landlord evidently had a passion for ancient books; their spines protruded on the shelves like the vertebrae of a living creature. The flat was better equipped with reading matter than with cooking utensils: Mitzi could peruse to her heart's content mystical poetry by Khalil Gibran, the mythology of ancient Egypt or Bruno Bettelheim's *The Uses of Enchantment*, but searched in vain for spatulas and sieves. Yet she'd loved the flat so much on first sight that its occasional impracticalities, and the busy road outside, had ceased to matter. Through its portals, she seemed to step back in time to a bygone world.

On the herringbone parquet sprawled orange, cream and cerise Turkish kilims, and on them stood worn, dark leather and wood furniture, some of it Edwardian or older. An antique square dining table of polished mahogany had pride of place in the bay window; she never dared eat off it without putting down two layers of tablecloths for protection. Still more books sat in the unusable little study, where the landlord stored superfluous papers, files, pictures and heaven knew what else in high-stacked cardboard boxes and plastic crates.

The low price had been startling – a sabbatical let – and she'd jumped at it, despite a fair amount of small print further down the contract. Now her battered little pine desk, at the back of the room, away from the sofa and a capacious green leather armchair with footstool, would seem incongruous if it were even visible beneath her computer – never mind the piles of magazines and newspapers to which she had contributed, a tall spike holding receipts to use for her tax return, and a tangle of leads for recharging electronic gadgets that the flat seemed ready to disown as anachronistic.

While the kettle gurgled in the kitchen, which opened off the living room through an archway, she drew the curtains behind the dining table and stared out at the view. The chestnut tree in front of the house, bare branches pointing twiggy fingers towards the sun. The stone wall, sprouting lichen, splitting chippings. Richardson Road was choked with traffic; bicycles zigzagged between the cars. But the grass on Solstice Green across the footbridge seemed bright today, the river was glinting back the early morning light, and on the water drifted a group of white swans. That was a good sign; she was sure there were fewer swans now on the river than there had been during her student days. Swans, proud of their poise, rising above it all. She prepared two mugs of coffee: his pale and sweet, hers strong, black and bitter.

He was padding about the bedroom in Cygnford United football socks, fastening his shirt buttons in front of the mirror on the antique wardrobe. 'I have to get the car home before work. How's the traffic?'

'Usual mess.' She sat on the bed, sipping coffee.

'Cool place, this. Big mortgage?'

'Renting. The landlord's an academic on sabbatical.' Mitzi kept the story short. 'I've only got it till July.'

'And then?'

She shrugged.

'You know, I could probably find you a good deal on a mortgage. Interesting offers at the moment – fixed rates, cashback, life insurance. Have a think, yeah? A nice return – you scratch my back, and all that...'

Mitzi's hand ached for violent contact with his nose. Instead, she forced a second-rate smile. 'No chance. Believe me, I've tried – I never know what's coming in from month to month.'

'How much roughly?'

She told him.

'Oh,' he said.

'I'll be out on the streets, I expect,' she tried to joke.

At the door he put an arm round her waist and his tongue into her mouth. She pulled away and said, 'See you, then.' Alone, she stood fighting nausea, listening to his footsteps clumping down the stairs; then the opening and closing of the front door. She leaned her forehead against the wall and breathed.

She was still alive, though, so she swallowed grapefruit and toast for breakfast, then took a long, hot shower before settling down at her desk to write up the news story she had been researching.

A large group of young Romanians were being accommodated by their 'employer' in a terraced house in a village not far from the potato fields and chicken processing plants of the flatlands that extended towards the sea. It was a short cycle ride out of town. Mitzi aimed for mid-evening, imagining they might have returned from the factory. Posing as a neighbour needing to borrow a power tool, she rang the bell and soon faced four lads who seemed rather happy to see a friendly blonde on their doorstep. 'Come in, please,' they invited her. 'Have some coffee...' Nervous, Mitzi followed them into a kitchen that stank of singed, reheated takeaway and something covered in grey fuzz, which turned out to be rotting cauliflower.

When she asked if she could look around, they showed her three rooms in each of which five sleeping bags lay side by side on the rough carpeting, and in what should have been the living room, seven. Clothing was piled against the walls: threadbare fleeces, tracksuit bottoms, hole-ridden socks. Black fungus spattered the window frames and the bathroom ceiling.

Where were the others, she asked. At work. Shifts. Some of them did 5am to 3pm, some noon to 10pm, depending. Money? Not what they'd been told. One shrugged. Another laughed. 'Money? I don't know this idea, that we get money for work...' Using body language as much as words, she told the tallest of them, whose hacking cough made his reddened eyes stream, that he must see a doctor, and gave him her GP's phone number.

After they'd waved her a cheery goodbye, she walked round the corner to where she'd left her bike, then rode home, fighting palpitations of fury.

Halfway through writing her article, her vision fuzzy with exhaustion, she paused to make more coffee – then deleted her draft and started again. The caffeine hit was intense; before she'd finished, her fingers were shaking, and not only in the icy draught hustling past the sash windows. Finally she tried to open her email. The connection was down. She was convinced that Cygnford's broadband gave up the moment the temperature dropped below five degrees.

Half past eleven. Copy deadline was midday. Fortunately not all her memory sticks had vanished into her Bottomless Pit drawer; minutes later she was pulling her hat over her ears and struggling with her bike lock, which had seized up with cold.

Pedalling down the towpath along the riverside, past the grand spaces of colleges that traced the centuries in a glance, she felt the wind dragging at her hair and clearing her mind. Life went on and Cygnford glittered with sharp beauty at Christmas. Outside the office, she chained her bike to some railings beside a notice that said NO CYCLES, then marched up to the reception desk to pick up a pass.

John Wilkins, editor of the *Cygnford Daily*, met her at the top of the stairs; from there he ushered her through a glass door into the office. The gust of air wafted random papers off his desk. She heard him mumbling expletives – behind his thick-framed glasses he had the look of a man who would explode if brushed with the finest Hungarian goose feather. 'Mitzi, have a seat. What can I do you for?'

She sat to his right, in front of his computer. 'My internet's buggered, so I've brought in the migrant workers' house piece.' She rummaged for the memory stick in her bag. 'And I had an idea I wanted to run by you. It's—'

The telephone on John's desk jangled. He grabbed it.

'John Wilkins. No. When? Take a look at the paper, madam, and you'll notice that our arts features only cover *forthcoming* events.'

Who'd be an editor, thought Mitzi, handing him a leaflet and thanking heaven she didn't work here full-time.

John glanced at it. 'What's this? Fairy tales?'

Mitzi knew John had children, but they'd be teenagers by now and out of touch with magic – assuming they'd ever been in touch. Sometimes she wondered what his wife was like. 'It's a folklore festival in Branswell. I know it's slightly out of our usual catchment, but it's something different and it's good for the diversity angle – a celebration for Christmas, with stories from all over the world.'

'Hmm.' John glanced up and down the leaflet, then, surreptitiously, up and down Mitzi.

She focused on the slatted blinds. She could see fingerprints in the dust. 'I can ring up the director, Robert Winter, but I've done a bit of research myself.'

'I thought you were a journalist, not a bloody student.' John didn't aim his newspaper at that element of the town, though it ran to thousands.

Mitzi counted to three. 'I think it'd be good. I mean, everyone loves fairy tales.'

'Why're you so keen all of a sudden?' He gave her a quizzical glance.

Mitzi cursed her perennial problem: a readable face. 'So, the thing is, Robert Winter is actually my landlord. But he hasn't asked me to do this. I don't know him at all, I've never even met him – I deal with his letting agent. It's just that the flat is full of these amazing old books and…'

John exhaled. 'Right-oh. Diversity does it, I guess. Heaven knows the readers hate it, but I think it's good to keep it going. Four hundred words and we'll run it as a preview.'

Mitzi, smarting inside as she usually did after seeing John, switched off her phone, then cycled towards the river, a long-limbed figure in blue jeans and purple fleece on a red bike, strands of her fair hair escaping her woolly hat and blowing into her eyes. A car honked at her before overtaking so close that her bike wobbled. She yelled and waved two fingers in the air, but the car had sped away.

At the towpath, she dismounted and began to walk, pushing the bike. She'd ridden beyond the turning for her home to enjoy the crisp air, which had been in short supply this dank December. On the river, rowing teams were training. A long, low boat sliced through the water; she could hear the cox shouting orders, and glimpse muscular figures at work, reddened faces, hands gripping wooden oars. Ducks drifted, curious, in the wake – and there sailed the swans again, minding their own business. Compared to the human river users, they looked serene, until one climbed out onto the bank, where its dignity disappeared as it waddled towards some bread that three little girls were scattering. The children all wore pink padded coats and descended in height like Russian matryoshka dolls.

Mitzi sat on a bench, rubbing her hands to keep warm, watching the birds and the family feeding them. She should go home and work – but her flat, with its tangled sheets and abandoned coffee cups, was the last place she wanted to be. Instead, she turned towards town and spent an hour browsing in the university press bookshop, which was nice and warm, and indulging in a triple chocolate muffin from a favourite bakery.

She was unchaining her bike from a set of railings, her new books in a blue canvas bag in the basket, when a plaintive thread of sound caught her ear. In some of the shop doorways, down the high street and around the market square, piles of cardboard and padded sleeping bags lay; here, some of Cygnford's homeless would take shelter from the cold. The number had increased through the year and while Mitzi had expected that winter would see them resort to hostels, it didn't seem to be happening. She'd got to know some of them through writing her articles for the paper. Last week one boy, to whom she had sometimes given sandwiches, had frozen to death in a supermarket car park.

The call she heard now was a woman's voice: high, probably young. Mitzi turned to gaze around until she spotted her, down a slip of side street from the bakery. She was sitting on the pavement beside the music shop doorway, a paper cup in her outstretched hand. She was fair haired and smooth skinned, no more than twenty, wearing jeans and a fleece, without hat or scarf. Mitzi tied up the bike again and went over, ice-numbed fingers hunting for her purse.

'It's so cold,' she said, giving her a pile of change. 'Are you OK? Have you got somewhere to sleep tonight?'

'Oh, I can't sleep at night. Too dangerous. I'll have a kip somewhere in the afternoon.' The girl's accent hinted at Yorkshire. She sounded so unbothered that Mitzi's curiosity was piqued.

She crouched. 'How long have you been living like this?'

'Two days.'

'What happened? Do you mind me asking?'

9

The girl began to tell her: it was a hideous story, but not untypical – and not without hope. A fight with her boyfriend, who was violent. A miscarriage after he punched her in the stomach. Discharged from hospital, she refused to go 'home'. All she wanted now was to get back to her dad in Ripon. He'd take her in, she was sure.

'There's a women's refuge three streets away,' Mitzi suggested.

'Nah,' the girl scoffed. 'I'd rather find myself the bus fare and get home to my dad. You can't do that if you're sitting in some kitchen, listening to people's stories and going, like, "Yeah, me and all". Like you know anything about their lives. Like they know anything about yours.' Her eyes were bloodshot with cold and stress, but her jaw was set and strong.

Mitzi unwound her own scarf. 'Please, take this. You need it more than I do.'

'Oh, I don't generally wear 'em,' said the girl.

'Please, take it,' Mitzi pressed. 'You could wrap it round your hands or your feet or your middle. This town's punishing in winter.'

'Yeah, they say the wind's straight from Siberia. Wherever that is.' The girl gave a shiver and accepted the scarf with a smile that was partly a flinch.

'You going to be OK?'

'I'm glad to be out of that situation, to be honest. I can get myself back on my feet now, if I can just reach my dad.'

Mitzi, who could never see her own dad again, pulled out all the cash she had in her purse – twenty-five pounds – and stuffed it into the paper cup. 'I don't know how much the bus costs, but it might help.'

Now the girl's eyes filled with tears. 'You're an angel, you. Thank you, darling. Merry Christmas.'

2

When Mitzi checked her phone, four messages were waiting. First, a call from a journal, *Nature Now*, with a commission – the sort of message she received with relief; even after five years of freelancing, she always feared her next feature could be her last. Then a message from an in-house corporate journal, which she loathed, but which paid well, wanting an article before the weekend. Third, her brother Harry's voice: 'Mits? Me. Catch you later.' No doubt he'd ring back or drop in.

Finally, the voice of her financial services date said, 'Hullo, sweetie, hope you've had a *wicked* day.'

After several hours of transcribing interviews, Mitzi switched both landline and mobile to voicemail. Her eyes were sore and the tendons in her wrists were twanging with tiredness. It was nearly 6pm. She poured a glass of wine and reached up to the bookshelf nearest the window for a well-fingered volume she had spotted there – tucked to one side, half concealed behind the velvet curtain, where it rubbed shoulders with sepia-edged copies of the *Mahabharata*, the Bible, the Koran, the *New Larousse Encyclopaedia of Mythology*, a black-jacketed volume called *The Book of Lies* by Aleister Crowley, and several tall, hardcover volumes of Arthur Rackham drawings. It was leather-bound, with gold embossed titling. The ivory paper felt as heavy as canvas under her fingers and the illustrations seemed ripe for Pre-Raphaelite celebrity. *Fairy Tales from Many Lands*.

> *Once upon a time, in a country far from here, there lived a king and queen who had no children. One winter day, when snow whitened the world, the queen sat by her window embroidering on linen across an ebony frame. Accidentally, she pricked her finger on the needle. Three drops of crimson blood fell onto the black wood and shone against the iciness outside. 'Oh,' cried the queen, 'how I wish I could have a daughter with skin as white as snow, cheeks as red as blood and hair as black as ebony!'...*

Mitzi lay on the leather sofa, pulling over her a blanket made of many-coloured squares her grandmother had crocheted; protection against the draught from the sash windows. One cheek against a cushion, she let the words spin filigree webs before her eyes. She knew the stories well, yet to read afresh the poetic words of 'Snow White', 'Rapunzel' or 'The Little Mermaid' sparked in her a sliver of longing that had no place in a local news rag or corporate journal.

The drawings, with sensual swirling outlines and distant washes of landscape, the trees and figures traced with the lightest of pens, were so vivid she could almost imagine stepping through the paper into them. If she did, would she ever want to come back again?

In these timeless tales, pumpkins could change into coaches and girls into trees; heroes proved their love through tests that should kill them, but didn't; witches and fairies watched over you, waiting to instigate harm or help, rewarding virtue, punishing evil. If you pursued a path of goodness, yet suffered for it, you might be rewarded with a better fate in the future or, sometimes, a merciful death, dissolving into foam like the Little Mermaid. If those you loved were to die, you might be consoled later, or even follow them into the underworld. The images multiplied, reflecting one another along a hall of mirrors in her mind. The pain of her father's death could still rise and grab her by the throat when she least expected it. She hadn't cried since the day of his funeral.

She put the book aside and wandered back to her desk, where a small sketchpad lay upended. Somewhere she had a soft 2B pencil – lurking under the spikeful of dog-eared receipts beside the computer screen. Finding it, she turned to a blank page and began to doodle. The backs of three be-coated children, like little matryoshkas, watching something beautiful by a river. The four towers of Duke's College Chapel, pointing upwards like the feet of an animal on its back. A face, large eyes with pale irises and reddened rims, sad and hopeful all at once…

Thinking of the girl outside the music shop, she let her pencil coax the image onto the page as if from deep beneath a blanket of dreams. She tried to count her blessings. Unfair that she should still feel as if an icicle had pierced her stomach, even though she had a beautiful flat around her, a warm blanket, central heating and supper. She'd done what she could – given her cash, her scarf, her heart. But maybe if she were to look up COACH FARE CYGNFORD–RIPON, then find the rest of the money and take it to the girl—

Two minutes later she had the answer. The journey would involve changing buses twice, once in Milton Keynes, once in Leeds. It would cost less than forty pounds. If only she'd given her just a bit more…

Mitzi threw on her coat and rushed out into the busy evening. The cashpoint was a ten-minute cycle ride away, in the market square. There she tethered the bike and queued behind a roll-stomached man puffing on a cigarette and three anxious-voiced American tourists trying card after unsuccessful card in the slot. A whiff of sour liquor struck Mitzi's nostrils as a wiry individual, stubbled and shuffling, approached the queue. 'Spare some change for a cup of tea…'

Mitzi was at the front. She pressed CHECK BALANCE. After paying rent, council tax, utilities, phone and her credit card bill, her account held £49.76. The *Cygnford Daily*'s pay round was next week – money for work she'd done two months ago, an arrangement that had somehow become standard in the industry. The corporate journal and *Nature Now* would pay at some point, when she got around to invoicing them. She pressed buttons and in a series of whirrs and bleeps the machine presented her with three quarters of her funds. She forced herself to ignore the drunkard and set off against the wind for the music shop.

Gone. As if she'd never been there at all.

Perhaps she'd already managed to plead the remaining cash. Perhaps someone had persuaded her to go to the refuge. Perhaps she'd been arrested. Or given up and gone 'home' to give her man one more chance to change…

If only she'd asked the girl's name. She could trawl cafés looking for a tired young woman tucking into a sandwich. She could enquire at the refuge; she could try the bus station and check the queue for Milton Keynes. Or she could go home and warm up, reassuring herself that, all things considered, she had done the best she could.

Safe inside again, anxious but helpless, Mitzi glanced out – a malignant stillness was settling in the air, as if it might snow. She dried her hair, put a potato in the microwave to bake, then glanced at her sketches. Awful. Never mind. Someday she'd learn to do it better. She could try again now; or she could dive back to the dream-world into which Robert Winter's capacious leather sofa and book of fairy tales lured her.

The potato, with a mound of cheese and salad, absorbed some of the wine, but not too much. She was just settling down again to read 'The Firebird' when a long buzz on the doorbell sent her scrambling for the entryphone.

'It's me,' came Harry's voice. Her brother had taken to arriving once a week with his washing. Mitzi pressed the buzzer, then nipped into the kitchen, through the archway from the living room, to make sure she'd remembered to empty the washing machine of her own load. Her feet and hands felt as lumpy as raw wool. Could she handle Harry tonight?

He bounded in with a flourish. 'Hey, sis.'

She reached up to hug him. 'Hey, Hal. Here's the soap.'

Harry dumped his jacket, cap and scarf on a chair before shunting his bulky canvas bag to the kitchen and emptying the contents into the drum. 'My thanks to you, good mistress Mitzi.'

'Oh, God, are you going for another Shakespeare?'

'I'm going to *get* another Shakespeare.' He bounced in his trainers towards Mitzi's fridge. 'They're doing *Twelfth Night* in June and the competition for Feste isn't exactly inspiring.'

'You want to play Feste?' Mitzi stopped herself. If her little brother wasn't good enough for the part, he wouldn't get it and he didn't need her to tell him so. She was meant to look after him, not criticise or doubt his abilities.

'Methinks my fair sister hath been at the bottle so wouldst not object were I to have a beer?' He spun round, ending with one ankle flexed in front of him, arms extended towards her, with his broadest grin. Mitzi smiled despite herself. Harry, two and a half years out of a performing arts degree, might be struggling, but knew how to work his own charisma.

'Bottom shelf,' she said. 'So, what've you been doing?'

'Auditions. Tons of them.' He straightened up, can in hand. 'I was in London for three days. Agents. Directors. Fuckers. If at first you don't succeed, and so on. But I met this seriously cute redhead on the bus coming back and we're going for a burger tomorrow.'

'You and your girlies...' Mitzi gave him an affectionate wink.

'It's quite demanding, trying to keep up with them all...' Harry raised an eyebrow. He had the same strong, level brows as their father, darker than their fair hair. There the resemblance ended: these days Harry, who was taller and thicker-set, boasted designer stubble and a tattoo on his right shoulder that showed Shakespeare's face above the words WILL POWER. He settled into the absent academic's green leather chair, with his feet up on the footstool, while Mitzi closed the curtains. It seemed a long time since she'd opened them.

She knew why girls gravitated to Harry. His frenetic energy might annoy her, but it combined with those self-mocking insights into the sort of charm she'd learned to avoid because it was so dangerous. Blue-eyed Harry, five years her junior, hadn't yet lost the glow of boys about to become men, or men who haven't quite ceased to be boys. By twenty-six it would be dwindling, by twenty-nine almost gone. It saddened her to think it might vanish from her brother so soon.

'Coming to see me be Oberon?' he asked. 'It was great yesterday. It feels so incredible, Mitzi, being up there, saying all those fucking fantastic lines – it's like you're – like you're—'

'King of the fairies?' said Mitzi. 'But why are the Shakespeare Players still giving you top parts when they're a student group and you're just hanging around in Stuart's house avoiding the Spectre of the Proper Job?'

'Oh, come on, Mits, you sound like Mum. It's not as if I'm not trying. I'm doing auditions every bloody week, more or less, I've got the audition speeches coming out of my ears and I've been crashing on pretty much every floor in south London... Anyway, *you* can't talk.'

On that, Mitzi had to concede.

'Actually, I don't know anybody who's got a "proper job",' Harry mused. 'Besides, it's all of two roles, and I'm bloody pleased to have them.'

'So, it's fine that Mum's helping you out and Stuart rents you the room cheap, but it can't go on forever. What happens next year? More student theatricals?'

'Dunno. Might do. Or I might do something else, like win an actual role through an actual audition. Or I'd apply for a postgrad course, maybe something at RADA...'

'Which you'll pay for how, exactly?'

'Oooh!' Harry shrank down in his chair. 'Here's my nose, Mits – go on, rub it in... But I can't do anything else, can I?'

'Most actors take other jobs when they're starting out. I've met ones who work in pubs and shops and restaurants and supermarkets and...'

'Yeah, and sometimes when they've been acting for decades... But look, I need to put in the effort right now. I've got heaps more auditions before Christmas and... well, it's an *art*, turning yourself into somebody else. Just grant me a fair go at it, for a bit? And if it changes, it changes, OK?'

'You should play Peter Pan. You'd look good in the Never-Never Land.'

The phone rang; the answering machine whirred and beeped. A now familiar male voice: 'Mitzi? You there?' A pause; a click. Mitzi yawned.

'No wonder you're Ms Grumpsville,' Harry remarked.

'It's not that,' said Mitzi.

'A bad Dad day? Oh, Mits.' Harry launched out of his chair and wrapped her in a bear hug. 'I miss him too. We've got to try and make the best of things, you know? Keep Carpe-ing the Diem, as he'd say. Honestly, he'd want you to. And he'd be glad we stick together.'

'I know.' Mitzi let herself hide her face against her brother's substantial chest for a minute. 'I feel so stupid being upset when there are so many people in so much more trouble. Another drink?' She made for the fridge to pour some for them both. 'I met this girl today who was on the street, begging – she wanted to get back to her dad. And I tried to help, but I've just been to look for her and she'd gone...'

'What did she tell you?'

Mitzi repeated the girl's story – abusive boyfriend, pregnancy, hospital – and watched Harry's expression morph from concentration to derision.

'And you believed it?' he said. 'Seriously, Mits, you believed that whole malarkey? She's got every trick in the book in that little speech. No wonder you gave her all your dosh.'

'What makes you think it wasn't true?' Mitzi rounded on him. 'How do you know? You didn't meet her. You never know what the stories are behind all those people in the cardboard boxes. They might be refugees, they might be addicts – it can happen to anyone if you're in the wrong place at the wrong time, breaking up, losing your job... How do you know what people could do, if they only had a chance?'

'You'd believe anything, Mits.' Harry gave a sigh. 'Look, you've been lecturing me, so I'm going to lecture you back. Let's say, for argument's sake, it's all true, about that girl. So, you did what you could. But you can't take everyone's troubles on your shoulders. She's not your problem.'

'But in a way, Hal, why shouldn't she be? We're all connected. We should all help each other, if we can.'

'You could also wonder why you work through every weekend and still you've never got any money,' Harry pointed out. 'You've got to draw the line somewhere... Be sensible. It's not your responsibility.'

'But...'

'Change of subject: how about I distract you? Can I sing you my audition song? They want us to sing "Hey Ho, the Wind and the Rain", trad version.'

'Go on, then.' Mitzi curled up on the sofa, clutching a cushion. Harry began.

> *'When that I was and a little tiny boy*
> *With hey ho, the wind and the rain,*
> *A foolish thing was but a toy,*
> *For the rain it raineth every day.'*

His voice was soft and direct, as if speaking, but at pitch.

'But when I came to man's estate,
With hey ho, the wind and the rain,
Gainst knaves and thieves men shut the gate,
For the rain it raineth every day.'

When Mitzi opened her eyes, his arm was round her shoulder, bringing her back to consciousness.

'Oh nooo, sorry… I didn't mean to fall asleep. I loved the way you sang.'

'You're well wasted,' Harry observed. 'Get some kip and I'll head home.'

'Yes, Mummy.' Mitzi gave only her second genuine smile of the day.

Harry bounced to the washing machine and retrieved his load. 'Mind how you go tomorrow,' he remarked. 'There's a storm coming, they say. A really bad one, from the east. It's got some fancy name. God knows why they give storms names. It's got to be an O. Olivia or Oswaldia or Odile…'

'Don't storms always come from the west?' Mitzi yawned.

'Not this one, it doesn't. Take care and don't go out unless you have to.'

Mitzi listened for the soft clop of the closing front door. Alone, she pulled off her clothes, gave her teeth a cursory brush and plunged into the wonderfully empty bed. There she drifted towards sleep, her mind still caressing the mournful tune of Harry's song.

3

By four in the morning, the rain was driving at the roof. By six, the gale had worked into a frenzy that shook the house with a roaring like the groans of a waking demon. At first light, Mitzi opened the curtains to gaze, disbelieving, at mustardy clouds scudding by, twigs and litter somersaulting along the pavement and the chestnut tree bending as if under a dead weight, its branches pleading, outstretched, for help.

The radio news admitted that the weathermen had underestimated the force of Storm Odile. The editor of *Nature Now*, when Mitzi phoned, was late for work and hadn't enjoyed her bike ride. 'It's hellish,' she told Mitzi in a shaky voice. 'The weird thing is that it's all the wrong way round – we don't *get* winter storms from the east. I'm asking our global warming chap to write something about it.'

By ten, raindrops still assaulting her window like paint flung by a furious artist, Mitzi prepared to make her calls for the corporate journal. She had to talk to the managing directors of Cygnford's top three accountancy firms about their favourite holiday destinations – the magazine's ploy for advertising revenue, of course, but the piece would pay for her groceries for a month. Everything was pre-organised for that day – and they were the sort of people, or at least the sort of men, who would make their journeys by car rather than bicycle and were unlikely to have made excuses to stay at home.

The third receptionist sounded bored when Mitzi phoned at two o'clock and asked to be put through to the managing director, who would have been alerted by the company's PR to expect a call. She realised, too late, that she had no idea what his name was.

'Please hold the line,' said the receptionist. 'I'll put you through to Peter Haddon.'

Mitzi almost dropped the phone.

She knew exactly where Pete Haddon liked to go on holiday. Together, once, they'd enjoyed a week in Rome, tripping over history on street corners, wandering in the shade of ancient archways in the Forum, savouring the evening air by the fountain in the Piazza Navona with a bottle of Chianti, and relishing long nights in which sleep wasn't a priority.

Paralysed, while the phone piped Tchaikovsky into her left ear, she wondered whether to ring off. Before she could, he was there.

'*Mitzi—!*'

'Pete? Hi. I, um, I didn't know it was you. I'm doing an article and, believe it or not, I need to ask accountancy MDs where they go on holiday.' She forced laughter.

'Mitzi, Mitzi… how on earth are you?'

'Fine. Chugging along. And you?'

'Oh, tickety-boo, thanks. I've been here a few months – I left the other company after… y'know… but I landed on my feet.'

'I'm really glad you're doing so well,' Mitzi tried to enthuse. 'It's really wonderful.'

'Good to hear your voice, Mitzi. How's life? Got a nice man?'

She didn't answer. 'When's the baby due?'

'Another month or so. Hopefully not Christmas Day…'

'Great,' said Mitzi. 'That's wonderful. Really wonderful. Now, I've got to ask you about your holidays…'

When she met Pete, who was ambitious and ten years her senior, he had everything, except a wife. The infatuated Mitzi, romanced by weekly flowers and cards containing her favourite poems, written out by hand, moved with alacrity into his shiny modern maisonette. She cooked him dinners, brought him coffee in bed, let him choose the weekend outings and did the shopping on her own, believing herself to be the happiest, most fortunate young woman in East Anglia and maybe soon to be married. Then one day her father, who had finally agreed to medical tests after losing a stone in weight, called to tell her the diagnosis. She'd wept in Pete's bed after visiting first the hospital, later the hospice, watching her father grow thinner, weaker, then insensible as the morphine dose was increased.

Pete came to the funeral and held her hand. A month later, standing in the kitchen, he told her he'd fallen in love with a work colleague, had been seeing her for a while, and she was pregnant, so Mitzi would have to find somewhere else to live. She'd been upset enough to grab hold of a nearby bread knife. Sometimes she'd almost regretted not using it.

And now here she was, listening to him describing some little Greek island, perfect in May or September, and uttering an occasional 'Yes', 'Really?' or 'Wow' when required. She stared at the red light on her voice recorder, resisting the temptation to throw both it and the telephone out into the storm.

'It's great talking to you, Mitzi,' he said. 'Why don't we get together and catch up? Come round for dinner and meet Sue.'

'That'd be really lovely,' Mitzi lied.

'Oh – and Mitzi? You can say one more thing. You can say Italy is my Mecca.'

Mitzi's innards gave a backflip. 'I will, Pete.'

The book of fairy tales still lay on the sofa. She sat beside it, absorbing the quiet, watching the clouds racing by and the rain hounding her window. Her heart was still thudding and her hands were clammy. The flat was starting to smell damp; there were leaks in the roof, but it wasn't her place to fix them without the landlord's say-so via the letting agent, the property management company and the downstairs neighbour – whom everyone called simply Professor Maggie – so if water came in she'd just get wet... Oh, God. She needed to calm down before attempting anything more. Deep breaths, five counts in, five counts out. Calm and focus. In and out.

Beyond the road and the river, something was flying in the wind – a curious triangle, pale as paper, expanding by the moment. A bird. A large bird, in trouble. Its wings, which must have been well over a metre from tip to tip, were offering no resistance; its black webbed feet were pressed back against its belly; its long neck was stretched, straining forward. Mitzi, still counting her breaths, recognised the yellow and black beak of a Bewick's swan, different from the musty pink of the mute swans that lived on the River Cygn. It flailed, flapping – then, as she watched in disbelief, it turned its back on the wind, set its wings, pointed its beak and dived, in control and with phenomenal acceleration, straight towards her house.

Mitzi leapt up, shielding her face with her arms, as the swan struck. The window imploded, the gale roared in with a geyser of glass and rain, and the swan thudded onto the table, blood trailing crimson in the water across its splayed wings. Its head lolled to one side. Unconscious? Dead?

Shaking, her legs like slush, Mitzi forced herself forward, step by step across the broken glass towards the creature. With one finger she reached out to touch the down on its neck, soft as fur, blotched with blood. Spots swam in front of her eyes and nausea gripped her – shock, she told herself, casting back for the sofa and slumping, head on her knees. Think, concentrate, remember. The swan is motionless – perhaps best to do something immediately useful before dealing with it? Broken window. Kitchen cupboard, scissors. Patch it up, fast. Fighting to control her breath, she pulled herself up. She had to hunt for packing tape and black bin liners, opening them up along the folds. Rain lashed her while she forced the improvised sheets against the gaping mouth of the window frame and the invading elements it was spewing into her room. In her panic, she fancied the storm was pursuing the unfortunate swan. And, oh God, the landlord... what on earth could she say to Robert Winter or his agent about the window?

It, though, was not alive. The swan needed her attention. 'A swan can break a man's arm,' her father used to say when they watched them together. An injured bird might become frantic even if you were trying to help it. Other people said birds were flea-ridden. Mitzi risked the parasites and stroked the swan's head. Was its eye following her? Watching, perhaps accepting her help? It had to be alive. She couldn't bear it if it were dead.

If she'd found a wounded cat or dog in the street she'd have known what to do – but a swan?

There was a vet's surgery further up Richardson Road, just a few minutes away. She looked up the number on the internet. The receptionist sounded as confused as Mitzi felt. 'A swan?' she echoed. 'I'm sorry, I'm new here, I only started two days ago, and the afternoon surgery's not open yet... but the thing is, Henry isn't really a bird vet. It's a different thing, you see... I don't really know the ins and outs.'

Mitzi's stomach seemed to plummet towards her knees. 'What can I do? Is there a vet who does deal with birds?'

'Ooh, I don't know… I heard there's a good one in south-west London…'

'Look.' Mitzi tried not to lose her temper. 'I've got an injured swan here, it's an emergency, I have no way on earth to get to south-west London and I don't know what the heck to do. Please, just this once, could you consider helping?'

'Well… I can ask Matthew, our other chap. He's in today – I'm not sure if he does birds, because we don't generally but maybe he'll try… It doesn't sound – well – usual. I suppose you'd better bring it in.'

'It's not usual,' said Mitzi. 'Thanks.'

That's right, just bring it in. A wild swan with a metre-plus wingspan. Assuming it was alive, if it would let her touch it then it might let her pick it up; it would probably be too weak to resist. Mitzi pulled on her raincoat and gloves and prepared to lift the splayed-out bird off the table.

She hadn't expected its weight, or the flop of its wings to each side, dwarfing her. She managed to manoeuvre it out of her door and step by step down the stairs. The swan's neck and head drooped over her shoulder, the wings spread across her body; it felt animal, living and warm, its heart beating in a way that seemed almost human. It smelled strange – rain, blood, salt. Could it have been in the sea? In the hall she admitted defeat and put it down.

It lay, helpless, in front of her. She pushed gently at one wing, then the other, encouraging them to fold. Now she could tuck the creature under one arm, supporting its lolling head with her other hand. Five kilos? Maybe six. Out on the river it would look in place and in proportion. In here, it was a pale giant from another world.

On Richardson Road, bicycles and cars flung spray from the puddles over the curb; Mitzi caught vignettes of astounded faces as people spotted her swan.

'Couldn't find a bigger pet?' a man muttered, walking past her too close. She pressed on, head bowed against the wind. She must look odd. A tall blonde in a purple raincoat, hair and face drenched, carrying a swan. A trickle of blood was seeping from one of its cuts onto Mitzi's sleeve, towards her hand; she felt a horror, as if the bird would be committing itself to her, becoming part of her, if its blood touched her skin. She averted her eyes; she didn't want to turn faint again.

By the time she reached the surgery, the swan seemed as heavy as a box of encyclopaedias. But thank goodness, Mitzi said to it, pushing the door open with one foot, thank heavens you're not dead.

The receptionist gasped. 'Oh, wow! Oh my God!'

'Quite a big bird.' Mitzi made for the nearest waiting-room chair.

'Oh my God, you're soaked through... Wait, I'll find something to put it down in – gosh, it is poorly, isn't it?' The girl disappeared into the offices while Mitzi waited in the warmth, thankful, stroking the swan, a rush of love for the unfortunate bird taking hold of her. Breathing in whiffs of animal food and some astringent antiseptic, she glanced at her wrist where a smudge of blood was beginning to dry.

'Here you go.' The receptionist placed a broad cardboard box at Mitzi's feet and fussed about, arranging a blanket patterned with paw marks for the swan to sit on. 'Matthew will see you in a minute. I checked with him and we do treat wildlife for free.'

Mitzi lowered the bird onto the fleecy softness. It was regaining consciousness at last, but showed no sign of panic; instead, it adjusted its wings, then kept very still. She backed away, fearing it might lash out.

'A swan can break a man's arm, you know,' the receptionist remarked.

'This one broke my front window.'

The receptionist's mouth formed into a perfect O. The swan sat, impassive.

'Ah, the lady with the swan.' Matthew emerged, striding over to shake her hand. Mitzi recognised him: a couple of years ago he'd had to put her friend Lara's cat down after its encounter with a Ford Fiesta, and Mitzi had gone along as her moral support. The memory still smarted. He had a kind face, though, and a touch that animals seemed to trust by instinct. She'd seen an injured pit bull terrier grow meek and compliant when he handled it.

'Let's get her in here, shall we?' Matthew lifted the swan in its box and led the way into the surgery.

'It's a girl, is it?'

'Let's say so for convenience.' He set the box on the surgery table. 'You know, of course, I'm not a specialist bird vet, but I'll do whatever I can under the circumstances. So, let's have a look. We're quite a big girl, aren't we...' He took a gentle hold of each of the wings in turn, extending them while closing his other hand firmly around the beak. 'Good, nothing's broken. Remarkable, really. Let's give those wounds a good clean, make sure there's no splinters of glass in there.'

He took some cotton wool and dabbed antiseptic onto it to swab the gashes in the swan's neck, shoulders and wings. At the first stinging touch the bird flinched; but perhaps Matthew's vet magic was working. Appearing to understand that she was being cared for, she settled back, cross yet accepting.

'Do you think she's going to be OK?' Mitzi asked.

'Amazingly, there's less serious damage than I'd have expected. But if we're not going to need the RSPB, it's a question of what to do now. Sometimes parks tag swans for identification, but we're a wild girl. We must have been blown off course in the storm.'

'I certainly hope my front window wasn't on her scheduled flight path.'

'Unusual.' Matthew sized up the bird. 'You don't often see Bewick's swans in Cygnford – though they do sometimes make their way to this neck of the woods. They live north – Russia, even Siberia, northern Scandinavia – and migrate round about October, after the breeding season. Could be that we've come south for the winter and somehow been separated from our friends. So, what to do... we've been concussed, but we're quite conscious now and remarkably compliant.'

'I do get the feeling she knows exactly what's going on,' Mitzi remarked, smiling – if more at Matthew's way of speaking about his avian client than at the swan herself.

'Now, I can call the RSPB.'

Mitzi pictured for a moment the swan being boxed into a wooden crate and carted off. 'Supposing I take her home with me?' she said. 'I live right by the river, so I could keep her overnight, make sure she's safe until she's over the shock, then pop her over the road to the water in the morning.'

'I take your point,' Matthew said, 'but don't feel you have to. It's a wild swan, not a human being in bird form. And just because we crashed through your window, that doesn't mean we're your problem.'

'But I'll happily look after her. I'd prefer that – I'd lie awake worrying otherwise.'

'Well – if you're sure, then I'll run you home with her if you like. There's time before surgery proper begins. Take the box and the blanket, and I'll give you some birdfeed that should sort out breakfast.' He filled a syringe and injected the swan. 'This is a tranquilliser, so hopefully we'll sleep it off…'

As the drug kicked in, the swan tucked its head under its wing to go to sleep. Mitzi followed Matthew out to his car; loading the box into the back, she glimpsed the scared eyes of the receptionist peering from the doorway after them.

4

When Mitzi had deposited the sleeping swan in its box in a warm corner of the living room, thanked Matthew and waved goodbye from what remained of her window, she busied herself with hunting online for a glazier and booking in her repair.

Matthew had said the tranquilliser would last well into the night. Mitzi felt a bolt of wonder strike her at the sight of the sedated creature beneath a shaft of lamplight, its neck curving backwards, the yellow and black beak resting beneath the feathers. An unusual variety of swan? An extra awareness and intelligence? Perhaps she could write an article about it, once her unexpected guest was back in the wild.

She fetched a dustpan and brush to clear up the larger pieces of glass, wrapping the shards in old copies of the *Cygnford Daily* – it had to be good for something – then vacuumed the floor. Robert Winter's precious mahogany table had to be checked for scratches; after a good polishing, a few tiny marks made by sharp edges were scarcely visible. As she could do nothing more for either swan or window, life had to go on; she retreated to her computer to attempt some work. Her phone call to Pete seemed months ago.

And now, of all things, she had to ring Robert Winter. That was her own fault for being so determined to cover his school's festival. At least she could organise the interview – as long as she took care to disguise her distress and pretend that all was well in his flat.

She listened, pleasantly surprised, to his welcoming voice – 'Hello there, Mitzi, it's Rob speaking' – which put her at ease straight away. 'How are you enjoying the river views?' he wanted to know.

'It's lovely,' said Mitzi, staring at the black plastic over the broken window. Breathe. In and out. By the time she saw him she'd have got her story straight. 'I'm really, really happy here. So, when would you have time to talk?'

'Hate to ask you to work on a Sunday, but why don't you come over for a spot of lunch, if you don't mind it being veggie? You could

27

see the pictures of the kids' projects – and I'd rather like to meet the person who's taking care of my flat! What do you think?'

'Great. I'm veggie too.' Mitzi liked his tone – the enthusiasm, the willingness to give up his Sunday lunchtime to talk to someone who was only going to write a short piece for a local rag. Besides, it would be good to get out of town. Robert had switched the flat for a small house in the area's sole hilly patch of countryside, south of Cygnford, close to the Iron Age fort. And she couldn't help being curious about her landlord and his books.

'About twelve thirty? I'll look forward to it. Thanks so much.'

Mitzi pulled herself back to the computer, pushing panic aside. Sunday was Sunday and by then everything would be fine, absolutely fine. The glazier would have finished, she'd find some way to pay him, the swan would be gone and surely there'd be no need to tell anybody about any of it?

She forced her brain to 'automatic' to start transcribing her interview with her former lover, listening back to his recorded voice, hearing the plastic sheet grunting in the wind and a rustle from the sleepy swan rearranging itself on the blanket. She thought about phoning her mother – 'Mum, you wouldn't believe how surreal today has been' – but Mum's first reaction would be excessive concern. Why inflict that on her? And then she'd want to know when Mitzi and Harry could come home for Christmas…

It was hopeless: she was wrung out with exhaustion. The wind had dropped and the steel-coloured sky was darkening to iron. Soon it would be dusk. She fought back; she had too much to do, she shouldn't stop now, but her eyes were closing of their own accord. She could have a nap and finish her work later.

She filled a large bowl with water and another with the vet's birdfeed, then put them close to the drugged swan. Minutes later she was under the duvet in the big wooden bedstead, falling through a kaleidoscope where she watched waterbirds hand in hand with somebody who had Pete's voice and someone else's strong, level brows, surrounded by splinters of shattered glass.

Mitzi awoke with a start.

Her heart thudded in her eardrums while she strained to catch another sound of the sort that had jolted her. The bedroom was dark; she'd been asleep for almost an hour. She'd locked the intact windows, bolted the door. Surely if someone had broken in, they'd have made more noise? Surely the jagged glass hole was too dangerous to climb through? Was it the swan moving about? But those sounds would have been different – rustles, maybe thumps of things falling over as it stretched its wings. What she had heard was a footstep: a person inside her flat.

She must have been dreaming. She exhaled deeply and closed her eyes – and the noise was there again, unmistakeable: in the next room, the creak of a floorboard beneath a foot.

Mitzi grabbed her sweater; her chilly hands fumbled with fright, trying to pull it over her head. What were you supposed to do when confronting an intruder? She had no alarm, no panic button, no object with which to defend herself, and she'd left her phone on the other side of the living room.

'Hello?' she ventured.

The footsteps ceased. Silence.

Mitzi swiped at where she thought the bedroom light switch was – it took several goes for her unsteady hand to find it – then pushed herself onward, round the corner, the light sliding out across the hall. Trying to steady her breath, she peered around the edge of the door, an image of a masked man with a gun hovering in her mind.

In a glint of streetlight through the evening gloom, she could make out a figure at the side of the room. Not the figure she'd expected. It was pressing against the wall as if trying to vanish into it. Not a man. A woman. Diminutive, bone-thin, in a pale garment, trembling from head to foot. There was no sign of a break-in; the window's black-bag patching was rustling in the gap, just as she'd left it.

'*Nyet – nyet—*' came a voice from the darkness.

'Who are you?'

'*Non – non—*' High-pitched. Scared witless.

'Do you speak English?'

'English?'

Her courage restored, now she knew the intruder was smaller than she was, Mitzi switched on the light. She blinked in the electric glare. As her eyes adjusted, the image came into focus.

The stranger was shielding her face with her bare arms, fists pressed to the sides of her head. Her black hair cascaded around her bony shoulders to her waist. Her skin was as pallid as starlight. She was wearing something that resembled a silky shift, perhaps rather an old one. Her feet, to Mitzi's astonishment, were bare.

'It's all right.' Mitzi controlled the tremor in her voice. 'What is your language? Do you understand?'

'I – speak,' the girl mumbled, behind her arms. 'I – Russian.'

Mitzi hunted for a vestige of tourist language. '*Privyet*. It's OK, I'm not going to hurt you – but who are you, and what are you doing in my flat?'

'I sorry. I sorry.' The girl's voice caught in a guttural accent, rolling the rs and rattling an involuntary 'ch' in her throat. Mitzi took a step towards her – and now she noticed with horror that her arms, all sinew and muscle, were covered in scratches and bruises, and her shift, torn in several places, was stained with fresh blood. Surely she hadn't tried to come in, or get out, through the broken window?

Mitzi glanced towards the swan's box. It was empty.

'Who are you?' Mitzi repeated. 'And what are you doing here?'

'I sorry, I not wish harm.' The girl was sobbing, perhaps with fear; in a rush of pity, Mitzi stepped towards her and gently took hold of one hand and then the other – tiny hands, which Mitzi's large palms swamped. She drew the injured arms away from the girl's face. A pair of deep eyes stared out at her. On her forehead under the wild black hair a red gash was oozing blood.

'Oh, my God,' Mitzi said, 'you're badly hurt. I'll call an ambulance. You must go to hospital.'

'No, no, no, I so sorry.' The pale hands clutched Mitzi's, the temperature freezing, the fingernails sharp as talons. 'Please, no hospital.'

Why such terror? Because a hospital would want details of who she was, where she lived, what she was doing? Whatever could have happened to her? Mitzi remembered newspaper stories she had written about Eastern European women escaping situations in this part of England far worse than those of her Romanian food-packers. 'Is someone chasing you? Do they want to hurt you?'

The girl stayed mute. Had she even understood? Or was she too scared to answer? She hadn't said yes. She hadn't said no, either. Why the hesitation?

She tried another angle. 'How did you get in?' How, for that matter, could the swan have escaped when the black sack was still exactly where she'd taped it? 'That glass is dangerous. A swan crashed through it this afternoon.'

'Yes. Is – me.'

Now Mitzi knew she was dreaming. '*What?*'

'I – am – your – swan,' said the girl. When Mitzi stared, speechless, she added, 'Please, you must believe, real truth. I not pretend.'

'I'm calling the police.' Mitzi pulled away, fast. This was not only an intruder, but a deranged and psychotic one. What was she? A traumatised refugee? An abused migrant? What had she been through? Or perhaps this was to do with the house Mitzi had written about? Maybe the criminal ringmasters had heard that the paper was exposing them and had sent the girl to threaten the reporter…

'No police! Please! Listen, you are kind to me as swan,' cried the girl. 'I am same being. You carry me in your arms to animal doctor, you give me food and water while I cannot talk. Now I talk, but you do not believe me.'

Mitzi flopped onto the sofa, her heart choking her. If this was the revenge of organised criminals, they'd chosen a bizarre way to go about it.

The girl surged forward and sank onto her knees. The gash in her forehead was just below Mitzi's gaze.

'You need a bandage,' Mitzi mumbled. 'Why are you kneeling?'

'I beg. I beg you listen to me.'

'Please, just get up.' She couldn't bear the sight of the seeping blood. Even if she were dealing with the Russian mafia, she couldn't be harsh when faced with this wound. However bizarre the situation, what was certain was that the girl needed her First Aid box, and fast. 'Come into the bathroom. I'll clean that wound for you and we'll put some bandaging on it. And you're shivering. I'll find you a jersey.'

The stranger walked after Mitzi into the bathroom, light on her bare feet; she sat meek and motionless on the side of the bath, letting Mitzi swab her wound with cotton wool and witch-hazel, and place a large strip of dressing over it; then wash her sinewy arms and put plasters on the worst cuts. Her odd, pale shift dress, Mitzi noticed, was made of fine silk. But it couldn't be. None of this added up…

The girl reached out, bypassing Mitzi, towards the taps on the basin. She turned each one on, then off, and Mitzi registered, with disbelief akin to shock, the astonishment in her eyes.

'This miracle,' the girl said. 'This magic…'

Had she not seen hot water – running water – before? How was that even possible, whoever she was, wherever she came from? She must be pretending, but if so, she was a fine actress.

'What's your name?' asked Mitzi.

'Odette,' came the reply.

'I'm Mitzi.'

'Thank you, Mitzi,' Odette said. 'You are very kind.'

Mitzi settled her warmest purple fleece around Odette's shoulders; the girl pulled it on and flashed a sudden smile at her. It took her breath away for an instant. The smile was impossibly brilliant, the dark eyes as serene and grateful as they had been petrified a minute before.

'Would you like a hot drink?' Mitzi asked, not sure what to do next.

Odette nodded, her eyes as trusting as a tame animal's.

In the kitchen, Mitzi poured milk into a saucepan, mentally pinching herself to see whether she really was about to make a cup of cocoa for a young woman who claimed to be a swan, appeared never to have used a tap before, and was intruding in her flat, covered in blood. If the gangster theory did not add up, what other possibilities were there? If Odette were an escaped mental patient, or driven mad by exploitation in the vegetable fields, or worse, perhaps she should deal with her by playing along.

Carrying the two steaming mugs back through the arch, she scanned the living room for any trace of the swan. All that remained were a few stray feathers in the box. She could see nothing physical to disprove Odette's words – and Sherlock Holmes' maxim came into her mind: 'When you have eliminated the impossible, whatever remains, however improbable, must be the truth.' But what exactly did 'impossible' mean?

'Now, sit down and tell me everything,' she encouraged, handing the girl a cup.

Odette, perching on the edge of the sofa as if ready to jump up and flee again, sipped her chocolate. A look of pure ecstasy suffused her face. 'Thank you,' she whispered. 'You have *no idea* how wonderful this is…'

'I'd like to understand, if you'll explain?' Mitzi, in the green leather chair, smiled as hard as she could to encourage some progress.

'Chocolate! *I* drink *chocolate*!' Odette's smile was so blissful that it spilled into laughter, an unearthly sound like a glockenspiel or – just how crazy was she?

'Odette, apart from the chocolate,' Mitzi prompted. 'I need to know who you are and what you're doing here, because otherwise I won't know what I can do to help you.'

'I tell you from beginning.' Odette sat back against the sofa's cushions, as if daring to let herself relax. She took a long draught and a deep breath. 'I am princess in Siberia. My father had terrible fight with family – you know – next estate.'

'His neighbour?'

'Yes, his neighbour, in English he is nobleman, Baron, I remember. This man, nobody talked to him, everyone was scared because he knew – you see – bad things, spells, evil, terrible things. My father argued with him over land that Baron said is his, but is ours; it had, you see, mine for precious stones, very rare type, which belong to us. Baron wanted this for himself. My father refused to sell it or to discuss it, so Baron cast a spell on me, my father's only child.'

Mitzi said nothing. What on earth? Oligarchs? Surely not. They'd sue each other, preferably in London, or employ assassins. They wouldn't cast occult spells over each other's children in deepest rural Siberia… would they? 'Tell me, how do you feel, generally? Do you have headaches? Do you hear voices – you know, telling you to do things?'

Odette shook her head. 'No voices. But at dawn I become swan, at dusk I become human again.'

Another test? 'What sort of precious stones? Diamonds? Or...?'

'Not diamonds. I do not remember English – I think...' Odette closed her eyes, concentrating. When she opened them again, their dark depths were filled with tears. 'I remember governess telling me,' she said. 'I think she said "charoite".'

'I've never heard of it,' said Mitzi.

'Very rare. Is purple stone, very beautiful... but so long ago...'

Mitzi could taste cocoa sweet and sticky on her lips, chocolate reality that could not be dreamed. She could see every crease and hear every rustle of the window's patching; in a dream, you wouldn't. She could hear traffic passing and identify the different engine tones of a car and a lorry. In a dream, you didn't. Though at such a moment you could wonder who was the madder: your intruder or yourself.

'Is complicated, because in winter we go,' Odette continued, as if encouraged by Mitzi's silence. 'We swans cannot survive Siberia winter, so we must go west and south. I go to island near Denmark – this is far west, and long journey, but every winter I go, and in spring return home.'

'You're enough of a swan to migrate?'

'I must, so I am there, and this day I am flying, but I am caught in storm. Is terrible, you cannot imagine – such wind, it takes you, you have no control – and then there is sea and I must fly over, I cannot live on sea with no land, because if night comes, then whoosh, I am girl again. And in winter, days are very short, and I am so tired, I cannot go on. When I reach here I am blown at window, I have no strength left and all I can do is try to stay alive, so I go with wind and break glass with beak.'

'How come you speak such good English?'

'I have two governesses as child—' Odette held out a hand three feet above the floor. 'One is French lady, the other is English. With my father and governesses we speak only French on Fridays and only English on Tuesdays, always. I still do. This way I know what day it

is, how many days, how many weeks and months, even if I do not
know how many years. You are too kind to say my English is good, I
know it is not…'

'How old were you when the Baron put the spell on you?' Mitzi
couldn't believe she was asking this.

'Nineteen years old.'

'And now?'

Odette shrugged. 'I not know about time. Years come and go, but
I stay under spell. Many, many, *many* years.'

Mitzi wrestled with the concept. Here was a lunatic in her lounge
– but Odette's directness, her straight, clear gaze, was just a little too
sane. She felt a chill on her neck. 'Do you mean you're nineteen
forever?'

'Until spell is broken.'

'And then? You'll be older all at once?' Mitzi vaguely understood
that if she wasn't dreaming, then she must be entering an altered
state of awareness, a condition in which she could almost accept this
preposterous notion. Giddy with shock, she wanted to disbelieve,
doubt and destroy. Yet another part of the Mitzi who sat mesmerised
by the swan girl was wondering if life was no longer as uninteresting
as she had thought earlier that day.

'I not sure,' Odette was saying. 'I think I will be at age I am when
bewitched; then I live normal life. But spell is hard to break.'

'But don't people give you advice, or try and do something about
it?'

'People?'

'People you meet. Someone like me?'

'I not meet people often. I live in forest near enormous lake, and in
winter on that island, always swan by day. I see few people in many
years. Sometimes in winter, in the migration.'

'My God. So how do you remember…?'

'… how to talk? My memory is always good, since I am little girl. I
find or build huts in forest, and once I go to castle by night and see my
father, once only did Baron allow me this, to see and speak to him –
and he gives me books in French and English. I talk to myself, always,
so I do not forget. And sometimes I must ask people for food… and

I must talk, but very little, because is dangerous for me. I always keep my hope that one day, like this, I talk with people again.'

'So you have to do what the Baron directs?' Mitzi guessed.

'If I disobey, he will kill me.'

'Why? What's in it for him?'

'Power – and life,' said Odette. 'My father is dead, the precious stones mine is taken by others, but still he will not set me free, because then he has lost. He lives today because of his power. If he sets me free, I have won, and then his power is gone, and his life will go too.'

Something was prodding at Mitzi's memory. A princess who turned into a swan? She picked up the book of fairy tales from the floor by her chair and rifled through it. Plenty of metamorphoses, but not that one. No – she'd read it in a children's book that belonged to her when she was six, a beautiful volume illustrated with delicate drawings, maybe Arthur Rackham's. She loved it so much that the page corners frayed with use, but her father gave it away to her younger cousin, thinking she'd grown out of it. How did the story go?

'How do you break the spell?'

'Spell is nearly broken, once.' Odette's eyes lost their brightness. 'A man must swear to love me forever, and keep his vow.' She surveyed Mitzi, one cheek brushed by a strand of her black hair. 'So far, only vow made to me was broken, very fast.'

'So... What happens now?'

Odette shrugged. 'I want to break spell, to be myself once more, but...'

'Presumably you also want to go home?'

'I do not know how. A long way, too long for one day without big wind – you see?' Odette made a flapping motion with her hands, then gestured stopping and falling. Her fingers were as flexible as willow branches and as expressive as music. Mitzi was about to suggest that Odette took a plane to Novosibirsk, or for the winter Aarhus or Stockholm, but then envisaged delays, a transformation at the wrong moment, consternation, crashes, and—

'Have you got a passport?'

'What's that?' said Odette.

'A document that lets you travel… oh no… and any money?'

'*Money?*' Odette shrugged.

'Do you have anything? Clothes? Shoes? Something that can prove who you are?'

'As woman I have nothing,' Odette said, shaking her head. 'I think you know who I am if you see me change into swan.'

No passport. No visa. No means. No proof of identity. No way to board a flight even if she could buy a ticket. At the same moment Mitzi realised that she must have accepted Odette's story. That was as incredible as the story itself.

'Well…' She wanted to say: 'You can't stay here.' She had work to do, and not enough money right now to support anyone, not even a fictional fairy tale character, not even for a few days. Resentment rose in her throat. Yet what alternative was there for Odette? She had nowhere to go – and at dawn, if she could be believed, she'd turn back into a swan. Worse, she was cold, injured and probably feverish. The dark eyes fixed on Mitzi, pleading.

'Look.' Mitzi's conscience took over. 'You can sleep in the study tonight, but you can't stay here forever. We'll get you better, then we'll think about what to do.'

Odette's face broke into a wide smile. 'Mitzi, you are beautiful person! I cannot believe, I crash upon window of most fantastic person in world!'

Mitzi squirmed. 'I can't just turf you out onto the street.'

'Thank you,' said the girl, her hands clasped. 'Mitzi, where is your husband?'

'No husband.'

'Truly? You are beautiful woman, you still young—'

'Thanks.' Mitzi gave a grimace.

Odette started, caught her eye and began to laugh, saying, 'Please forgive, I not mean—'

Mitzi laughed with her, to her own surprise. She'd never heard a laugh quite as infectious as Odette's: clear and free as a bird in flight.

'But someday.' Odette reached out and pressed her hand.

'Maybe.' Mitzi drew away from the touch, too warm, too human. 'Now, would you like something to eat? I'm going to have some supper.'

Odette shook her head gently. 'Thank you, but I feel strange.' She held up a hand and moved it clockwise.

'Maybe it's the tranquilliser. Come on, I'll sort out somewhere for you to sleep.'

Mitzi took her into Robert Winter's 'study' – the cubicle of a room at the back of the flat, which she was not supposed to use; anything he had not taken to the cottage with him and that was not for the tenancy was somewhere in there now. Among the heaped-up boxes and crates, there was just enough room to fold out the camp bed he had left behind. Mitzi fitted it with pink cotton sheets. In the morning, she thought, smoothing them, I'll find it was a dream. But if she's still here—

'When you wake,' said Odette, 'I will be swan.'

'Yes… well, you're welcome to stay in the swan box if you like. With the paw-print blanket. And tomorrow evening we'll decide what to do.'

'You are so kind,' Odette stated simply. 'I thank you from bottom of heart.'

The quiet words tugged at Mitzi. 'That's OK. I'll say goodnight and leave you to get some sleep.'

'Goodnight, Mitzi,' said Odette. 'May a hundred angels guard you and rest you.'

Mitzi, turning her back, made for her computer and sat for a long time staring at the screen, taking in nothing. Eventually she persuaded herself to Google 'Siberia' and 'charoite'. In front of her there materialised images of high mountains; rivers as wide and winding as satisfied pythons; the shores of Lake Baikal with powder-blue hills on its distant horizon; bright-coloured churches like French wedding cakes with conglomerations of onion domes; tumbledown wooden huts with slatted brown sides and long fronds of grass up to their skew-sided windows; frozen landscapes where shining ice and metres-deep snow blazed in the light. And deep lilac, opalescent stones, polished and glowing in Russian antique jewellery.

She had to be dreaming. She would wake up and start her day anew, without this insane nightmare unfolding in front of her. Wouldn't she? Supposing, as the chocolate stains on the two mugs suggested, this was not a dream? What if the impossible really were happening to her, in her own home? Down Mitzi's back trickled something she realised was a sweat of fear.

5

When Mitzi floated up from the bottom of a lake of sleep, the clock showed eight thirty. It was all a dream. Everything. 'Thank almighty God!' she said aloud.

A crash threw her dream away from her: something falling and breaking in the next room. In an instant she was on her feet and in the kitchen where, squat on its short black legs, the injured swan was standing. It had tried to jump or fly onto the side of the sink, toppling the drying rack to the floor. Water glistened in the washing-up bowl, but the swan's dish was empty.

'Poor old thing!' Mitzi exclaimed, before she saw her favourite breakfast mug, a present from Pete once upon a time, on the lino in shards. The swan gazed at her as if guilty.

'Princess indeed.'

It *was* a dream, wasn't it?

She ran to the study. The camp bed's pink sheets had been slept in – and on the carpet, beside the discarded purple fleece, lay a single white feather.

Fetching her well-used dustpan and brush, she gazed at her bird visitor. 'Odette?'

The swan waddled towards her, stretching its neck out to touch her elbow with its beak. So gentle. And it was thirsty. Mitzi filled a bowl with water and put it on the floor. 'Odette? Is it you?' As she watched, the swan seemed to her to be nodding, before it bent its head to drink.

Mitzi breathed deeply, too deeply – was she hyperventilating? Was her imagination in overdrive? What was wrong with her? Her eyes felt heavy, her mind paralysed with dismay and confusion. She was reaching for the kettle when the telephone rang – the chief sub on *Nature Now*, chasing late copy.

'I've had some problems with the flat,' Mitzi told her. She wondered how one explained the interchange of swan and girl to anyone, let alone someone sane, let alone herself. Restricting her story to the window smash, plus a plea for a deadline extension, she headed back to her cafetière.

With a great rustle of feathers, Odette settled onto the dog blanket in the box. Mitzi folded away the camp bed, then tried to concentrate on work. She could almost taste her heartbeats. What could she do? Who could she tell? Who could help? And who would ever believe her? Mum, in Dorset, had a hard enough time without having to worry about this. Harry would laugh at her and tell everyone in the play and the pub and they would laugh at her too. Perhaps it wasn't the mysterious intruder who was crazy, but Mitzi herself. She'd be dragged away, screaming, in a straitjacket.

The doorbell signalled the glazier's arrival. Mitzi froze. She couldn't let a wild bird be seen in her flat, especially not a wild bird that was really a woman.

'Odette? Come on, we've got to hide you. Someone's come to fix the window.'

The swan shook herself and padded to the study, where Mitzi placed the box in a corner, ushered her into it and closed the door.

The glazier was curious about what had happened to the window, but, while he worked, seemed more interested in telling Mitzi about his next job. It was at St Mark's College, he said. One of the dons had been involved in a fight. 'Apparently over a girl,' he remarked.

'St Mark's?' Mitzi said, feeling her face redden.

She'd been standing in the queue at the Arts Cinema with Lara when they'd begun to chat to the young man behind them, who turned out to be a junior research fellow at St Mark's. It took Mitzi, who'd broken up with Pete a few months before, twenty seconds to decide he was The One. He was cultured and well-spoken; he loved cooking. She pictured them together in a pristine kitchen, stirring and laughing, listening to clever quiz games on Radio 4. 'You'll have to come over and sample a Stephen special,' he remarked, while her mind galloped. Lara, who'd been with the same man since she was twenty and was now engaged to him, tapped Mitzi's ankle with a pointed toe.

'Watch yourself,' she hissed, once Stephen was out of earshot and they were finding their seats for the film.

'But he's lovely!' Mitzi scrambled over a row of knees.

'I'm not worried about him. I'm worried about *you*. You've been getting through them, you know…'

'They just didn't work out. This one's different.'

'Aren't they all?'

'How'd you know? You've been with the same guy for nine years…'

Two nights later a text message delivered Stephen's invitation to dinner in his college rooms. His suite overlooked the river from huge windows.

'It's great because you can feed the ducks,' he remarked, chopping pieces of red mullet in his kitchen. 'You're not one of those veggies who doesn't even eat fish, are you? I'm told my bouillabaisse is the best in town.'

Later, once the bowls were stacked in the sink, fishy dregs congealing round the rims, Stephen dimmed the lights. Mitzi needed no encouragement to sit with him on the sofa. And even if she hadn't meant to stay the night, stay she did – wishing she'd gone home instead.

It wasn't that she hadn't enjoyed it, but why the hurry? Had she led him on? Why couldn't she be firmer? But wasn't this what people did these days? Meet someone, go on a date, shag them? Wasn't it supposed to be normal? So why did she feel… as lonely as she had on the first day her mother took her to school and left her there. How can you feel more alone in bed with another person than when you're truly alone?

Soon he was snoring, his body well satisfied. Mitzi lay awake until dawn, asking herself questions, finding no answers. At last she slid out from under the duvet, dressed quietly and slunk away from St Mark's College via the back gate.

When he phoned, she was asleep; her machine took the call. She rang him back and promised to try again the next day. She hadn't seen him since, except once in the distance at Sainsbury's fish counter.

'I thought he was The One,' said Lara, sardonic. 'Mitzi, seriously, can't you get a grip?'

'Don't I try…'

'Maybe you try too hard,' said Lara.

The window was mended, boasting a spotless new pane – conspicuous beside the grainy patterns of dust and limescale on the old ones – and the glazier had gone. Mitzi bundled the black plastic into the bin, then awarded herself extra coffee while she worked on her piece for *Nature Now*, which was more than a little late.

Finished at last, she was able to do what she'd wanted to all day: plunder the ivory pages of the fairy tale book for any trace of transforming swans. Coming back out of its world, she seemed to see the room from a great distance, from a land of woodcutters and witches, forests, fields and magic carpets, which made Cygnford on a Friday afternoon seem remarkably insignificant. She looked across at the great white bird, reinstated in the living room. 'Odette?'

The swan lifted its head.

'I've got to go shopping. But supposing we go out this evening and I show you the town? Assuming, that is, that you are indeed going to turn yourself back into a human being at sundown.'

The swan gave a protesting honk.

'I'll treat you to a good dinner,' Mitzi promised. 'See you later.'

Mitzi zipped around Sainsbury's, avoiding students' trolleys of baked beans, peanut butter and beer, then through the market for fresh fruit and vegetables. She eyed the various doorway sleeping bags for a gleam of fair hair and a glimpse of a plum-coloured scarf that used to be hers. No trace. Perhaps her friend had made it to Ripon; at least it was accessible by cheap bus, unlike Siberia...

Cycling home, she took her favourite route along the riverside, earthing herself with the familiar bike-ache of her thigh muscles, and trying to guess the faculty destinations of students as they pedalled over the hump-backed bridge. This was her town, her home by choice. She'd find a way to make her unusual visitor welcome, on her own terms.

Her phone rang; she pulled over to the side of the towpath to answer.

'Hey, Mits. I'm pissed off.' Her brother sounded petulant rather than sorrowful. 'I've been dumped. Not so much as a thanks-for-the-burger. Where did I go wrong? I gave her tickets for the play and everything!'

'You're at a loose end, then?'

'There's a show this evening, but yeah, tomorrow's a bit empty. And Chris fixed me free tickets to this Christmas charity ball he's playing at on Tuesday, and now I've got nobody to go with.'

'Come for supper tomorrow, then. Can't have you sitting around feeling sorry for yourself.' Odette would have moved on by then. She would have to; the alternative was unthinkable.

'You're a star, Mits. Coming to the Shakespeare tonight?'

'I'm sorry, Hal – something came up. Next time.'

'Next time. And there *will* be a next time. I'm off to the theatre to get ready.'

Harry paced about in the wings, trying to warm his hands, which were icy. His fingers were long and straight, his palms wide, the thumb curving back in what he'd been told was a sign of a strong will. It was in his hands that Harry's emotions first manifested. Anger would arrive as a hot reddening in the centre; performance nerves made the blood rush away, turning his fingertips blue. He thanked heaven he wasn't a musician like his housemate, Chris.

Demetrius and Helena had gone; now Puck was on stage, with a test-tube of herbal tea that represented the magic flower juice; then came the atmospheric rumble Chris had composed to accompany Oberon's lines. Harry took a breath, then stepped into the patch of fuchsia-pink light that awaited him.

Oberon – in the plumber's overalls in which their production clad him – circumnavigated the set, spiralling in towards Puck and her motorbike goggles. Because of the glare of light in his eyes, he couldn't see the audience, but an instinctive energy seemed to draw the speech up though his feet, from the core of the earth. Their first conversation came and went; now he seized Puck by the wrist, pierced her with his eyes.

'I know a bank where the wild thyme blows,
Where oxlips and the nodding violet grows,

45

Quite over-canopied with luscious woodbine,
  With sweet musk-roses and with eglantine…'

His hands were warming. He drank Shakespeare in like mulled wine. The speech sprang forth; not for a moment did he fear forgetting it. The director had decreed that Oberon would be portrayed as the head of a plumbing company that underpinned the lives of all the humans. Somehow it still worked. No amount of reinterpretation could scratch the words of Harry's beloved Bard. The way that that man had arranged language lifted him more than music, more than drugs; he lived each second on stage with an intensity he couldn't reproduce away from it, where he was never as happy or as free. Here Harry Fairweather knew, for three hours, exactly who he was.

Mitzi waited for dusk, wondering what would happen when it arrived. Outside, the sky was deepening from ivory and ghost-grey to violet and gold. She glanced at the swan. She'd believe the transformation when she saw it, not before.

The streetlamps glowed as the last daylight dissolved; the swan stirred, shook itself alert, then made its way out of the room, swaying on its webbed feet. Mitzi waited, trying to remember how to breathe. A minute later, a girl's voice called her name from the bathroom.

She found Odette in her white shift standing in the dark, gazing at her dim reflection in the mirror. Mitzi hovered, trying to take in the fact that not only could Odette resume her human form as simply as putting on a different dress, but she had even gone delicately into the bathroom to change. Mitzi switched on the light; the swan girl blinked in its harshness.

'Good evening, Mitzi.' She was pushing her hair back from her forehead to examine the gash.

'Hello there. You look better,' Mitzi remarked. 'How do you feel?'

'So much better!' Odette clasped her hands together. She peered at the range of bottles on the shelf. 'What are these?' But for her wounds, Odette's skin was as fine as a child's. She removed the lid of a small tub and sniffed the contents, which gave out a scent of honey and rose.

'It's to make your skin soft and keep you looking young.'

Odette's eyes widened. She reached out a finger to stroke Mitzi's cheek. 'But so soft your skin.'

'So, it works.'

Odette began to giggle. 'And what this?' She pointed at a bottle marked Peppermint Foot Lotion.

'To soothe your feet after a long day out.'

'*Da!* And this?'

'That's shampoo.'

'Sham-how?'

'For washing your hair.' Mitzi began to giggle too – an unfamiliar sensation. Odette, fascinated, was dipping her finger into potion after potion.

'This so funny! I have not touched such things since I was princess. I had silver box of skin oil and cream and rosewater. Many years ago.'

Mitzi wondered just how many years Odette was talking about. 'I was thinking, if you would like to try it, we might go out to eat tonight and I can show you Cygnford. It's so pretty at the moment with all the Christmas lights and I'd love it if you could feel welcome here. Do you know what a restaurant is?'

'I remember! Thank you, I like very much.'

'What do you like to eat?'

Odette's peal of laughter was so loud that Mitzi wondered how much Professor Maggie downstairs would hear. Professor Maggie was deputy head of the economics department, six foot tall, black-stockinged and blonde, and would see through attempted deception in a quarter of a second. It would be all the better, under the circumstances, if she could take Odette around Cygnford as a 'normal' human being – 'My friend from Russia's staying for a bit,' she rehearsed. Going to a restaurant would be a good start.

'I not eat in restaurant for a long time,' Odette declared. 'I like to try. I like to try everything!'

'You must have tried a lot in your many years?' Mitzi ventured.

'Swan food,' said Odette, giving a wry smile. 'Plants in lake. Sometimes I find food from tavern that is not eaten, or kind people give to me. Now all of this new. So kind of you, Mitzi, to think of me.'

'You've had to beg for food?'

'Sometimes when nights are longer and colder, before we go west. Even then it is terrible to feel winter beginning.' Odette shrugged. 'If the lake starts to freeze, soon I cannot dive.'

'Is it Lake Baikal?'

Odette's eyes lit up. 'You know this lake?'

'I've heard of it. You must tell me more as we go. I just remembered...'

... that of course they couldn't go anywhere with Odette clad in nothing but an antique silk slip. 'We need to find you something to wear.'

'Mitzi?' Odette pressed her hands together. 'Please – may I use sham-how to wash hair? It has been a long time...'

Mitzi showed her how everything worked and left Odette to enjoy her first-ever power shower.

A quarter of an hour passed, with steam filtering out around the bathroom door. When Odette emerged, wrapped in a large white towel, Mitzi fetched a comb and the hairdryer and escorted her to the big mirror on the bedroom wardrobe, plus a nearby electric socket. Odette's fingers curled around the comb handle and she began tentatively to work on her wild hair.

Mitzi watched as the swan girl, perhaps responding to long-ago muscle memory, made cautious progress with strand after dark strand. A tear glimmered in the corner of one eye. 'I had comb at castle. With pearl...' She pointed at the black plastic handle. 'But it is lost in forest...'

'Well, this one works fine – you look fantastic,' Mitzi encouraged. A little attention and her house-guest would be a beauty. Mitzi switched on the hairdryer, demonstrated its method and, taking the comb, began to help her smooth out what the book of fairy tales would have termed her 'raven tresses'. Under her fingers, Odette's hair as it dried was turning as soft as fur.

Hunting through her wardrobe, Mitzi knew her jeans would be too long for her diminutive guest, so she gave her a new pair of black tights and showed her how to put them on. Over them went a short black skirt, kept up with a belt, and a scarlet jumper with a v-neck. A pair of shoes that pinched Mitzi were too large for Odette, but didn't fall off when she walked.

At last Odette stared at her own slender form in the mirror, the red jersey vivid against her pale skin, and her dark eyes enormous, fringed with curled lashes – and now, instead of the tears, the side of her mouth twitched and she began to laugh. 'Swan,' she said. 'This, a swan!'

'Please don't tell people that. I'll find you a coat – but listen, Odette. You must promise me that when we're out of this flat, you won't tell anybody about the, um, the spell and the swan?'

6

'So what's it like, flying?'

Mitzi and Odette were walking along Richardson Road, purple and red together. Mitzi felt clumsy beside the delicate girl who looked as if she'd stepped out of a fashion magazine, even with shoes that didn't fit, and an old crimson coat around her so large it would have concealed her hands had Mitzi not folded back the cuffs and fixed them with safety pins.

'Flying,' Odette echoed. 'Yes. I like flying.'

'What does it feel like?'

'It feel—' Odette frowned, seeking words. 'It feel – you know, air is wide and deep and you can *go*. You depend only on wind; and sometimes it is for you, sometimes against. Here we may go—' she pointed forwards, backwards and along a side road. 'But there are no paths in air. You go wherever, up, down, on, back. It is difficult, because so many ways you can choose, but always you must fly, you cannot stop.'

At the crossroads, Mitzi paused, but Odette did not; Mitzi grabbed her arm as two bicycles and a National Express coach trundled in front of them.

'So big, these carriages,' Odette remarked, gazing after the bus.

Mitzi took a moment to explain buses.

'And these?' Odette pointed at another bicycle. 'That is *amazing*. Is difficult?'

'Not really. You have to practise, but once you know how, you know how.'

'Like flying. Can I learn?'

'Of course,' said Mitzi, wondering if Odette would be in Cygnford long enough to try.

The pedestrian precinct was filled with shoppers and Christmas partygoers, ambling or prancing along underneath strings of light that traced out the shapes of angels. A seasonal motif of a golden tinsel star gleamed in every window. Odette wanted to stop and stare at each one. 'I see shop only when I was *leetle* girl. Long, long ago. What is this?'

'Cameras and lenses.'

'Cameras?'

'For taking photographs.'

Odette looked blank.

Mitzi opened the zip section of her handbag and pulled out a piece of card. 'This is a photograph. Of my father.'

Odette smiled, surveying the image. 'He is like you. He has kind face. These pictures so smooth – by a painter so very good!'

'They're not painted, that's the point. It's like… a trick of the light. You've never seen this before?'

'Never.'

With a renewed shock, Mitzi tried to remember when photography was invented. So Odette was… *how old?*

'Where is your father now, Mitzi?'

'He died, quite recently. In April.'

'I am sorry – please forgive.' Odette seemed embarrassed. 'You miss him?'

'I'll always miss him. Even though he never seemed to approve of anything I did.' Odette's manner had been so straightforward and frank that Mitzi found herself responding in kind. 'I think he always wanted something better for me than what I had or what I was doing. Nothing was ever good enough, and that could be difficult.'

'I understand. He loved you, so he wanted best for you.'

'For someone who's hardly seen a human being in decades, you're pretty sharp.'

'My father was also like this. I watch him from forest as he grow old and die, but I can do nothing because Baron's spell, his revenge on my father, forbids me to go there. I miss him also.'

'But when you are human, you can't still live in the castle?'

'It is a ruin. As if it is dead itself.' Odette gave a sigh. 'I found empty hut for shelter, deep in forest and close to lake. Once some wicked people, some hunters I think, burn down my hut. So I build one.'

'But – how?'

'Hard work. I tell you later,' Odette smiled.

They walked on, silent; Mitzi was fighting the sensation that Odette could see into her heart better than any of her permanently human friends. Mitzi was the only one of her circle who had experienced such a loss; at the time some retreated or vanished, too frightened to help her – including Pete. She pictured Odette as the swan circling a remote castle, unable to reach her dying father – and she longed to bring her peculiar new friend the consolation that she herself had missed. Instead, she quickened her pace towards the Lansdale Shopping Centre, a handy shortcut to the market square, looking forward to a substantial drink.

She led the way through the red-brick mall, past shoe shops, stationers and boutiques festooned with signs declaring EXTRA 20% OFF, and past groups of youngsters loitering on the edge of the desultory fountain beside the escalator, the girls with short skirts and bare legs despite the December chill, the boys with baggy jeans and hooded sweatshirts. Odette hurried in her ill-fitting shoes to keep up with Mitzi. Someone wolf-whistled.

'Told you you looked good,' Mitzi teased.

Odette glanced round, searching. 'Who is that?'

'Just ignore it. I guess there are more wolves than wolf-whistlers in Siberia.'

A youth was pacing towards them across the mall; Mitzi, imagining knives, drew back on reflex, but Odette met his gaze head on. Mitzi fidgeted with her handbag strap and put her weight onto the balls of her feet, ready to run if necessary. If she had nearly taken Odette for a trafficked sex worker on first sight, what might these local lads be thinking?

'You on holiday, love?' he grinned into Odette's face. 'I could show you the town.'

Odette stared up at him, smiling.

Mitzi experienced a flash of understanding: Odette, for all her insights and empathy, must have lived in such isolation that she hadn't the first clue how to handle this. How strange to be so old and wise, yet at the same time so young and innocent. 'Bad luck, mate, she's new around here,' she announced, grasping Odette's arm.

'Bloody Polish,' came the boy's voice behind them. 'Too stuck up to do the jobs? Go back where you came from!'

'Let's get out of here,' Mitzi growled to Odette, who showed no fear, only bemusement.

'But I'm Russian,' she protested.

Safely out in the open again, Mitzi realised her knees were shaking. She steered Odette towards the nearest restaurant, which happened to be Mexican and sported a window in which Christmas trees alternated with images of sunshine, sombreros and garish drinks. It wasn't quite what she had envisaged for Odette's first evening in Cygnford, but it was cheap, fun and would forestall any further trouble.

At the door Odette stopped.

Mitzi tugged at her sleeve, to no avail. 'Odette, what's the matter?'

'He has gone!'

'The yob?'

'What is yob? English word for man?'

Mitzi felt sweat rising on her forehead. 'A yob is a particular sort of man – like – well, like them.'

'But I not understand!' Odette protested. 'This man – I see he is rough, but he seems interested to know me...?'

Mitzi hesitated. Someone, somewhere, was missing the point.

'Evening, ladies!' A cheerful waitress was at their side, menus in hand.

'Table for two, please?' Mitzi said. The girl ushered them towards a spot in the middle of the busy restaurant, but Mitzi suggested a corner instead – quieter and, perhaps, safer. She wondered what Odette might make of Mexican food.

They settled down, a candle flickering contrasts of gold light and shadow onto Odette's face. 'What is it?' Mitzi prompted, tucking her handbag under the table and getting her breath. Her hands were still unsteady.

'You see,' said Odette, her fingers interlaced, 'is very important man must love me.'

'Surely you don't think just because someone tries to pick you up in the street that he's about to be the love of your life?'

'But why he do it? Why he so angry if he not want me?'

Mitzi clutched the cocktail list, letting the edge of the card dig into her hand. 'He was only trying his luck, to see if he could get off with you, and don't you ever, *ever* go with anyone who does that unless you know exactly who he is and you like him. I thought you said it was dangerous for you, talking to men at home?'

'With them, you know at once,' Odette said.

Mitzi despaired. Not only was Odette not a sex worker, but now it was obvious she had never even had sex – however old she really was. How was that even possible? What about life as a swan, amid nature red in tooth and claw? What about the evil Baron, who presumably could do as he pleased with her if he wished? And she'd had nobody to help or advise her, no mother or sister or friend... 'I need a drink,' Mitzi gulped. 'Do you know if you like cocktails?'

'Chicken-tail?'

'Cocktail.' Mitzi took another breath. 'I'll order for you, shall I? I expect you'd like the Pina Colada, everyone likes those.'

'I try anything!' Odette beamed. 'Is chicken cooked how?'

'It's a drink.' Mitzi waved at the waitress. 'One Pina Colada, please, and one Sloe Comfortable Screw.' She didn't explain the double entendre to her guest. 'Now, how about food? Do you eat meat or do you prefer vegetables?'

'Very long time since I eat this way,' Odette explained, inclining her neck with grace. 'You must choose for me, please, Mitzi.'

'All right.' Mitzi selected a vegetarian enchilada for Odette and a burrito for herself.

'They have no blinis?'

'Blinis? In a Mexican restaurant?'

'When I little girl, I eat blinis all time, but not since then.'

'This is food from a different country.' Mitzi patted her wrist. 'Don't worry, Odette, I'll get you some blinis. They sell them in the supermarket.'

The drinks arrived, Mitzi's tall and pale golden, Odette's frothing over a wide glass, a pink paper umbrella perching on its rim. Odette's face registered astonishment and delight. Mitzi took a long draught and let the alcohol flash to her head. She shut her eyes for a moment.

She could simply pretend that everything was normal and that she was having an evening out with her visiting friend from Russia…

A giggle brought her back to earth. Odette's Pina Colada was almost gone.

'Heavens! Don't drink it all at once, it's very strong,' Mitzi warned, much too late.

'But tastes – mmm!' Odette laughed. 'Not much like green swan food and lake water.'

'I bet.'

Odette copied her, leaning back and closing her eyes; Mitzi spotted two men nearby staring across at her. 'You know,' Odette said, 'it feels good, being human.'

'But you can't fly,' Mitzi teased her gently.

'As swan you fly, but drink lake. I prefer to walk and drink this!' She let out a peal of laughter, which broke off in a feathery hiccup. 'Mitzi, you eat here always?'

'No, no – just sometimes on special occasions. Usually I cook at home.'

'So is special occasion tonight? You are kind, wonderful friend.' The girl grasped Mitzi's hands across the table. 'I not enjoy anything so much since I meet prince.'

'Prince?'

Odette's eyes filled. 'You see, Mitzi, this is only way to break spell. When man swears he will love me forever, and he keeps his vow, I am free. Until then, not. And I meet prince. He finds me in forest, many years ago, he says he loves me and will break spell. Baron cheats him so I cannot escape. He makes his daughter to look like me. Prince does not know and becomes betrothed to magic girl and because is daylight, I am swan, I cannot tell him is not me.'

Mitzi felt the urging of a heated memory. 'There's a ballet… with music by Tchaikovsky… I think I saw it once on TV.' A childhood image of an old screen and a ballerina in a white tutu flooded into her mind. 'But—' Her head spun as she calculated the timing. 'That ballet is over a hundred years old.'

'What year is now?' enquired Odette.

'Two thousand and eighteen.'

'Two-oh-one eight? This means—' The horror in Odette's face shattered into a fit of laughter. 'This means I am one hundred and eighty-five years old! Me! I nineteen!'

'*Hush*,' gasped Mitzi, noticing curious glances from other diners.

'How old are you, Mitzi?'

'Thirty. Here comes our food.'

'But me, I nineteen always. I one hundred and fifty-five years older than you and eleven years younger, together!'

'Thank you,' said Mitzi loudly as the waitress, bringing two laden and steaming plates, looked on, bemused. 'Enchilada there, burrito here, please.'

Odette seemed to be enjoying the unsubtle aroma of spicy beans and guacamole. 'This very interesting.'

'Something more to drink, ladies?' asked the waitress. Before Mitzi could say anything, Odette answered, 'Oh, yes, drink like this!'

'Tap water, please,' said Mitzi.

Odette took a mouthful of enchilada. 'Hot!'

'You don't like it?'

'Is wonderful, but so hot.'

'Take it slowly.'

Mitzi was finding it difficult to swallow, trying to absorb Odette's latest tranche of information. Odette, though, was tucking in with joy. The waitress, arriving with the second Pina Colada, grinned at her rapt expression as she placed the glass ceremoniously in front of her. By then Mitzi was wondering whether she had given Odette the treat of her life or made a terrible mistake.

'Are you serious?' she ventured. 'That a man has to vow to love you forever, and that will break your spell?'

Odette nodded, her straw in her mouth.

'So when the prince let you down – that must have been horrific.'

'Yes, but under spell,' said Odette. 'Both of us under spells.'

'I'm sure that was a very convenient excuse for him.'

'But love is obvious.'

Mitzi stared at her.

'Is difficult, because to break spell I must be loved,' Odette explained. 'But now my prince is dead more than hundred years. In hundred years, nobody else like him. There has been no other love like this love.'

Mitzi put down her fork.

'I think you know too?' Odette leaned forward. Mitzi saw her own features reflected in the swan girl's dark irises.

'There was someone I loved very much,' she said. 'The standard's set, and no one lives up to it.'

'Was long ago?'

'Not very.'

'He died?'

'He married someone else – the person he left me for – and now they're having a baby.' Mitzi fought the lump in her throat.

'But you not have spell, so what happened?'

'It's a long story,' said Mitzi. 'Because of other things – my father became very ill and then he died – I can't have been much fun, and all my attention was going to my dad. So then he met this woman, at work...'

'But if you both love, is not that biggest thing?'

'How do you mean?'

'Love is most important thing of life,' Odette stated. 'Why other things get in way? Your father dying is terrible, and man should know: if he loves you, is most important thing and so he must help you.'

'You make it sound very simple.'

'Should be simple, yes? If he does not do this, he does not love you.'

Mitzi, to her horror, felt something warm and wet forming in her eyes.

'Oh no! Please forgive, Mitzi, I not mean you to cry!'

'It's OK,' said Mitzi, who never cried and couldn't stand the idea of doing so. 'But I still spend half my life wondering where all that love went.'

'I know so well. But for you, someone else is coming, sooner or later...'

'What about you? Can you look at other people?'

'Spell means I must, or I remain swan always. But if there are men in forests at home, they are often dangerous, I hide from them. They have guns, sometimes, and dogs. The animals, Mitzi, you would not believe the animals. I must hide from dogs, wolves, bears and very dangerous big cats with ears like—' She gestured.

'Lynx?'

'Yes, lynx. And tigers. There were many tigers, long ago. Not so many now.'

'Is it really true that someone has to swear to be faithful to you?' Mitzi challenged, with caution. 'Because, to me – to anyone now – it sounds completely crazy. Sure, we all want to find love, but nowadays you don't *have* to do that in order to have a good life.'

Odette shrugged. 'Yes, is true. If I find another like my prince, one who swears to be faithful, but betrays me, then all is lost and I become swan forever.'

Mitzi was silent, weighing up words to no avail. How can you alter a spell that was cast according to the values of... If Odette was nineteen when she was bewitched, and she was born 185 years ago, that meant... her spell – her kidnap, one might say – was in 1852? The 1852, moreover, of a Siberian wonderland by Lake Baikal where the powers of nature encompassed everything. Mitzi kicked her own ankle under the table. Spells that turned women into swans would be no more logical in nineteenth-century Russia than they were here and now, in—

'Mitzi, what is this town called?'

'Cygnford.'

Odette repeated the name. 'But this is famous city. It's old?'

'Very old, parts of it. It's famous for its university.'

'But the scientists my father knew, some of them travelled here to study! Some from Cygnford come to Siberia to meet him and see his library.' Odette's eyes were brilliant in the candlelight. 'Here I find my love, I know. I feel it here.' She wrapped her arms around her solar plexus.

'So that's our aim for you in Cygnford?' Mitzi said. 'To break your spell?'

'My aim is always to break my spell.' Odette beamed. 'Here, perhaps it happens.'

'Right...' said Mitzi. 'Look, do you want something else to eat? Something sweet?'

'I think no space,' Odette laughed. 'Oh, this feels funny – I eat people food for first time in years, it is greatest, greatest joy, and I have no space!' Three women at the next table glanced, smiling, at the laughing girl. Mitzi caught the waitress's eye and asked for the bill. She admired Odette's confidence that Cygnford might provide her with the right man, willing to swear eternal love. Her own experience suggested this quest was not so easy to fulfil.

By the time the waitress arrived with a chip-and-pin machine, Odette had fallen silent. She was holding her forehead with one hand. 'The room, it revolves.'

'I told you not to have that second drink.'

'Is not me, is room.'

'Is *not* room, is you. When did you last have alcohol?'

Odette gave a hiccup.

'All right,' Mitzi soothed. 'We're going soon, I just have to pay.' She handed a credit card to the waitress.

Odette rose to her feet, then sat down again. 'The room, it goes fast.'

Taxi home, thought Mitzi, smiling at the waitress and taking the receipt. Odette held her arm and they made for the door. Idiot, Mitzi castigated herself. She'd wanted to make Odette's first experience of modern restaurants exciting and enjoyable – but how stupid to feed someone used to weeds and lakewater a hot Mexican meal and two cocktails. Odette began to sing quietly, in Russian. Mitzi speeded up their exit.

Outside, Odette leaned against a wall and gulped in the icy air, her eyes closed in some strange ecstasy. Flashing Christmas lights above them lit up her tipped-back forehead with alternating patches of ruby, amber, jade and sapphire.

'Swan,' sang Odette, 'I am not swan! Oh, Mitzi, I feel so happy. I live as real girl, not swan. I feel never like this before. So beautiful, this night, this city! And here I'll find my love and break my spell.'

The road opposite the Lansdale Centre was hardly Mitzi's idea of beautiful Cygnford – but overhead, beyond the brash decorations, winter stars were glistening on a dark satin sky and a new moon cast a benevolent sliver of light. Odette was singing a Russian folk song. Mitzi was surprised that her voice was so strong and expressive. She wondered, with a pang of confusion, when exactly Odette would last have seen or spoken to another human being. She took her arm and walked her towards the next street where, to her relief, the taxi rank held a waiting car. Odette protested, wanting to stroll under the stars, but Mitzi pointed out that were she to pass out halfway home, they'd be in trouble.

'But I never feel so good,' insisted Odette.

Mitzi opened the taxi door. 'Richardson Road, please…'

Odette gazed out at the passing town: low, terraced, pale brick houses, a parade of shops along a side street bedecked with strings of flashing lights, the new blocks that housed the university computer laboratories, then the darkened market square and distant towers of Duke's College.

'You've seen cars before, haven't you?' Mitzi asked, under her breath.

'Seen yes, not ride in.' Odette turned to her, eyes glowing. 'It go fast. Is like flying but on ground!'

'Where you from, then, love?' asked the driver.

'She's on holiday from Russia,' Mitzi said, before Odette could respond. The driver was glancing at their reflections in his mirror.

'No cars?' he said. 'Just goes to show, dunnit, can't believe a word you hear on the bloomin' news. All fake nowadays, innit. Now, you take that Mr Putin, for example…'

Mitzi listened to the driver rattling on while Odette sat back, eyes shut, the engine tone mingling with her gentle humming. Luckily the ride was short. Mitzi thrust a ten-pound note into the cabbie's hand and hauled Odette out after her.

'Tomorrow,' Odette murmured, as much to herself as to Mitzi, 'tomorrow I fly away.' She was climbing the stairs to the front door one at a time, pulling herself along the banister.

'I thought you were going to meet the man of your dreams right here in sunny Cygnford,' Mitzi reminded her. To the right, she glimpsed the sheen of Professor Maggie's bottle-blonde ponytail as she peered at them through a gap between curtain and window frame.

'Yes, but I must fly, I must fly away.' Odette half-sang her words. 'I love to fly, I love to be free. Sometimes, you know, to be a swan is not so bad. You are wonderful, Mitzi, but I must not disturb you more, and I must go.'

'Hush.' Mitzi ushered her in. Upstairs, she unlocked the door of the flat. Odette wandered ahead and flopped onto the sofa.

'Thank you,' she said. 'Thank you for all, my wonderful friend.'

'So, er, what happens in the morning?' Mitzi felt awkward.

'I must leave,' said Odette. 'You will let me fly out of window?'

Mitzi couldn't name the emotion, part relief, part a slam of rejection, that struck her as she nodded her agreement. 'It's been lovely having you here.' She meant every word. 'Are you sleepy?'

'I am happy never to sleep again!' Odette threw her head back and laughed. 'I am so happy.'

And if she left in the morning, if she were gone… Mitzi settled onto the green leather armchair and said to Odette: 'All right, then. Don't sleep, not yet. Come on, tell me everything. There's so much I want to know…'

Odette breathed for a minute. 'Where shall I start?'

In the morning, after a scant few hours' sleep, her head still humming with images from Odette's multiple revelations – stone and wood, sky and sea, building alone by moonlight, flight across the spreading woodland, mountains, steppes and archipelagos – Mitzi came back to the living room to find a white swan slumbering on the sofa under the blanket. Its wounds had almost healed, though she could barely imagine what kind of a hangover it might have. Clothes and shoes lay askew on the floor. As Mitzi moved around the kitchen, clearing up, making coffee, the swan stirred, then rustled across to her, large body swaying over short legs. It pressed its head softly against Mitzi's arm and clattered its beak in the direction of the shiny new window.

Mitzi opened it as wide as possible; in the flow of cold air, she hoisted the swan onto the sill. It glanced at her, then faced forwards and sprang. She watched as it soared up over the river and the green; and the steady swish of its wings faded away into the sky.

7

Saturday in Cygnford, just before Christmas, and Mitzi had to brave the town centre. A muddle of cars oozed along the one-way systems; families with buggies and scooters jostled among students and trundling tourists wielding selfie-sticks, on precarious pavements from which they could not spill onto the road for fear of speeding cyclists.

Mitzi forced herself onto her bike to join the throng, touring the market for good mozzarella. She'd cook pizza for her brother; it would probably be the one decent meal he'd eat all week. Harry and his housemates, Chris and Stuart, lived more on drink than food; what there was of the latter usually came from the chippie or the burger bar. The market was swirling with the mingled scents of mulled wine, stale cigarettes, garlicky olives and musky incense from the New Age stall, and every stand seemed to be pumping out a different saccharine Christmas album. Mitzi heard slivers of singing, American twangs, distant strings and guitars: crooned-out dreams of snowy surroundings mingled with hearts given away and admonitions not to cry or else.

Frantic the place might be, but what a relief to escape the flat and the white-feathered vestiges of these past days. At noon, she headed for the health food café where she and Lara had arranged to have lunch. Enjoying stir-fried vegetables and tofu with her down-to-earth friend, Mitzi found it strange to be chatting about work, Lara's forthcoming wedding or new films as if nothing unusual had happened, as if she had not spent the last two days with someone who was half swan and half crazy teenager, partly naïve, deluded stranger and partly the wisest person she'd ever met. Someone who kept track of days by speaking English on Tuesdays and French on Fridays to trees and wild creatures, wandering by moonlight through billows of deep pink *bagulnik* flowers in the vast forests of the Taiga. Someone strong enough to build a hut from logs with her bare hands, and quick enough to escape danger by climbing the highest pine or running the longest path; civilised enough to play the most demanding piano pieces, be coached by the greatest of composers, and devour the literature of Victor Hugo and Pushkin, yet without hope of breaking her spell...

'You're a bit peaky,' Lara remarked, munching salad. 'It didn't work out with your financial man?'

'Who? Oh – him. Sorry, I've been a bit out of it the last few days.'

'Why, what happened?'

'Not a lot.'

'You don't look like not a lot. You look like a force ten hangover, a wasps' nest in your roof and seventeen articles by this afternoon.'

'Not quite – but a swan crashed through my window, and I had to sort it out.'

'God, Mitzi, that's not "nothing". What did you do?'

'Well, it broke the glass and knocked itself out...' It would sound so matter-of-fact: a swan crashed into my flat, turned into a young woman and got drunk on two Pina Coladas... 'It was still quite dopey when it came to, so I got it over the road to the river and off it went,' she lied. 'And the window's been mended, but please, don't ever, *ever* tell my landlord.'

Mitzi, cycling home, made a mental list. Phone Mum, do laundry, cook pizza. Odette's guttural accent lingered in her mind's ear, describing the continuity of forests and seasons. Frozen air, frozen ground, frozen lake. Long winter nights on the island in which her human self endured for extra hours of darkness, or in a chilly spring or autumn in her home forest, building fires sparked by striking flint, or huddling for warmth under a bear pelt she had skinned on her own from an animal's corpse. Sometimes on the migration she flew with other swans, but every night she would have to leave them, hiding in the places she had learned to find shelter, year after petrified year.

The flat felt much larger, empty and silent without Odette's laughter ringing out, or any white feathery heap in the cardboard box. Mitzi found herself glancing out of the window for a glimpse of a swan winging over Solstice Common – but today, there was none. Nor were there swans on the river, only some mallard ducks and a few coots.

Her flat was silent but for the patter of Professor Maggie's radio downstairs, some politician blustering on the news about the sunny uplands that would welcome the country once it left the European Union. 'Rubbish,' chimed in another commentator. 'You're talking fairy tales, unicorns, baloney…' The swan's box was upended beside the bin. In the bare branches of the chestnut tree, Mitzi glimpsed something moving. She peered out for a closer look: surely the rotund body and globe-like head that she'd thought she saw could only belong to an owl?

She unpacked her shopping and took out her phone to call her mother. After dialling, she thought better of it and switched off again. Mum would hear the strain in her voice and would insist on interrogating her.

Where was she going to spend Christmas anyway? Did she have to go to Dorset? For Mum's sake, of course she did. Yet being in the house without Dad, she would feel like the Little Mermaid, treading on knives with every step.

She sat at the computer, catching up on her admin and invoicing. When she logged in to her bank account, blue figures on the screen showed her that an article for the *Cygnford Daily* that would once have paid her £200 now paid £120. There must be some explanation – a misunderstanding between editor and accounts? Or else they'd cut the article and paid her for what they ran, rather than what she wrote? She'd have to check on Monday, unless the accountant had already departed on her 'annual leave'. Mitzi had not given herself a holiday for four years. She could have used some time off after her father died.

Outside, the traffic spelled Saturday afternoon, the forebodings of Christmas adding a hint of static to the air. At three, she made some tea, then realised she'd forgotten to buy milk. She pulled on her boots and set off down the stairs.

As she opened the front door, something seemed to be pushing it in towards her, something heavy and soft. At her feet lay a heap of white feathers, bloodstained.

In an instant Mitzi was on her knees beside it. Odette the swan had not crashed into another window, but her feathers were ragged and there were bloody streaks on her wings and neck. Her beak was hanging slightly open. Mitzi tucked her under one arm and sprinted back up the stairs.

Her teeth clenched against the sight of the blood, Mitzi swabbed Odette's wounds with antiseptic. Whatever could have happened? These cuts were not clean-edged, but jagged tears, raw and varied, some superficial, some vicious rips in her skin. Perhaps an animal had attacked her – a dog or a fox? She was lucky to be alive.

She retrieved the box and the vet's blanket from her recycling corner; the swan sank into it. Mitzi stood by, taking in the shape of her snaking neck. Looking after a sick animal was one matter, but…

'All right,' she said. 'I took care of you last time. I'll take care of you now. But what are we going to do next?' The bird – no doubt shocked, frightened and exhausted – didn't react. Poor thing. Mitzi stroked the feathered head with one finger. She left her to sleep and forced herself back to her work. Harry could pick up the milk later, on his way over.

And what if Odette were there when Harry arrived? It wouldn't be easy to hide her. Her transformation was due at sundown, which was getting earlier by the day… Mitzi thought fast and grabbed her phone. He didn't pick up his mobile, so she called the house instead.

'Oh, is Harry there? It's Mitzi,' she said to the housemate who answered.

'Hold on, Mitzi,' said Stuart. Like Harry, he and Chris were involved with the Cygnford Shakespeare Players: Stuart looked after lighting and admin, while Chris wrote the music. Chris also played jazz piano and taught harmony and counterpoint for the university, earning a meagre income that was still significantly larger than Harry's. The house belonged to Stuart – or more accurately, to his mum.

'Sorry, he's out…' said Stuart.

'No worries, I'll text him.'

Tapping out her message, she pondered the big deal that a simple question about milk and timing had abruptly become.

At dusk, the ailing swan woke, roused itself and made unsteady headway towards the bathroom. Mitzi stopped herself from following. She longed to witness the moment when bird became woman, but Odette had managed to push the bathroom door closed, and it seemed kindest to let the mystery remain the secret of its owner, or victim.

A second later Odette, in her white shift, threw her arms around Mitzi, in tears.

Mitzi hugged her. 'It's OK, you're safe now. What happened?'

'Mitzi, please forgive – but this time you not forgive, I know, oh, I beg you, forgive.'

'Hush, Odette. Was it a fox?'

Odette, crumpling onto the chair, shook her head. 'Swans.'

'*Swans?* Your own species?'

'I am a stranger. Here swans have different beak from mine, they have pink beak.'

'They're mute swans. You're a Bewick's.'

'So I am different, and they do not like strange bird on river.'

'So they attacked you?'

Odette covered her face with her hands. 'I not know what to do,' she said into her palms. 'I am not swan for swans, not person for people – I am nothing, Mitzi, nothing at all...'

Mitzi gave her a tissue and sat beside her, awkward, while the girl mopped her streaming eyes. 'Odette, you're beautiful and wonderful and people love you. You're from somewhere else, that's all. The swans would be the same with any stranger on their territory. Humans behave like this too, you know. It's horrible, but it's not personal, it's not about who you *really* are. They don't look that far.'

Odette's eyes were bloodshot. 'What shall I do? How can I go home?'

Home? To the log hut she'd built on her own? To those desperate winters and long, lonely migrations? 'Don't try and think about it now – you're in shock. I'll make you a hot drink and you must rest. My brother's coming over later and I'm cooking for him, so you can join us, but it'd be best if... if you didn't tell him anything. Remember your promise?'

'I say nothing – but what we *will* tell him?'

'I'll think of something. Now, do try and stop crying.'

'Is relief to cry.' Odette half smiled. 'As swan, I cannot cry. Is such relief.'

Mitzi turned away to put on the kettle. She never cried. Perhaps that was why the pain never went away... She knew this theory perfectly well, having heard it enough times from a tweed-jacketed bereavement counsellor. Acting on the advice was less simple.

Equipped with sweet tea, tissues and the camp bed, Odette was soon ensconced again in the study, amid Robert's crates and boxes, where she quickly fell asleep. In the kitchen Mitzi began to chop vegetables and mozzarella to make pizzas for three. Under her knife, onions fell into split layers and tomatoes into flat ovals, thin juice coating her fingers. Tears or none, Odette was back. What was she going to do about it?

It's not as if she's a paying lodger with a contract and a job, Mitzi thought. She's a hundred per cent dependent on me, just because it happened to be my window that got in her way... The lodger idea was useful. That was what she would tell Harry: she had advertised online and found—

The bell rang, Harry's usual insistent press. Mitzi said a silent prayer, then let him in.

He bounded up the stairs, two at a time. He was wearing his old leather jacket, jeans, his usual cap and a black t-shirt emblazoned with a skull, and in one hand he brandished a carton of milk.

'You got the message, then.'

'Better still, I got the part.'

'You're going to play Feste?'

'For the sun it shineth every day! You didn't come to the *Dream*, Mits.'

'I wanted to, but like I said, something came up. Let me get the dinner on.'

Harry headed automatically towards the fridge. Mitzi, wondering how to raise the topic of her new flatmate, caught her breath as Harry's foot missed the edge of the swan's box – but his mind was elsewhere.

'It's in St Mark's Theatre. New venue, state of the art technology, the works.'

Mitzi began to load the three amply filled pizza crusts into the oven. Harry did a double-take.

'Three? Your new financial whatsit chap's coming over?'

'No way.'

'You haven't – um – invited someone for me?' He leaned towards her, eyebrows working hard.

'Harry, um, this has happened rather quickly, but I've got a sort of a lodger and she's joining us later.'

'A *what*? Madam Mitzi Live-Alone? You didn't have one of those the other day.'

'Her name is Odette and she's Russian.'

Harry's mouth fell open.

'She's not feeling too good at the moment. She came off her bike,' Mitzi improvised. 'She's not used to cycling.'

'Is she pretty? How old is she? I want to meet her!'

'She's in the – her room – sleeping.'

'When will she wake up, then?'

'Harry.' Mitzi, arms akimbo, growled against her brother's grin. 'She's not for you. Got it?'

'How do you know?'

'Take my word for it.'

At that moment there came the sound of soft footsteps behind the study door; it opened a slit into the lamplit little entrance hall. Odette herself peered out, cautious as a shy cat, her hair spreading around her shoulders, the cuts and gashes on her face dim in the soft light, but defined against her pallor. Mitzi saw Harry's eyes widen and heard him draw in his breath. He seemed temporarily, and most unusually, lost for words.

'Odette,' she gulped, 'this is my brother, Harry. Would you like to come and eat with us? Harry – meet Odette…'

'*Ochin priatna*,' declared Harry, swinging into performance mode and flashing his widest smile.

Odette, eyes fixed on Harry in apparent amazement, mumbled the Russian greeting in return.

'It's so very lovely to meet you.' Harry assumed his most polished, musical tones. 'My dear sister didn't even tell me that someone was moving in with her.'

'Hal, will you check the pizzas?' Mitzi interrupted. 'Odette needs to get dressed and she's a bit short of clothes, so I need to find her something of mine.'

'Madam, thy wish is my command! Cry God for Harry, England and Saint George!' Harry swung away towards the kitchen.

'That's my not-so-little brother,' remarked Mitzi. 'He's an actor.'

Odette gazed after him, eyes luminous.

Mitzi hurried to her bedroom to find the red jumper and black skirt. Soon Odette, wearing them, emerged slowly into the lamplit living room, blinking. Harry, who was still holding the oven gloves after swapping pizzas between shelves, nearly dropped them.

'That's the best-behaved pizza anyone could hope to meet on an average day,' he remarked. His gaze settled on Odette and lingered.

On the table where the swan had made her crash landing, Mitzi arranged a green and white cloth, with padded undersheet to protect Robert's precious mahogany, plus white crockery and her best Ikea wineglasses. She rummaged under the sink for two candles, matches and a silver candlestick that had not been touched since she moved in, associated as it was with Pete. Over the sink, the flames warmed her face and hands as she twisted the wax stems deeper into the holders. She glanced round, trying to catch Odette's eye – to find that the swan girl and Harry had sat down opposite one another, gazing wide-eyed over the plates. The candles, placed between them, cast gold-flushed light onto both faces; Mitzi tried to memorise their expressions for later reference, possibly sketching. A whiff from the oven reminded her that the pizza, if not attended to, would burn.

'And once again,' said Harry as Mitzi dished out, 'no meat? Not a scale of fish? Not one feather of poultry?'

'You know there isn't.'

'I don't know how you survive on green stuff all the time. I'd be worm-feed in two minutes. What about you, Odette, are you veggie too?'

'I eat mostly plant,' said Odette uncertainly.

'You see, you vegetarians just don't get enough protein, so you waste away to skin and bone. What you need is a big Christmas dinner with roast turkey or goose or swan…'

'Harry!' Mitzi protested.

'You think me too thin?' Odette looked so hurt that Harry recoiled.

'I think you,' he said, 'the most beautiful girl I have ever seen… The thing is, I'm a bloke, and I'm hungry and – Mits, you could have cooked that kamikaze swan that tried to kill itself on your window. Good dinners for a week there.'

Odette, who appeared more than reassured, was trying to suppress a fit of giggles.

'It's illegal to eat swans – they all belong to the Queen,' said Mitzi. 'Now, why don't you tell Odette about the play?'

'What one, play—?' said Odette.

'I've just been in *A Midsummer Night's Dream*. Shakespeare. Do you know Shakespeare in Russia?'

Odette sat up and closed her eyes for a moment; then she let forth a stream of Russian, declaiming in a strong, beautifully articulated tone. Harry's eyebrows shot upwards.

'What's that?'

'From *Gamlet*. To live or to live not, he says. But me, I not understand Gamlet. I think if you alive, you must live. Is wonderful living – I love living!' Her face had begun to glow with the joy of being human in congenial company. Mitzi, her heart sinking into her slippers, could almost see Harry's mind twirling faster and faster. She couldn't remember the last time he had dated the same girl for more than a fortnight. And Odette needed someone to break her spell.

'You are always actor?' Odette asked.

'Well, right now I'm looking for an agent and doing some auditions in London. Otherwise, I hang around Cygnford and do what acting I can, and I work regularly with the Shakespeare Players. But this summer's looking good. I'm going to be Feste in *Twelfth Night*, and we're taking it to the Edinburgh Fringe. Next year we're going to do this huge Shakespeare project all over town. What about you? What brings you to Cygnford?'

Odette bit her lip. 'Is by chance... I land in Cygnford. I like, I think maybe I stay here.'

'I see... well, I'm very, very glad you decided to land on my sister. So, what else have you been doing? Apart from falling off bicycles?'

'Mitzi and me, we go eating – and we have wonderful drink named chicken tail.'

'Cocktail,' said Mitzi.

Harry pushed back his chair and gave a roar of laughter. Odette joined in. Mitzi wished she could stop worrying for long enough to be part of it too.

'So, look. We must do things, you and me, and go places,' Harry offered, while they made good progress with Mitzi's best pizzas to date. 'If you want to do anything, anytime, just call me. Mitzi will give you my number.'

Presumably, Mitzi reflected, munching, Odette had never used a telephone. Thank heavens he had offered up his number, rather than asking for hers...

'How long are you staying?' Harry asked.

'Is difficult. You see, I not know how to go home.'

'And where's home?'

'I live in Siberian forest. Very beautiful place, no people. I live there long, long time.'

'You don't look old enough to have lived anywhere long, long time,' Harry smiled into her eyes. Odette blinked.

'Please excuse,' she said, pink-cheeked, and rose to go to the bathroom.

Harry gazed after her, breathing in as if the air were preserving the perfume of innocence that lingered around her. 'My *God*, Mits,' he said, as soon as they heard the bathroom door close. 'Where did you find her? She is *unbelievable!*'

'True.'

'But... bloody hell.' He sat up, gazing after her. 'Seriously, I think I'm in *love.*'

'Harry—'

'Come on, don't wet-blanket everything! Give me a chance!' He flopped back in his chair, eyes glazed, long legs extended. With his mud-tinged trainers, faded jeans and high-cheekboned face – open features, blue eyed, fair skinned – could he really resemble the new-look prince Odette was hoping to find? Mitzi's very own, infuriating little brother? Surely not?

'You go for a different girlie, if not two, every week,' she reminded him. 'And you always want the ones you can't have. Odette's got enough to worry about without you pestering her.'

'Just you wait. If I ask her to the Christmas ball at Bardingley, you'll see, she'll say yes *at once.*'

'That,' said Mitzi, 'is exactly what I mean.'

Odette was back a moment later, and Harry fixed her with his broad smile.

'What are you doing Tuesday?' he said. 'Because I was wondering: would you like to come to a ball with me on Tuesday evening?'

'A ball? Wonderful! Mitzi also?'

Harry caught Mitzi's eye with a quick 'told you so' wink.

'I've got something on,' Mitzi said.

'It would be the two of us, plus some friends of mine, who you'll love. It's a special fundraising do, a charity for preserving some of the ancient sites in this area, but I've got freebies from my musician housemate because he's playing. We can stay as long as you like – it's an all-night job.'

'Music? Oh, I love to go! And on Tuesdays I always speak English anyway.'

'*Da!*' Harry encouraged, despite his surprise. 'I'd take you out tomorrow too if I wasn't rehearsing. You won't change your mind?'

'Oh, no. I never change mind.' Odette beamed at him.

'Can I have that in writing?'

Mitzi rose to draw the curtains. Some rearrangement was taking place in the darkness behind the branches of the tree: the silhouette of a squat body and the silent ruffling of feathers. 'Look,' she said, 'there's that owl again. Harry, did I tell you there seems to be an owl living in the chestnut tree?'

'Where?' Harry peered out.

'Did you see it, Odette?' Mitzi turned.

Odette was standing behind them, her shoulders sagging. 'Owl?'

'They're not so common round here.' Harry took in Odette's expression. 'Scared of them?'

'Where is owl?'

Like an optical illusion bringing the tree to life, the creature separated itself first from the trunk, then from the gnarled branch; silent, it launched a wide wingspan and took to the air, gliding out of sight towards the river. Mitzi and Harry gasped in joint admiration.

Odette seemed to be shielding her face with her arms, almost as she had when Mitzi first saw her.

'Odette? What…?'

All she said was, 'Please excuse – I need to sleep.'

'Of course. You've had a rough day.'

'Goodnight, Odette.' Harry went across to her. 'Don't forget our Tuesday date. I'll pick you up around seven.' He reached for her shoulders to kiss her goodbye.

Odette backed away, pallid, then gave a nod, her gaze still turned to the window, as if following the invisible trail of the disappearing owl.

A little later, after Harry had bounced away down the stairs, Mitzi glanced into the study, where Odette, sitting on the camp bed, was combing her hair with slow, meditative gestures. Something about her eyes told Mitzi this was not the time to ask what had frightened her. If she wanted to talk, she would talk; if not tonight, then maybe tomorrow. And Odette would certainly be there tomorrow.

8

In the morning, soon after sunrise, the swan greeted Mitzi with an enthusiastic honk. The air smelled of frost and across the bare branches of the chestnut tree drifted the ringing of diverse, distant chapel bells, tangling together in a gleaming chorus. Mitzi knelt to examine the swan's wounds, which seemed to be healing well. At least she had no fear now that the bird would lash out at her.

'You want to go out?' she asked. 'I'm off to do an interview, I'll be back this afternoon.'

The swan clattered her bill and flapped her wings; Mitzi ducked the outstretched snowy power of them. After opening the window, she lifted Odette onto the sill; the swan paused, judging the air, then sprang. Mitzi watched her gain altitude. There was no sign of any owl in the chestnut tree – only Professor Maggie downstairs emerging to untether her bike at that very moment and watching, incredulous, as the swan soared up towards the clear sky. Mitzi dived away from the window, wondering if Professor Maggie had any contact with Robert's letting agent. And now she had to go and see Robert himself...

Shortly before twelve Mitzi unchained her bicycle, buckled on her helmet and programmed Robert Winter's address into her phone's sat-nav app. He had given her detailed instructions about how to find the house, but it seemed so complex that a backup wouldn't hurt.

The streets were still relatively quiet, though the pavements were well populated with strolling tourists. Mitzi veered to the left, past the front of Duke's College and its chapel, the grey Grecian colonnade of the art gallery and, soon, the little brown signpost to the station. Her bag jumped about in the basket each time she struck unevenness in the road. She tried to focus on the questions she must ask her landlord, rather than the topics she had to be careful to avoid.

The hospital came into view close by; she navigated the roundabout and pedalled on, out into the countryside. Her legs began to twinge with extra effort: the flat landscape was giving way to undulating hills dappled with woodland. It was somewhere here that Robert Winter lived. Mitzi enjoyed the deepening quiet, the clarity of the air, the still brightness of the morning's last dusting of frost on hedgerow twigs.

Mitzi knew she was still a country girl at heart. She and Harry grew up in Dorset, in a village that Thomas Hardy was rumoured to have depicted. Although as teenagers the two of them grumbled with their school friends that there was nowhere to go and nothing to do, Mitzi had never wholly adjusted to city life, not even Cygnford, which couldn't be called a grand-scale metropolis. She visited London only when work demanded it. With Pete, she'd spent more time there, visiting galleries and theatres and talking about whether they might, hypothetically, someday, set up home in one of the more affordable – on Pete's salary – outer suburbs. Mitzi nevertheless knew that she was not for London, or it for her. She would awake to find she'd been dreaming of open fields, sunken ancient lanes between dappled green hedgerows, the sea in the distance and her father carrying her on his swimming-broadened shoulders towards the beach for an afternoon playing on the sand.

She stopped herself thinking about her father; she had a job to do. She passed the entrance to Anderbury Wood and swept down a wide, curving road into the valley. At the next cluster of houses she found a half-concealed left turn and followed it through a low avenue of beech, oak and hawthorn trees, which in summer would form a green tunnel, but for winter was an elongated basket of tawny twigs, luminous with melting frost. She had never seen this road before. Gradually it was narrowing and growing bumpier. Mitzi jolted in the saddle, but now she could glimpse the terracotta hint of a brick building through the barren trees.

Robert had told her to turn right at the white fence; there she dismounted. The road became a gravel track, then rounded a bend and at last she saw the house: a bungalow covered with a tangle of creeper stems. In front lay a well-kept patch of garden and to one side a building that looked like a garage, though an old red Mini was parked outside rather than inside it. Mitzi gazed at the scene for a moment, then went forward to ring the bell.

'Mitzi,' said the same voice she had heard on the telephone, now even warmer and more affable. 'You found your way perfectly.'

Mitzi fastened the lock onto her bicycle wheel. 'It's wonderful out here, I can hardly believe it.' She turned, flushed from bending, and smiled at Robert Winter.

She'd been expecting a man of fifty, but her landlord appeared to be in his late thirties, dark and big-boned, wearing a chocolate and cream chunky sweater and immaculate, well-pressed trousers. Smile lines webbed the corners of his dark eyes.

'What can I get you to drink, Mitzi?'

It took Mitzi a moment to utter the words, 'I'd love a nice cup of tea, please.'

Following him, she stepped across the threshold. The cottage was virtually an extension of her flat. The living room's longest wall was coated from floor to ceiling with abundant bookshelves; she noticed, at eye level, three more leather-bound volumes of fairy tales, just like the one she had found in the flat. Here they were rubbing shoulders with copies of the Talmud, Sufi poetry and the complete works of Sigmund Freud. The top shelf held a row of large clay pots of various sizes, glazed brown, green and blue. They looked almost alive. She could imagine them bending, twisting, assessing the goings-on in this room like birdwatchers observing the human world instead.

'How about a herbal tea?' Robert suggested. 'Come and choose one. And do call me Rob, by the way – everybody does.'

Mitzi selected lime blossom from his kitchen cupboard, then set up her voice recorder on the coffee table in front of the open fire, where the young flames were stretching out experimental fingers between fresh logs. Woodsmoke, warm and delicious, reached her nostrils; behind the scent, a hint of damp seemed to be hiding. The armchair was saggy and soft, with a blanket draped over it, perhaps to conceal the places where the fabric was wearing thin; piles of paper and towers of books dotted the place like molehills, while plants hunting for air and light took up every windowsill. There was no sign of a television and the computer on the desk was dark and inactive. This house felt unworldly, removed from mainstream life; a feeling, Mitzi remembered, that might indicate someone living there alone.

'You left your lovely leather chair in the flat,' she noted.

'I can take it away if you prefer.'

'Oh, I love it,' she said quickly – the last thing she wanted was to lose her comfortable furniture. 'I'm just surprised you didn't bring it here.'

'It's a bit college-y for this place,' he mused. 'And it wouldn't fit in the Mini. So, what would you like to do? We can eat first, then be professional, we can talk first and then eat, or we can talk over lunch. What do you think?'

'Maybe we can do the interview first, then eat, and if anything else comes up later then we can record some more.' Glancing along the nearest shelf, she spotted Jung, Marx and Krishnamurti. Something told her this was going to be a longer interview than she'd expected.

'I love the pots,' she remarked as he handed her a mug that matched them.

'Thanks.' He settled down opposite, legs extended towards the fireplace. 'That's my main subsistence beyond academia – I'm a potter. I teach a bit, I sell a few pieces and I'd like to do more, but I do it because I enjoy it. If it were commercial, it wouldn't be so much fun. At least I don't have to make egg-cups shaped like chickens.'

'How do you fit the teaching in with the lecturing?'

'I've only started since the sabbatical. I have a couple of adult education classes, a few lessons in one of the choir schools and a day a week in the Branswell school that's doing the fairy tale procession. But actually, I'm testing my wings. I want to see if there's a living to be made at this. It gets me back to the earth and away from all the infighting and college politics and if it works out, I might stay. We'll see.'

'And the building I thought was a garage—?'

'That's my studio. Wheel, kiln, the works. Tell me, how are you enjoying the flat?'

'Oh, it's great. I love it there. I hope you don't mind, but I've been reading some of the books.'

'That's what they're for. Otherwise, everything working OK? No problems, no issues?'

'Not a thing,' Mitzi beamed as hard as she could, an image of the glazier at work and the swan in its box flashing through her mind. 'So, shall we talk fairy tale festivals?' She leaned forward to press the red button.

'Right...' He turned self-conscious, as people often did in front of the microphone. 'What can I tell you?'

'Let's start at the beginning. How did the idea come to you?'

Rob began to talk, hesitating over his words at first; but as he described the events he'd planned, the excitement of persuading the children to do their research, selecting and voting on the best ideas for the floats, his face became animated with a glow that wrapped around Mitzi like a warm scarf, making her smile, making her relax, making her forget. The fragrance of the golden-coloured lime blossom tea was seeping up her nose and through her lungs, like a flavour long lost and unexpectedly rediscovered. It seemed to be lulling her into a heat haze of pure happiness. Perhaps there was something else in the teabag – chamomile, lavender, turmeric or...

'Some people have been asking what the big deal is about fairy tales,' Rob said.

'Tell me?' Mitzi forced herself back into journalist mode.

'A lot of my academic writing has been looking at various theories that fairy tales are good for children's development, because they address unconscious fears in an indirect way. They help you recognise that you'll be able to get along with your own qualities, like kindness or ingenuity. There's an integrity to them, values we forget about – being courageous, being generous – I don't want to sound pompous, but I think they're about how to be human. Maybe through rediscovering lost innocence, in some way... Jeez, I'm probably talking crap, but I promise it's honest crap!'

'I don't think it's crap at all.'

'Which are your favourites?'

'Lots. I like "The Little Mermaid", "Cap of Rushes" and "Hansel and Gretel".'

'Have you got a brother?'

'Yes. Why?'

'A younger brother? Please forgive me if this sounds arrogant, but do you feel you have to look after him and maybe you think you've failed somehow?'

'What?' Mitzi was floored for a second. 'How did you...?'

'Just a hunch. The two children are lost in the forest, they eat the witch's house and the witch puts Hansel in the cage to fatten him up for dinner. Gretel has to get him out. You see?'

Mitzi saw. 'Poor Mum thought she was having a bad time with Harry because he got some tattoos, which she hated – she's, like, a bit conventional – and he's always wanted to be an actor. And she expected me to help shunt him back towards some sensible pursuit – which of course I haven't. He's a good actor and it makes him happy. But she worries about him and...'

'Where do you think your mother might be, in the story?'

Mitzi thought. The mother figure disappears, and in her place you get—

'The *witch*? Oh no, not our Mum! Is that Freudian or something?'

'Nothing like that.' Rob reached out to give Mitzi's elbow a reassuring pat. 'I get sick of the way different schools of psychology are always at one another's throats. None of them can be right all the time. So... that's one reason I'm here and not in college.'

They caught each other's eyes and began to laugh.

'I can't really put that in an interview for the local paper,' Mitzi remarked.

'I'm loving this, whatever you do with it. Let me make you some more tea.' He started towards the kitchen.

'I'm interested in the fact that you keep your fairy tale books alongside religious ones,' Mitzi remarked.

'That's where they belong,' said Rob, opening cupboards. 'The religious ones, I mean. They're all fairy tales, aren't they? The whole world spins on fairy tales. Everything's about what people choose to believe. You want to fight a war? It'll be about what you *believe* to be true, whether political, religious, racial or economic, but it mightn't *be* true at all.'

'By the way... do you know a story...?' Mitzi hesitated. If anybody could shed light on her Odette problem, it would be Rob. But... not that she could tell anyone and expect to be believed, but if she did, her landlord was the last person who should ever learn what had happened in his flat during this weirdest of weeks. 'A story,' she ventured, 'about a girl turning into a swan and having to be rescued by someone swearing eternal love?'

'Oh, *Swan Lake*?' Rob said, as if it were the most natural thing in the world. 'Have you not seen the ballet?'

'Maybe once, when I was tiny...' The words came out faintly.

'It's beautiful. Rather like "The Little Mermaid"... Oh, Mitzi, I'm sorry, I didn't mean to psychoanalyse you, talking about your mother and all that. You're not upset, are you?'

'No, no...' Mitzi realised her face, as usual, must be showing more of her thoughts than she'd hoped to allow. 'I'm fine. Absolutely fine.'

'Let's eat.' Rob leaned over her shoulder and switched off the voice recorder. Mitzi had forgotten all about it.

'Remind me – what happens in *Swan Lake*?' she asked, while they made their way to the kitchen. A big pot of spice-scented soup was glooping over a low flame, and on the table a wooden salad bowl waited, filled with green leaves, cubes of feta cheese, red and yellow peppers and black olives.

'OK.' Rob set out plates and soup bowls, with Mitzi's fresh tea beside one placemat. 'The prince is coming of age and his mother wants him to get married. She's invited some princesses to a ball and he's supposed to choose a bride from among them. But the last thing our prince wants to do is grow up and face his responsibilities. He goes off hunting and spots a flock of swans. He corners the leader and is about to shoot it – when it turns into a princess called Odette who says she's been bewitched and can only be rescued by a man who swears to love her forever. The prince says he will, and tells her she must come to the ball so that he can choose her. But Odette is a swan by day and only becomes human after dark, or at midnight, or something. The wizard watches her, I think disguised as an owl, and the prince tries to shoot the owl, but Odette stops him... Mitzi? What is it?'

'An *owl*?'

'This all has some terrific significance, hasn't it?'

'I'm sorry.' She couldn't meet his gaze. 'It's nothing, really nothing.'

'That's OK. Don't worry... Let me give you some soup.'

'What happens in the end?'

'Well,' said Rob, ladling out lentil soup, 'the wizard disguises his daughter as the swan princess, but wearing black instead of white, and takes her to the ball. The prince is fooled and swears eternal love to the wrong girl in front of everyone. Then he sees the swan outside the window, realises he's made a terrible mistake and rushes after her. Now the only way for them to be together is death, so they throw themselves into the lake; and their deaths break the spell and destroy the wizard.'

Mitzi couldn't look at him. 'She dies?'

'Yes?' He waited.

Mitzi couldn't face it. It was now or never. She chose... never. 'The stories are great and I love them, but – aren't they misleading?' she heard herself gabble. 'Isn't that why some parents won't read them to their children? Because life isn't like that?'

'Oh, but life is *exactly* like that, at its deepest level, the symbolic level.' He gave her a giant smile. 'And magic? People only ever believe whatever they want to believe. As I said, the whole world is based on fairy tales. I believe in magic too, Mitzi, but a different kind. An everyday magic, when people are their best selves and all things become possible. Try this: everything's symbolic. Think of something. Any ordinary thing you do every day.'

'Food shopping?'

'OK, let's turn shopping symbolic. You go to a supermarket, there's all that choice, but what you buy is up to you. You can pick up healthy things like fresh fruit and pulses, or you can get what people expect, perhaps bacon and eggs or baked beans, or you can find weird and wonderful combinations of spices and be incredibly inventive. You see?'

'Yes, but... About *Swan Lake*, Rob, what do you think a psychologist would say about it?'

'So...' Rob, blowing gently on a spoonful of soup to cool it, seemed to be thinking over Mitzi's question. 'There's the prince who's shirking responsibility and always wants what he can't have. He can't have the swan princess because she's a swan, and he can't have the magician's daughter because she's an evil spirit, so by running after one impossibility after another he destroys his own chance of happiness. Then there's Odette. Usually the same dancer plays her and the magician's daughter, Odile – white swan and black swan – so maybe they're two aspects of the same person, or forces pulling the prince in opposite directions: the unattainable white swan, innocence, purity, goodness, versus the black swan, sex, fascination, temptation, evil. The wizard could be a predatory older man, or even the girl's father, which is why she won't let the prince shoot him. His hold on her is so strong that she can't grow up and have a real relationship. She's been forced to remain an innocent little girl, instead of becoming a mature, seductive woman like Odile. She has to break his hold.'

Mitzi crunched through her salad, her mind spinning. Rob's eyes seemed to drill a tiny but direct tunnel straight into her subconscious. She felt she should have learned something tremendously important, yet had no idea what it could be. What on earth was in that tea?

He glanced at her. 'Sorry, I've been spouting a load of crap and I'll shut up now,' he said. 'Tell me about you. Did you study journalism?'

'No, English. I worked for a while as a subeditor, but I prefer writing. There was a huge layoff of staff and I was one of them. But I was so pleased to be free of the place that I didn't look for another job, I just set up as a freelancer.'

'That's brave.'

'My mother thought it was idiotic! Sometimes I think so too. But my father died last April and since then I've felt life is too short to spend it doing things you hate. Right now, everything seems a little aimless and I never know whether I'll—' She stopped herself: not a good idea to tell her landlord she was always convinced her income would dry up in two months' time.

If he noticed, he didn't pursue it. 'You know, you may not feel there's a direction, but that doesn't mean it isn't there.'

'That's a nice thought.'

'What else do you enjoy?'

'Sketching. Nice food. Reading, galleries, seeing Harry on stage – when he has anything to act in. I missed his latest play. What about you? How long have you had this place?'

'I bought it as a wreck about seven years ago – it was nothing but a few bricks and a spiders' conference centre. I started doing it up at weekends, by way of a nice distracting "project". Then when I took the sabbatical I thought I'd try living in it and renting out the flat, instead of vice versa, while I see which way things are going to go.'

Mitzi let him pile more salad onto her plate. 'I don't know how I'm going to turn all this into four hundred words. You're much too interesting for your own good!'

'Could I see it before it goes into print? Is that allowed?'

'Mostly not, but...' Mitzi thought fast. John would flay his journalists alive for sending copy to an interviewee in advance. But was this a ruse to stay in touch? Why not? 'Well, it's not exactly political dynamite, and I'd like to get things right,' she considered. 'I could email it to you tomorrow or Tuesday?'

'I'm just curious. I promise I won't start rewriting it. But I don't do email – that computer is dead in the water, so to speak, and my phone is a mere phone.'

'Um... I could read it to you on the phone?' Mitzi was looking at his hands: thick palms, long, straight fingers, calloused from holding a garden fork. The hands of an artist, a thinker, a gardener.

'It's a deal.' Rob reached out a hand to shake hers – a jokey gesture, but she felt a gentle current of connection slip between them.

The image of him waving goodbye from the cottage door seemed fixed behind her eyes while she cycled home, a small bundle of the lime blossom tea bags that he'd pressed upon her jigging about in her basket. She should be used to this side of her work – meeting someone, talking to them, glimpsing their world, saying goodbye. But the world she'd entered today was the same as hers, expanded and idealised. It was not just because she lived in Rob's flat that she felt she'd stepped into her own house and turned away from it.

Lost in thought, she made slow progress back to town. She seemed to have travelled a great distance since that morning.

9

Later, when Mitzi settled down at her desk to begin her article, Rob and his house still hovered in her mind – the woodsmoke, the dusty books, a tang of walnut oil, fresh basil and honeyed, perfumed tea. She typed:

'If you go to Branswell on Saturday you're in for a big surprise. If you go to Branswell on Saturday you'd better go in disguise....'

A soft swishing noise pulled her away from the words. Outside, a large white swan was flapping towards the house. Mitzi opened the window and let her soar in to land in a heap on the kilim. She was stunned afresh by the creature's beauty, and her heart turned over as the swan settled into its box and prepared for sleep. Without its dazzling whiteness, the rustle of feathers, the occasional quiet clatter of its beak, the front room would seem bleak and sterile. Odette, whether as swan or woman, cheered her up simply by existing.

She wanted to write about choosing spices instead of sausages, about the scent of fresh herbs and winter fires, the shape of a perfect vase, or the colours of a frosty morning in the woods. Instead, she sat there writing jolly dross. Evening was approaching. She'd leave it for now and check over her final version in the morning, she decided, pouring a glass of wine and hunting down her sketchpad beneath the receipts spike.

By the time the glass was empty, dusk had set in. Odette roused herself and waddled off towards the bathroom. Mitzi barely saw her go; she was still trying to capture on the page Rob's face, his kind eyes with their crinkle lines, the cheekbones – oddly, she realised they reminded her of Odette's. Perhaps he had some Slavic roots?

Mixing with the drag of her pencil on the pad, there came the sound of Odette's footsteps pacing about, and of cupboard doors opening and closing. When she appeared, she was in an Indian cotton dress that Mitzi had not worn for years.

'This dress looks so beautiful!' Odette bounded colt-like across the room and sat down beside Mitzi. 'These colours, pink, purple, gold thread.'

'It's nice,' Mitzi agreed. 'But you'll freeze. We're going to have to buy you some proper clothes if you're going to stay in Cygnford. And you have to wear something lovely for the ball.'

'This? Cold?' Odette gave a peal of laughter. 'You come to Siberia… Mitzi, you draw?' She glanced towards the sketchpad. 'May I look?'

'Oh no, no… they're dreadful.' Mitzi covered her work. She didn't want Odette to know she had been sketching the landlord.

Odette's gaze was straying to the window, where the chestnut branches were catching shadows in the evening air.

Mitzi drew the curtains. 'Is that better?'

'How you know?' Odette stared after her as Mitzi poured a second glass of wine for herself and some apple juice for her guest.

'I met a very extraordinary man today. He knew your story, though I didn't tell him why I wanted to hear it. He mentioned the owl.'

'He follow me, the owl. I not know how, but he find me. Mitzi, I am scared.'

Mitzi handed her the glass. The girl's hand brushed against her own, icy. 'Odette, there *are* owls here,' she began. 'This might be any old owl. Why do you think it's him?'

'If he find me, I not escape. I lose my prince because he trick us. I have last chance to find man who love me and who makes vow. If he find me, he will stop me.'

'Odette,' Mitzi ventured, 'is the Baron – your real father?'

The swan girl's eyes widened in bewilderment. 'My father dies more than hundred years ago,' she said quietly. 'Baron is neighbour, big enemy, he and father hate each other. Why you think Baron my father?'

'In the story,' Mitzi began, afraid of putting her other foot in her mouth too, 'it says that you stopped the prince from killing him.'

'Stories.' Odette shrugged. 'Stories are not real.'

'Wouldn't it have broken the spell if he'd killed the owl? Can the owl be killed? Or is he… immune?'

Odette bit her lip. 'I do not know,' she said. 'I imagine he is immune, but this is not certain…'

'Let me show you something.' Rob's books were eclectic in range. Mitzi stood on a chair to reach the top shelf and found what she wanted: *British Birds*, a full-colour volume in which the difference between a mute and a Bewick's swan was made clear, as well as the differences between barn, screech, snowy and tawny owls and, hopefully, the mysterious creature lurking outside.

'See him?'

Odette examined the pictures, then pointed. 'This one.'

'A tawny. That's English. Wouldn't your Russian Baron turn himself into a Russian species?'

Odette shook her head. 'He come to England, he become English owl. Not like me, I always same swan. Mitzi, owl means I am prisoner!'

'Odette, you're *not* a prisoner – can't you see? That is an ordinary, common-or-garden English tawny owl that hoots at night and eats small rodents. It has nothing to do with you and until you stop believing it has, you're going to think you're in its power.'

'Because of Baron I turn into swan every day for more than a hundred and sixty years,' Odette stated. 'What you say is not for me. Is for you: about what you believe, not about what I must do.'

'You're too clever to be a swan half the time.' Mitzi felt discombobulated. Rob might analyse the story on its psychological level, but its heroine didn't know it had one. For all his insights, he hadn't left Mitzi equipped to deal with a fairy tale character sitting in her living room taking everything at face value.

'Odette, why does he keep you? What does he *want*?'

'Like I say, this is a question of power. He wants to be most powerful of all men and of all who know magic, and if he releases me, that means I have won and so his power has gone.'

'And that's it? Sheer bloody-mindedness?'

Odette was quiet for a few moments. Then she seemed to be forcing out some words: 'It is more than this… but very, very hard to explain.' The gleam in her eye was enough to puzzle Mitzi, and to cast one of those increasingly familiar cold rushes across her neck.

'What happens if you do break the spell?' she asked. 'If you find the right man and he doesn't mess it up?'

'If a man swears to love me forever, and keeps his vow, I am free. But not so easy, you know.'

'Yes, I do know.'

'Your brother...' said Odette, not looking at her.

'Odette,' Mitzi began, 'please be careful with Harry. He's attractive, I'm sure, but he's no prince. He's got his head in the clouds and he has no idea you're anything but my lodger and possibly an illegal immigrant. I don't know what he'd do if he found out...'

'He would have fright. Imagine how he look – like this!' Odette turned her eyes and mouth into immense saucer shapes, then broke into shouts of laughter.

Mitzi smiled despite herself. 'Oh, Odette, what are we going to do with you?'

Odette shook herself slightly, as if smoothing her feathers, then stood to approach the bookshelves, her eyes shining. 'Go ahead,' said Mitzi. 'Explore as much as you like.'

Odette pulled down book after book, flicking through the pages. 'Very clever, to use paper cover... How I wish my English is better, to read them all.'

'I can find you something in Russian,' Mitzi offered, 'though you'll have to help me. We can download some Russian books and you can read them on my tablet.'

Odette's bemusement reminded her that she needed to explain this – and having thought her guest's eyes could not grow wider or more amazed, she soon found she was wrong. 'Is *magic*,' Odette breathed.

'That's rich, coming from you. Which writers do you like?'

'Pushkin,' said Odette at once. 'Polish poet Adam Mickiewicz in translation, and I love novels of George Sand in translation – you know, is really a woman writer – something extraordinary! – and they say she was Chopin's lover, according to Monsieur Liszt. And...'

As Odette rattled off a catalogue of literary celebrities from the 1840s, it dawned on Mitzi that she would never have heard of...

'Tolstoy? Dostoyevsky? Pasternak? Great Russian writers from the late nineteenth and early twentieth centuries. You haven't read them, have you?'

'As good as Pushkin?'

'Some would say even better.'

'Oh, Mitzi! Please, show me?'

Mitzi pulled a chair to the computer for Odette. Web pages for the novels of Tolstoy emerged before their eyes, downloadable e-books in many languages, lists of '100 Greatest Russian Novels Of All Time'… and Odette's eyes filled with tears. 'Is all right,' she told Mitzi. 'I cry for joy. This miracle machine! Where I start?'

'Show me which Cyrillic words translate as *War and Peace*,' said Mitzi, 'and I'll download that one for you. It's very long and it'll take a while to read, but I think you're going to love it.'

Moments later the download was complete and Mitzi was switching on her tablet to show Odette how to work it. Taking the machine, running one pale fingertip along the screen and inadvertently highlighting the words, Odette could have been handling a newborn kitten, such was her expression of rapture.

By the time Mitzi was too tired to stay awake any longer, Odette had mastered the tablet and was in the leather armchair, legs tucked under her, riveted to *War and Peace* in Russian. Her hair spread around her like a cloak and over the borrowed thin dress she had wrapped the crocheted blanket for extra warmth, at Mitzi's insistence – though, sure enough, she seemed not to feel the cold.

'I'm worn out,' Mitzi admitted. 'I have to go and sleep.'

Odette gave a nod, not lifting her eyes. 'I read some more…'

The next morning, while Odette sat in her swan box preening her feathers, Mitzi plugged in the tablet to recharge it. The battery had run down almost to nothing; overnight, Odette – starved of the written word for more than a century – had devoured chunks of Tolstoy that would have taken Mitzi a week to read. Forcing herself back to work mode, she polished what she had written the day before. Then, gathering her courage, she dialled Rob Winter's number, half hoping he'd be out.

'Mitzi!' came his voice, before she'd spoken one word. 'How are you? How's it going?'

'Good, thanks. Shall I read you the piece?'

'Fire away.'

Mitzi read. Now the language flowed and all the information she wanted to include sat snug within the word limit.

'I don't know what to say,' Rob declared at the end. 'It's beautiful and you used all the quotes I hoped you'd choose. Will you let me buy you dinner to say thank you? Are you busy tomorrow?'

'Um—' Mitzi swallowed. The next day, Harry was taking Odette out. Mitzi was anxious about the possible outcome. On the other hand, she could do nothing about it. 'Thanks,' she said. 'That'd be great.'

The swan had swung her large body across the room to the window and was staring out through the bright new glass. Mitzi pushed up the sash and Odette, still not used to taking off from heights, hesitated on the sill, spread her wings and launched herself. She reeled briefly, then gained equilibrium and headed upwards and out of sight.

Mitzi watched the bird vanish. She would go into town to work off her confusion and do some errands. At least the corporate journal had paid up and she was solvent again. She cycled to the marketplace and joined the crowds of Christmas shoppers. In the midst of this morass, she had to buy Odette some clothes for her big evening out and normal evenings in.

Among the market stalls, she browsed through woollen dresses and skirts with intricate floral patterns in many colours. Her mind felt like used cotton wool; she had to force herself into focus. Odette was the issue – human Odette, petite, jet-haired, snow-skinned. She bought an Indian dress like her own, but smaller and made of thicker material, bright red with black and gold embroidery. At a nearby stall she picked up three t-shirts, green, red and blue, some basic underwear, a warm white jersey with a zip and hood and a pair of skinny jeans, extra small. That would give Odette a basic wardrobe, but for—

'Oh God,' said Mitzi aloud. 'Shoes.' A passing woman turned and smiled at her. Mitzi walked towards the pedestrian mall, wondering whether she was beginning to unhinge.

She found a cheap shoe shop that had a 2-for-1 deal on ballet pumps, so took it up. Emerging with two pairs in size 3 – one black, one white – and socks to match, she remembered that she, too, had a dinner date. Did she have the funds now to buy herself a new dress? No, that would be far too extravagant, and anyway, Rob simply wanted to take her out to say thank you for the article, which might look quite different in print once the subeditor had cut it, so there was no need to dress up.

'Spare a little change, please,' came a female voice from nearby: a pale woman, cheekbones protruding, thin hair scraped into a ponytail, was sitting on the ground near a set of bins and a cashpoint, a paper cup in front of her. Mitzi scooped her loose change into it.

She was about to head home when strange noises caught her ear: voices excited or anxious, running feet clattering over the cobbles, shouts echoing off the façades of the shops and colleges on Duke's Parade. Mitzi dashed back to her bicycle and pedalled off to investigate.

10

The swan soared high over the spires of Cygnford. Overnight, in her human shape amid the study's cardboard boxes, she had slept little; instead, she'd alternated between reading that astonishing book by Lev Tolstoy, and pondering the difference between herself as a young princess with a boudoir full of exquisite jewels and ball dresses, and herself today, trying to find her feet in a new town, longing for something even slightly nice to wear to this modern ball.

She circled, watching the swarms of people around the city centre, as tiny from the air as soldiering ants. They'd walk into shops under the arching Christmas angels, searching for gifts for their families; later they'd come out carrying large, shiny bags. She couldn't do this.

Or could she?

Odette cruised over the town centre until she spotted a quiet portion of pavement, beside a small chapel. It was difficult for a swan to land except on water, or occasionally crashing through somebody's window. She had mastered Mitzi's flat, though sometimes the kilims slid on the floor under her weight, taking her with them; and leaping into the air from the windowsill was not ideal, but could be managed, with care. The paved ground was another matter. Still, nothing ventured… Odette lowered her wings a jot, letting herself glide gradually downwards. The grey slab of pavement approached and she extended her feet to take the weight, balancing with her wings to lessen the shock. The impact, when it came, was horrible, a sharp jolt of unyielding stone that sent a tide of pain through her joints, but after it subsided she found she was unharmed, safe and where she wanted to be.

She began to shuffle, laboriously, along the pavement. Her head, when she raised it, was level with most people's waists or hips. Faces bent towards her, smiling and indulgent. 'Look, Mummy, there's a swan!' cried a child, about Odette's own avian height, running up to her. Odette reached out her neck towards the little girl, but the child's mother marched over to scoop her away. 'Ellie, stop it. Swans are dangerous.'

Dangerous? Odette watched Ellie being pulled along by the wrist and scolded. Her human heart ached within her swan's body. A small boy took something sticky that he'd been chewing out of his mouth and threw it at her.

Odette, dodging, shook her feathers and reminded herself of her task. Swaying over her webbed feet, she made her way along the mall, pleased that most people avoided or ignored her, until she reached a window behind which stood statue-like figures wearing attractive red, purple or charcoal garments. The fashions, miraculously free of corsets, petticoats and stockings, were so much simpler than those of her girlhood that her task should be easy. Inside, she could see a black skirt similar to the one Mitzi had lent her. She turned towards the open door and waddled in.

A buzz of astonishment went up as she stepped onto the wooden floor, but she managed to stay focused, hunting for the skirt. There it was, on a hanger amid an assortment of dark clothes, and she headed for it, beak outstretched.

'Hey!' An explosive noise made her jump and lift her wings: someone clapping her hands close beside her head. 'Get off! Shoo! Get out of here!'

Odette extended her neck and hissed. The shop girl took a step back, hands flailing, trying to usher the swan towards the door. Odette dug in her claws and in one swift movement tugged the black skirt from its hanger.

'Does it belong to somebody?' another girl demanded. There was a shaking of heads among the customers, all of whom were standing as if spellbound. Odette, skirt in beak, edged towards the door. The garment dragged her head downwards, heavier than she'd hoped.

'Hey!' The scared shop girl grabbed the skirt by the hem. Odette flapped her great wings and pulled.

'Gosia! Help me!' called the girl. A pair of long, black-trousered legs approached Odette and even as she backed away another young woman stepped out from behind a till. Somebody grasped her body and a hand caught hold of her beak and forced it open. Fingers adorned with blue, sparkling painted nails prised the skirt from her; mortified, she felt the material slip from her grasp. Someone was coming at her with a broom; the bristles flared into her face like a mad dog. Odette cut her losses and fled. Behind her she heard a peal of laughter as the glass door swung shut.

The swan retired to a quiet corner of the street to nurse her indignation, taking it out with a hiss on a group of pigeons who were strutting about too close to her. She needed to change her strategy.

Back in the comparative safety of the air, she noticed one important difference between the shopping street and the marketplace. The shops were protected by windows and doors; the market stalls were not. At some of these, clothes were hanging on high pegs, well away from the ground. Odette wheeled back towards the river. She wanted to practise her hovering technique.

A little while later she cruised above the market, surveying the options. One stall held familiar clothing: a rack of men's black jackets, the sort that would have been worn for dinner at her father's castle, though these were less well cut, and made from seriously inferior materials. Opposite them sat a rail of dresses, many short and made of shiny stuff patterned with sprigs of flowers or trimmed with lace; and two that were long, full and floaty, one pink, one blue. The bodices were simple and the skirts like clouds. On a wire hanger, high on the stall's frame, was an identical dress, as white as her feathers. It bore some resemblance to the one she had worn for her first ball when she was fourteen years old, give or take some details – the neckline was rather plain, the satin less fine, the stitching cruder, it required no underskirt and there were no diamonds – and it was not only attractive, but accessible. The approach was clear; she reckoned that all she had to do was stay in the air, no matter what happened.

She set her wings for her attack. A woman beside a fruit stall was pointing her out to a friend. The swan ignored them, fixed her gaze on her target and dived.

White satin loomed ahead and for an instant her feathers caught in the net skirt as it blew about in the turmoil of her flight. Hands grabbed at her; a large object, a briefcase or satchel, glanced against her right flank. Through the shouting and screaming she kept her nerve and her focus. She dodged the bag, dealing a flap in the face to its astonished owner, then grabbed the wire hook and rose into the air, the dress dangling beneath her as she hauled it towards the river. It was heavier still than the black skirt and she had to strain her wing muscles to stay aloft. This hadn't occurred to her; it felt more weighty by the moment and, worse, a crowd of onlookers was gathering to follow her lumbering flight. Desperate for breath, she made for the largest building she could see: a chapel made of pale grey stone with four ornate carved turrets, an enormous stained-glass window and a high, vaulted roof. Beside it lay a tidy stretch of green lawn, bordering the river.

Fluttering beneath her as she winged over the chapel, the dress suddenly would move no further. She was being jerked out of the air; hard, slanting stone caught her as she plummeted downward. The gutter stopped her falling off the roof altogether. Gathering her ruffled dignity, she sat down, folded her wings – then wondered what in the world she could do now. The dress was trapped on a stone pinnacle atop one of the corners, billowing above her like a flag. Below, a small throng had built up to watch.

Despondent on the chapel roof, Odette began to feel worried. She'd be fine as long as she didn't move. But swans were designed to land on and take off from water – beautiful, clear, flat stretches of fresh water – not towering rooftops. She had learned to launch herself from Mitzi's window, she realised, because it wasn't too high and therefore not threatening. There was security behind her both ways, and a river opposite, and once she was aloft all would be well. If she were to leap off the chapel roof there was no guarantee she'd be able to take to the air. Yet if night fell and she was still up there—

She noticed, far below, men in red uniform on a large, scarlet lorry propping up a gigantic ladder against the chapel; it was rising towards her, apparently of its own accord. Beside it stood the middle-aged woman whose angry voice identified her as the owner of the dress stall. Odette edged along the gutter and peered down into the crowd.

Mitzi was pedalling over the cobbles of Duke's Parade when she saw a fire engine pull into a side street that was too small for it, and people running, excited rather than scared, towards the main gate of the college. She thought she could see Lara among them – Lara who would never leave her desk but for a quick sandwich at lunchtime.

She spotted the dress at once, flapping on the corner of Duke's College Chapel, but it took a few minutes before she could make out the shape of a swan cowering at the base of the roof. She let out a laugh before anxiety struck her. She tried to jot a few words in her reporter's notebook – swan on roof, dress caught on gargoyle, firemen as heroes – but her mind was racing. The fireman would rescue the dress, but he wouldn't know that this swan needed rescuing too and he might leave her there. But if he didn't leave her, then he'd have to carry her down, and then there might be calls to the RSPB or a university research department, or… Beside Mitzi, half the crowd were filming the goings-on on their phones. She pushed her way forward – the word 'Press!' usually helped – making as much noise as she could.

Odette heard a familiar voice and scanned the crowd for Mitzi. There she was, distant and tiny in her purple fleece, and Odette had never been so pleased to see anyone in all her many years. But how would Mitzi know it was her, not any common-or-garden swan? Odette rose on her webbed feet, flapped her wings, tried to shout to her – and with a honk, tumbled off the roof.

Mitzi dived forward as the bundle of white feathers cascaded head over webbed feet past the stained glass and gargoyles. The force with which the swan fell into her outstretched arms knocked her flat. Grass in her mouth, feathers in her eyes, she registered that the bird was alive and unhurt. And Lara in her high heels was there, ready to help.

'God,' said Lara, while Mitzi picked herself up. 'You do have bad luck with swans, don't you?'

The swan was on its feet and Mitzi heard someone in the crowd saying: 'Call the RSPB!'

'Fly,' she hissed at the swan. 'Go on! Go home.'

The swan stared up at her. Exasperated, Mitzi scooped her up and, with a strength she didn't know she possessed, threw her into the air. Odette spread her wings, as she had been too shocked to do during her fall, and rose upwards on a welcome current that carried her towards the sky. A second later, she had disappeared over the chapel roof. A smattering of applause sounded behind her.

Mitzi dusted herself down, retrieved her notebook and walked, head held high, back towards the college gate.

'Hey miss, you shouldn't have done that.' A departing fireman accosted her. 'We were just getting the RSPB.'

'They'd have done the same,' Mitzi replied. 'The poor thing's had a nasty time and probably wants to get back to the river.'

'Yes, Mitzi, how did you know what to do?' asked Lara.

'When I was a kid, my dad once rescued a swan that was caught in some wire, and that was what he did.'

'At least Mrs McSwidden got the dress back,' Lara said. 'I must find out what the legal position is if one's stock is stolen by animals.'

'Act of God, I reckon. I must go and write this up for the paper. See you!' Mitzi escaped, giddy with relief.

'Act of God?' echoed Lara as Mitzi paced away.

'We're all His creatures,' the fireman said. 'Though I doubt Mrs McSwidden would agree.'

'You have to *buy* things,' Mitzi said, for the fifteenth time. She was sitting opposite the unapologetic Odette, arms folded, trying to impress upon her that one could not simply swipe a dress from the market and fly away with it, hanger and all. 'That book online was free, but that's different…'

'I know, but how can I? I have nothing,' said Odette, also for the fifteenth time. 'I want beautiful dress to wear to ball.'

'Of course, but that's not the way to get it.'

'So I get how?'

'I get for you.' It was difficult not to lapse into Odette's speech patterns, especially when infuriated.

'Not right for you.'

'No, not right. So we find some work for you to do, yes?'

'I work, so get money, so can buy.'

'Exactly. Speaking of which, we need something for dinner. Come down to the corner shop with me?'

Odette put on her new shoes and the warm white jersey to follow Mitzi cautiously down the stairs.

'So what I do?' she demanded as they walked.

'It's tricky because you don't have any papers, work permits and so on – you're not a legal immigrant. That means you're technically an *il*legal immigrant. Now, I don't like this any more than you do, but you'll have to find some kind of work in which people will let you get away with it and will pay you cash, but won't treat you badly because of it. If you could learn to type and improve your English at the same time it'd be a good – Odette? Are you listening?'

'That dress. So beautiful…'

Mitzi knew that in the morning she'd be going to the market to try and buy the dress for Odette. She pushed open the shop door; Odette jumped when the bell jangled.

Mitzi made for the cartons of soup while Odette stood and gazed as if mesmerised at rack upon rack of foodstuffs in multicoloured tins, packets, tubes and bags. She picked up a bottle of tomato ketchup and tried to open the lid.

'Odette, leave it alone.'

'Must buy first?' Odette gave a sigh. 'Is red paint.'

'It's not red paint,' whispered Mitzi, avoiding the gaze of the shopkeeper, Uma, a frazzled but motherly woman in her forties who was her friend. 'This is a food shop. That's a sort of sauce made from tomatoes.'

Odette replaced the bottle and peered into a lighted freezer compartment. Mitzi explained the concept.

'Oh yes!' Odette cried. 'Once I fly over this land that is always frozen and I find dead bear. This bear, it dead long time, but no smell or sign of death because of ice. Me, I think I am as if kept in ice by spell…'

'Hush…' Mitzi saw Uma, behind the counter, looking on in astonishment.

'And this?' Odette picked up a packet of prawn-cocktail-flavoured crisps.

Mitzi outlined the making of crisps.

'But this is miracle!' said Odette. 'Tell me, why crisps not frozen?'

'It's more convenient like this, because you can open them anywhere and eat them right away.'

'We try?'

Mitzi never touched crisps. She popped the packet into her basket.

'Prawn cocktail,' Odette mused, her eyes excited. 'Is like drink?'

'No, is nothing like drink. Prawns are shellfish.'

'Then is not cocktail!'

Mitzi groaned softly, but Odette's eye had already been caught by something else.

'Mitzi! Carrots! Potatoes! Look! Look! Where is earth, mud?'

'Our vegetables are cleaned and sent to us in the very best condition,' Uma said from the till.

'But this I never see! This is best shop in Cygnford.'

'Glad you like it.' Uma flashed a white-toothed smile.

Odette, clutching a potato, glanced a second time at her. 'You are from where?' she asked.

'Bradford. It's up north, in Yorkshire. You don't know England well?'

'Uma, meet my Russian friend, Odette,' Mitzi intervened. 'She's from Siberia, she's never been here before and there are lots of things she finds a little... strange. Would you mind telling her a bit about your background, please?'

'Ah, I see. Well, my family were Indian, but they lived in Kenya, in Africa,' Uma explained. 'My parents came to this country in the 1970s and they set up several shops just like this one, which is now mine.'

'They can? This possible?'

'Yes, a lot of people did this. It's a family business and I hope I can build it up more so that my daughter will inherit something even better.'

'So I could come here and work too? I need work if I stay.' Odette stroked a pale, clean potato.

'It's complicated – you have to go through the right official channels. You need proof that you're here legally. Can you get that? Have you got a permit in your passport?'

'It's a tricky sort of situation,' Mitzi said, 'and a very long story, but basically at the moment Odette has nothing at all, no passport or papers or money or anything, and that's why I'm trying to help her.'

'I was just reading your article,' said Uma, 'about the Romanians in the village house. It's appalling. They make people live in such terrible conditions.'

'She's not connected with that, I promise. It's... hard to explain.'

Odette's face fell. 'Can I not work as I am? Is difficult, Uma, because Mitzi uses her money to buy things I need. Is not right. I feel so bad for her, I don't know what to do to help.'

Uma's eyebrows twitched upwards; Mitzi could see that Odette's somewhat unusual sense of responsibility had made an impression. 'Hmm... Look, I wouldn't normally think of doing this, but evenings are always a tricky time to find people to help out and it's difficult for me with the children. If you're looking for some night work that doesn't have to be official, I could use an assistant in the shop a few times a week. It would have to be very informal and I can't pay a lot, but it might help, yeah?'

'Oh, Uma, that is amazing! This shop, this paradise!'

Mitzi paid Uma for the groceries. 'Maybe a trial run...?'

'Possibly,' Uma said. 'Yes, Odette – why don't you come and try a couple of hours and see how you get on?'

'That's very kind. We'll make a plan.' Mitzi felt like an overprotective mother. 'Come on, Odette, let's go home. I have to write up your escapade at the chapel for the newspaper.'

11

The next morning the *Cygnford Daily* website featured a large photo of a white dress flapping from the tower of Duke's College Chapel, plus several zoom-lens close-ups of the swan cowering by the roof gutter. But John, with the words, 'Front page stuff and this is all you can do?' had thrown Mitzi's own paragraphs back at her by email. The final story had been sexed up, with short and superfluous words, by someone who hadn't even been there. Mitzi logged off, fuming. Why hire journalists at all if you only ask unpaid interns to rewrite the copy? More productive than feeling angry, she decided, would be to head for the market to buy the dress.

Of course, it had gone.

'Snapped up first thing,' said a satisfied Mrs McSwidden. 'All that fuss.'

'Have you got anything else like it?'

'Have a browse. Take your time.'

Mitzi spotted the pink and blue versions of the dress; neither colour seemed right for Odette. But there, at the end of the rail, hung a faithful replica of cocktail dresses from the 1920s, its white material emblazoned with metallic Art Deco shapes, fringed at the hem and studded with intricate beading. The shape would suit Odette's bony figure and it was unusual enough to suit her personality too. As for size, they could work some magic with safety pins. 'I'll take this one...'

Odette, striking human form again around 5pm, ran her fingers over the beading, her mouth open with joy. 'This is so beautiful! When you say this design is done?'

'It's a vintage thing, based on the 1920s.'

'Is not like our dresses in Russia, is funny shape...'

'Try it on and see how it looks.'

Moments later, Odette came back from the bathroom with the dress shimmering in the lamplight, its embellishments reflecting back from her eyes. She was going to be difficult, very difficult, for Harry to resist. 'Let's just take in the shoulders a tiny bit,' Mitzi said, and set to work with the safety pins, trying not to give away to Odette quite how extraordinary she looked. Perhaps it would be safer – for everyone – if she had no idea of the power of her own beauty.

'When you go out?' Odette wanted to know.

'About seven. I think Harry's coming by then for you too. I'm going to have a bath...'

'And I have time to read!' Odette declared, bounding across to the armchair.

Running her bath, Mitzi threw some rose-scented oil into the water. She basked for ten minutes and washed her hair. In her dressing gown, she stood by the wardrobe wondering what to wear. She settled on a blue dress that matched her eyes. She probably shouldn't have been dressing up for her thank-you dinner with Rob Winter – it was just an ill-motivated habit. From the living room, silence. When she glanced round the door, Odette was still in the leather chair, bare feet tucked up under her, motionless but for her eyes, which were drinking in words with a joy reserved by others for vintage champagne.

'This amazing person,' said Odette, without looking up. 'This man, Tolstoy. I have never seen a book like this before.'

'Nor have I,' Mitzi admitted. 'I should read it again too, but only in English.'

'I teach you Russian,' Odette beamed. 'And you teach me English.'

'Sounds good,' Mitzi said, part of her imagining evenings with the mysteries of Cyrillic unfolding in front of her, or explaining the past imperfect tense to Odette – and another part wondering just how long Odette might be considering staying here.

The bell rang at two minutes past seven. Mitzi opened the bay window and waved down to Rob on the front step. 'I'll just be a moment!' she called. All of a sudden, she no longer minded leaving Odette to her own devices with Harry.

'Shh,' she whispered to Odette. 'It's Rob – he doesn't know you're here... I'm sure Harry will be along soon, so have a good time and do be careful.'

'What you tell Rob?' asked Odette.

'Nothing. Don't worry…'

Outside, Rob was leaning on his propped-up bike, gazing up at the window, his face all but hidden by a dark woollen hat and a red scarf wrapped several times around his neck and chin. 'Just feels so funny to be back here,' he said, while Mitzi set about unchaining her own bicycle. 'I've always left everything to Cygnford Estates. Don't worry, I'm not going to nose about to see if you've wrecked the place.'

Mitzi fumbled with her bike key. Was this perhaps one of her sillier ideas – agreeing to a dinner date with her landlord, when she'd repaired a window without telling him and had acquired an unofficial lodger with no identity papers or…

'Where would you like to go?' he was asking her, as if that was all that mattered. As far as he knew, it probably was. 'How about that French place opposite the green?' He made no further remark about the flat, and Mitzi, pushing off from the curb, changed the subject and chattered about her newspaper. She found herself staring at his back as he rode ahead. The sight was soothing, reassuring, rather like the effect of the lime blossom tea. She watched his feet moving round on the pedals, felt her own assume their rhythm and was conscious of passing cars, bare trees and groups of strolling people nearby in the chilly air: a wintery world in which the motion of wheels and the presence of a friend were the only specific sensations.

Odette, lost in Tolstoy, remembered just in time that she, too, had to prepare to go out.

She pulled on the white dress that Mitzi had bought for her, taking care not to move the safety pins, then combed her hair for five minutes, working out the last traces of feathers and the tangles usually induced by the force of her transformation. Her face in the mirror was odd yet familiar, herself yet not herself, and pale as ice compared to Mitzi's healthy colour.

Odette had seen Mitzi brightening her cheeks with blusher and enlarging her eyes with liner pencil and knew that these accessories were in a drawer by the basin. She opened it and looked through the boxes, brushes and colours, wondering where to begin.

Ten minutes later the effect was definite, if not quite what she had expected; at least it was better than her unnatural pallor, the result of more than a hundred and sixty years in which her skin had never been exposed to sunlight. She felt better, more confident; when Harry rang the bell she bounded down the stairs, filled with hope.

'Hey there.' Harry stared, nonplussed, at his companion for the evening.

'Harry, great pleasure to see you!'

He picked up her hand and kissed it. Odette was transformed. Carmine cheeks? Silver eyeshadow? Who would have thought that such a natural, charming, unsophisticated girl would slap on the warpaint like that? But of course, she was like him: an eccentric, a free-thinker, born simply to be herself. She was wearing a white, beaded, low-waisted cocktail dress, twenties-style, with an old red coat that was a couple of sizes too big, slung on top for warmth. He recognised it as one of Mitzi's. Odette hadn't fastened it and her throat rose from the dress's white and gold neckline, long, slender and pale, like a swan's.

He held the taxi door open for her, imagining her without the dress. The idea brought him a surprising stab of guilt as well as the intended excitement. This gorgeous, daffy girl was beautiful, yet unaware of it. She was sexy, yet he'd guess she scarcely knew what the word meant. She was different. She was... innocent. And Harry realised, while the taxi pulled away, that he was having trouble with certain words and their meaning himself.

In the restaurant next to the green where, in summer, Cygnford would play cricket, Mitzi was eating fish, sipping cold French wine and listening to Rob talk about the day he walked out of his City job.

'I'll never forget it. All that agonising, and suddenly it was over and I never had to go there again.'

'You just walked out? After that long?'

'Crazy… After I'd been thinking I hadn't planned enough, I needed more security first, I just couldn't take it any more. I must have gone a little nuts.'

'I don't think it's crazy,' Mitzi said. 'It worked out fine, didn't it? You did your doctorate and you've ended up on a lovely academic sabbatical!'

'I'm a lucky ducky.' He smiled across the glasses at her. 'You were brave yourself, going freelance so young. Don't you mind living and working alone?'

'It's funny,' Mitzi challenged him. 'If a man lives and works alone, everyone thinks he's strong and self-sufficient. If it's a woman, everyone thinks she must be lonely and neurotic.'

'But I never thought that,' he protested.

'I enjoy having some space to myself.' Mitzi sipped her wine, unobtrusively kicking her own ankle. The restaurant had dark wooden round tables, each bearing a small vase of blue and yellow primulas, and prints of Matisse cut-outs adorned the walls. A Carole King recording was swinging along in the background. The whole should have added up to a relaxed place to be with someone whose company you enjoyed, but she felt coiled with stress, thanks to the cumulative effects of John the editor, Odette the swan and the effort of maintaining her composure when she would have preferred to run into a field and scream her lungs out, rather than risk falling head over heels for her own landlord.

Afraid of talking too much, she encouraged Rob to talk instead. He'd obliged, but even so he was now three quarters through his risotto, while Mitzi, who had mainly been listening, could find little appetite; most of her lemon sole was still on her plate. Rob seemed to be considering his next move. Then he leaned forward to stare straight into her eyes.

'I'm confused,' he said. 'It's great, sitting here talking; and I so much like being with you – but you seem rather tense. Is something the matter? I wish you'd tell me.'

Mitzi put down her glass. Rob's gaze was so intent that he reminded her of the ophthalmologist she had once had to visit after walking into a tree in the Dorset garden. A deep light in his eyes tugged at her heart and larynx.

'It's all right. I promise it's nothing to do with you. It's – well, I've got to know a girl here who really confuses me. I'm trying to help her.' She put her right heel over her left foot and pressed. What the heck was she doing and saying? *Do not tell him she's been staying. Do not tell him she has so much as set foot in Richardson Road…*

'Yes?' Rob waited.

She cast about for inspiration. 'It's just that – well, it's all because of this article I've been doing about Eastern Europeans who've been trafficked or abused in Cygnford, and she's from – from somewhere out east – and people keep thinking she'll be like them, but she really isn't. She's so unworldly, I can't think of another word for it, unless it's "innocent". "Naïve" sounds wrong. It's something more profound.'

'You strike me as quite unworldly yourself,' said Rob.

'But in her case, it's sometimes that she literally doesn't know how things work. I've been showing her stuff – but everything, *everything*, is new for her. She's adorable, she's such fun, but I'm spending so much time worrying about her. And I feel guilty, blaming her. I don't know what I can do to help her – other than giving her *War and Peace* to read, because she's never read it before and she's crazy about it.'

'I believe you.'

'Thank you…'

'Not only that. I think you're a wonderful, strong, brave woman and you do yourself down too much. How many people would ever be kind enough to give a stranger that much help, just because she's there?'

Mitzi felt lost for words. She could glimpse a tempting panorama in which they were together and could share life by instinct, because they understood everything in the same way, streamlined and unspoken. She also knew that most such panoramas vanished as quickly as they'd appeared.

'I get the feeling there's a lot I don't have to explain to you,' she said, deciding to meet directness with directness.

'Like what?'

'Things about trying to put traumas behind you. Trying to turn yourself into the best person you can be, and it's maybe easier said than done.'

'And having a solicitous mother a long way off, a younger sibling with – well, directional difficulties – and having lost your father. I didn't tell you earlier. I wanted to see if you'd guess.'

'Tell me?'

'My father died long ago and my mother moved away to live near her sister.'

'And you have a younger brother?'

'Sister. She's four years younger and also not following the path Mum would like. She lives in an ashram in New York State.'

'Doing what?'

'Landscaping the gardens, for nothing, and getting close to God. But she's happy, as your brother is, and we have to leave them to it. You see, we have more in common than you thought. And like I said, it's all fairy tales, all of it, except to the people who want to believe in their own particular kind of magic.'

She saw his hand move, his fingers uncurling from the knife and extending across the table towards her own. Detached, she watched her own hand loosen from the wineglass and allow Rob's to meet it. How peculiar their fingers looked, interlaced. How strange it felt: warm, soft and full of energy.

They walked back to Richardson Road, pushing their bikes, talking little. The temperature had dropped several degrees while they were in the restaurant and Mitzi's nose and ears were beginning to hurt with cold. At the front gate they stood, trying not to catch one another's eyes.

'I'd ask you in for coffee, but it's quite late and I haven't tidied up,' Mitzi gulped.

Rob leaned over his bicycle and kissed her cheek. 'Thanks,' he said, 'and no worries – I should be getting back. There's a frost starting already and the roads will turn icy. Next time, perhaps?'

'Next time.'

Locking her bike, Mitzi watched him cycle away towards the crossroads. It was only a few minutes afterwards, when she looked about the empty flat, that it struck her she hadn't expected to return alone – nor had she wanted to, but for the need to keep Odette out of Rob's way. 'Come on, my girl,' she told herself. 'Tea, book, bed.' And she began to wonder how Odette and Harry were getting along at the ball.

12

Odette sat beside Harry in the taxi, watching the houses rushing by, thrilling with the speed of it. She was pleased to see her cavalier for the evening was wearing the black jacket, trousers and bow tie that reminded her of her father's formal gatherings at home in the old days.

She was remembering another occasion, long ago, when, deep in the forest, her prince had begged her to come to a ball where he would swear fidelity before the entire court. It was summertime, though, and Odette's nightly transformation had become disturbed, triggered as it was by light. During the white midsummer nights of June, she often remained a swan almost until midnight. The full moon would rise alongside the setting sun, but she would see it only from her lakeside haunt. She waited on the shore, wings folded, shivering, watching the fiery malingerer sink, the sky around it turning from aquamarine to gold to lilac, moment by slow moment. She felt in her blood the interference of the Baron's spell.

At last she could stand it no longer. She launched into the water and prepared for take-off. The lake surface lifted and scattered under her wings as she broke free into the air, soaring over the woods towards the hill crowned by her prince's castle.

She wheeled down towards an arched window lit from within by the flickering of a thousand candles. From the great hall a melange of sound – laughter, music, dancing – escaped into the night that was no night. Her prince, arm in arm with a young woman in a black dress, was talking to a bearded man whose face she knew as if it were part of her own body.

She battered the window with her wings and cried out with all her strength, but either the court orchestra drowned the swan's call or the Baron had ensured by enchantment that she would be neither seen nor heard. The prince's whole form was turned towards the girl in black, his expression lost and powerless. Odette knew this woman was her manufactured double; and the prince had fallen under the spell, transfixed, obsessed. Feathers tore from her wings as she drummed harder and a diamond-shaped pane shattered, a splinter gashing her side. The nobility within ignored her from their haven of candlelight and warmth. She retreated into the forest, aching for the human expression of grief in tears she could not shed.

The prince came to find her, human again, too late. When the storm blew up, dawn had broken. Odette the swan rode on the rising waters as he drowned.

In the taxi, Odette pushed her memory away. That was all over; she had been granted another chance. Harry was no prince, but here, in her second new century, that seemed not to matter. The important thing now was apparently that they could talk to one another and that when he touched her wrist it tingled. She looked at his long body, fair hair and lively eyes and felt proud to be beside him, picturing them waltzing together later on. Perhaps they would be invited to lead the polonaise. In her mind she rehearsed steps she had not danced in company since her days as a princess – though she had never been above practising them alone by night, when the spring moon was high and shining. She'd deck her hut with clouds of pink *bagulnik* blossoms and imagine the candles, the orchestra, the dancing partners.

Bardingley Hall, a stately home turned adult education college in the countryside, bore little resemblance to a castle, but when Odette walked beside Harry up a long drive lined with flaming torches, surrounded by glamorously clad couples, her heart filled with satisfaction. She recognised the house's architecture as sixteenth-century, familiar from drawn illustrations her governess had shown her in her father's leather-bound books. Around the little complex of buildings there stretched deep expanses of parkland and, beyond those, the fields.

Waiting in a queue to leave their coats in a cloakroom, Odette was taken aback when she heard the music that was intended for dancing. She could see no musicians anywhere, just some huge black boxes through which thudded a sound unlike any musical instrument she knew, and much louder, too. Instead of the spacious, civilised aspect of the balls that her father used to hold, this one was packing people into the foyers in such numbers that there was little room to move.

'Where orchestra?' She had to shout to make herself heard.

'There'll be live bands later,' he yelled back. 'Too noisy?'

'We find place more quiet?'

'Let's get a drink. You like cocktails, don't you?'

Harry held her arm and steered her through the crowds, past a tall Christmas tree, along wood-panelled corridors where multicoloured streamers and tinsel dangled from the ceiling and great bouquets of lilies and irises stood in china urns in the corners. Soon they came to a room where several musicians – each of whom oddly wore a red hat trimmed with white fur and a pom-pom – were plucking and blowing on guitar, double bass and clarinet. To one side, an antique card table topped with green baize bore a silver punch bowl full of something aromatic. At the end of the room, an empty bay window seat seemed to beckon them. Harry filled two glasses to the brim and they settled there on plush cushions to listen to the music.

'You like this?' Harry asked.

'I like very much, but what is it?'

'Jazz.'

'How?'

'J-a-z-z.'

'Tell me about it?'

Harry found himself describing the origins of jazz among African-Americans; Dixieland, the Mississippi, the roaring twenties after which Odette's dress was modelled. She listened, riveted, apparently incredulous. Happy to have such an attentive audience, he kept talking, and the more he talked, the more she soaked in the information, like some exotic variety of deep-sea sponge.

After another glass of punch she wanted to dance, and a 1940s-style big band was starting up in the main hall. Harry glanced around at other women, who wore long, sequinned gowns, short black shift dresses, or designer numbers with odd tufty skirts and overexposed shoulders.

'You're the best-looking girl here and the best dressed too,' he told Odette.

'Dress is gift from Mitzi.' She beamed at him, holding up her arms in ballroom posture.

'Where did you learn to dance?' He was intrigued by the old-fashioned but expert way she moved.

'I have lessons as child. I learn waltz, mazurka, polka, polonaise. I love polonaise. We dance polonaise tonight, perhaps?'

'Er, we'll see... You haven't danced like this before, then?'

'This?' Odette laughed, he thought a trifle contemptuously. 'This is too easy. Nobody does steps, they only jump here and there. No skill.'

'Well, some of us have two left feet.' Harry experimented, holding up one arm; Odette twirled beneath it, back and forth. 'You're a gorgeous dancer,' he said, both hands settling on her slender waist.

The first number finished and the band struck up 'A String of Pearls'. Odette wanted to keep on dancing; and so she did, Harry discovered, at the end of every number. His brow was turning sweaty. He longed for some ventilation, despite it being December. You'd have thought this girl hadn't had a dance for decades. Obliging her, he was out of puff and much in need of a drink by the time the Cygnford Swing Orchestra finally dismantled itself. He thought some of the players, whom he knew from drama productions, were watching him and laughing. Odette, tapping her feet as she hummed the last tune, looked at him and laughed too.

'Some girls might've flaked out after all that. You're fit as a fiddle, aren't you?' he said.

'Yes, oh yes! We dance more?'

'Later. Let's see what else is on. Another drink now, *da*?'

'Hal.' Chris's sand-coloured hair and red-framed glasses appeared; he was fighting his way upstream against the torrent of departing dancers. 'Enjoying yourself?'

'Chris, say hello to Odette. Odette, this is Chris, my housemate. He's a musician and he's playing the piano later. He fixed us the ticket – for which thanks upon more thanks, mate!'

'So you're the amazing Odette.' Chris looked approvingly down through his spectacles.

She smiled back. Why did they need a ticket to go to a ball? They used to be by invitation.

'I've heard a lot about you,' Chris was saying.

'Things good?' Odette beamed.

'Er, just a bit. You're Russian? *Ochin priatna!*'

Odette, delighted, echoed the greeting.

'When are you on?' Harry asked.

'Over breakfast. So we've got the whole night to not get pissed, just great... And I'm doing my solo at midnight – Gershwin, Porter and stuff, plus some bits and pieces of my own.'

'We'll be there. Where've they put you?'

'Quiet, boring room where no one goes. See ya later.' Chris vanished among the milling guests in the corridor. Just then, Harry saw Odette's expression take on an even more puzzled look and as he was about to turn to see why, his vision was blotted out.

'Guess who!'

A pair of female hands had clamped over his eyes.

'Mademoiselle Olivia! I didn't know you were coming!'

'Oh, Daddy bought tickets for us all.'

The red-haired actress–student Caroline, who was to play Olivia in *Twelfth Night*, was dressed in a brief, sea-green, silky number that showed more flesh than it hid. Now she was interposing these bared limbs in all their sparkle-lotioned glory between him and Odette. Harry liked redheads. His gaze snapped onto her cleavage, familiar after a few occasions in the past year when they'd had a few drinks together and got a little too close.

'Thought I told you Olivia wasn't quite the part, darling.' He rubbed her bare back and smacked a large kiss on her cheek. 'For Olivia you need to be a little, well... less, um, is more. This is my girlfriend, Odette – she's Russian. Odette, say hi to Caroline.'

'How lovely to meet you.' Caroline forced the corners of her mouth upwards. 'Darling, I must fly, I've left Roddy to the tender mercies of some unspeakable harridan...' And she whirled away as fast as she'd appeared.

Odette glared after her. Harry put an arm around her and felt her tense, presumably with anger. 'What's up?'

'Who is she?'

'We act together. She's in *Twelfth Night*. Performing Arts student, third year... Odette, what *is* it? D'you seriously mean you don't like me talking to other girls at all if I'm out with you?'

'But – is not *talking*. Is—' She searched for words and resorted to gesturing the stroking of an unclad back, and kissing.

'The English word is *flirting*, darling. Caroline's just my pal. Don't you ever – I guess you don't…'

'You love her?'

'*Love* her? I love everyone.'

'What you mean?'

'Odette, it's midnight. Let's go and hear Chris.'

Odette followed him along the corridor back towards the jazz room, where Chris was hauling a protective cover off a baby grand piano. A few couples in small groups were sitting around the low tables, many drinking coffee in tiny white cups. By some miracle, the window seat was still free. Chris waved to them as they settled down there; then he fidgeted with the piano stool's height before striking up some quiet Gershwin. Odette shifted around to make herself comfortable against the cushions. Her movements reminded Harry irrationally of a bird settling into its nest. Leaning back, he studied her face, her body language – and a new stillness. Her eyes were fixed on Chris.

'Piano,' she breathed.

'Didn't you see it earlier?'

'No. Oh, Harry, I not see piano for so long. And this music, so beautiful!'

Chris played through several songs with piano improvisations to match; Odette shifted forward to the edge of the seat, humming along whenever she picked up the tune. When he'd finished Gershwin's 'Someone To Watch Over Me' she could contain herself no longer. She jumped to her feet and bounded across to him.

'Chris, please, please, may I play? I play piano not for many years, I not even see piano so long.'

Chris peered up at her in astonishment. 'Well – I don't know – the thing is, I'm under contract to play, and if you haven't played for years—'

'But I play very, very well, truly. I cannot bear to see piano and not touch! I love so much.'

'If it really means that much to you, then,' Chris faltered. 'But just for a minute, OK?'

'Thank you, *thank you*!' She slipped round the piano and sat down on the stool. Chris, standing beside her, and Harry, from the window, watched in surprise as she adjusted the seat, then brushed one fingertip along the top of the keys.

'I love so much,' she whispered. She found a chord; soon, hesitantly, a soft Chopin prelude, the one in E minor, began to emerge from the piano's innards, its slow, pulsing chords shifting note by note under a long, languid melody. Her playing was so heartfelt that Harry caught his breath and felt an uncomfortable pricking sensation behind his eyes. As the piece finished, he saw that tears were clinging to Odette's cheeks as well.

'That's incredible.' Chris stared, bemused, at Odette's transfigured face. 'Harry didn't tell me you were a pianist. Did you study somewhere?'

'I have some lessons from Hungarian pianist who visit my country,' Odette told him, her eyes damp and dreamy. 'He very beautiful man, very famous musician, his name Franz Liszt. I have only a few lessons – I travel all the way to Kiev to meet him and study – but I think he teach me everything.'

'*Franz Liszt*? That's a good one! Seriously, Odette, who did you study with?'

'With Monsieur Liszt,' Odette reiterated.

'Hey, Odette,' said Chris, 'Liszt died in 1880-something. Come on, be sensible.'

'*Is – true*! Why you not listen to me? I travel for *three weeks* from my home to Kiev to meet this man!' Several heads turned among the couples around them.

'Listen – Odette – you have a beautiful speaking voice. Do you sing too?' Chris switched the subject, fast.

'Sing? But *yes*, I sing, I love to sing. At my father's parties, I always sang for the guests...' Relief spread across her face. She had forgotten her need for discretion.

'Know any Gershwin?'

'Any who?'

'The music I was playing before, d'you know any of that?'

'I never hear before, but I like very much.'

'Can you sing at sight?' When she nodded, Chris tipped her off the piano stool and thrust some pages of music into her hand. 'Let's try this one. "The Man I Love." One of Gershwin's best – you'll like it. Ladies and gentlemen! Please welcome my special guest star – all the way from Russia, let's have a big hand for the lovely *Odette!*'

Polite applause dotted through the room. Odette, finding herself the centre of attention, stood professionally beside the piano, her back straight, the music held in one extended hand. Harry watched, astonished, his arms folded. Odette could have been singing operatic arias, so precise and pure was her soprano, so assured its vibrato. At first she hesitated over the 'blue' notes in the melody, but as soon as she grasped the tune and realised what the words were about, her heart took over. Harry felt almost sorry for her as she sang, with immense longing and an impossible Russian accent, about what the man she loved would be like and when she might meet him.

'I won't ask who you studied with.' Chris winked at her as they finished, perfectly together. 'But you're a great singer. You were really listening. Your style's a bit classical, but if we worked together I could help you get the feel of jazz, help you relax into it. What do you say?'

'Oh, I love,' sighed Odette. And Harry wondered why her eyes were so sad.

'Cool. I'll get your number from Harry and we can meet up and go through some stuff. You'll need to project more if you're going to do gigs with the band, but that'll come.'

Odette stroked the piano's wood as if it were a living animal. Harry, crossing the room to her, thought he could still see a tear lingering on one cheek.

'Darrlink.' He slipped an arm round her waist. 'You want to dance more? There's a big jive band next. I reckon you'll like them.'

They walked along the corridor to the hall, which under its vaulted wooden ceiling was teeming with laughing, inebriated couples; a 1950s session was about to begin. The lead singer was wearing a sequinned white suit.

Harry let out a snort. 'Oh God. It's an Elvis tribute band.'

'He look funny with hair that way,' Odette remarked.

'You never heard of Elvis?'

'Who?'

'Heck. Franz Liszt indeed... I can almost believe it. Don't take this wrong, but you're at least a hundred years behind the times!'

'That is cruel. I cannot help that things are strange to me. Is hurtful to laugh...'

'OK, OK, I'm sorry. Let's dance, that'll cheer you up. Now—' as the band launched themselves into 'Rock Around The Clock', 'just follow me and try and do what everyone else is doing.'

A few minutes later, Odette was breathless, dizzy and confused.

'This is taking enough skill for you?' Harry teased her.

'Is too fast! It is not elegant to dance so fast.'

'Elegant? Forget "elegant". Just have fun!'

There was a roll on the drum and 'Elvis' took centre stage.

'Now then, everybody, we've got one of your fave slow numbers comin' right up,' he announced, a Yorkshire accent lurking under the phoney Deep South twang. 'But there's a-somethin' I'd like y'all to do for me, all you lovin' couples. We're gonna pretend we're real well joined together.'

A collective hoot went up from the dance floor. Elvis waved an accusing finger.

'Uh-uh, not that way. I want y'all to pretend that your partner is *part of you*. Part of you, yourself. Get it? Y'all cuddle up and yer know that lovely guy or gal ain't nothin' but some other part of yourself. An' I think you'll find your dancin' won' never be the same again. Ready?'

'Fucking hell,' said Harry. 'A Yorkshire *mystic* dressed up as Elvis Presley?'

'Oh, but I like.' Odette held up her arms. 'I think it is beautiful idea. We try, *da*?'

'Gotta play the game...'

The lights lowered and the band began a slow waltz in which the singer told his girl that he couldn't help falling in love with her. Harry put both arms around Odette and held her close; their feet moved in unison, and as they concentrated, their steps seemed to blend into one movement that sank into the melody and merged with the rhythm that was holding all the dancers together in one vast, hypnotic ritual. A peculiar, unfamiliar and unfathomable ache seemed to rise in his heart.

'So what part of you am I?' he whispered to the Russian girl, warm and fragile against him. Her hair smelled of fresh shampoo and some strange, exotic flower he didn't know.

'You are part of me that I miss.' Odette swayed from foot to foot. 'Part has not been there, but I seek it, now I find it. You are man I seek, man who really living and in world. You understand? I not speak very well.'

'You're amazing.' He pulled her closer, stricken. Now to feel her cool, bare arm beneath his fingers was almost too much. Could he take her home? Might she let him pull that crazy dress off her? He lowered his face and pressed her cheek with his own, feeling her catch her breath.

'Mmm,' she muttered into his shoulder. 'Feels like wonderful thing in drink.'

Harry held on to her, puzzled. He was aware that not only was he not sure how to read her signals, but she didn't know how to read his, which were considerably clearer.

'What part of you I am?' She was moving her feet in perfect time with the music. He forced his own into harmony with hers, lost in her warmth.

'You know… there's a part of me I want to reach and hold, but it always gets away. Every time I think I have it, it's gone. I sometimes feel this on stage, but… It's something better than me, so much better than me. And that's you. Do you understand?'

'But I am here!'

'And now I've caught you and I can keep you. Can't I? Come on, give me a kiss.'

He bent and pressed his mouth against hers. She wobbled, as he'd hoped. To his shock, he was starting to tremble too.

'Harry,' she whispered as Yorkshire Elvis warbled about joining hands and lives. 'You will love me forever, perhaps?'

'Of course… I told you, I love everyone.'

'But me?'

'I'm *crazy* about you!' Harry wrapped her hand in his. 'How about this: I won't let go of you again for the rest of the night. Promise. Do you promise too?'

'I promise!' Odette seemed to be laughing against his chest. 'Harry, we keep playing this game? Everyone is stopping, but I think is wonderful.'

'We'll keep going as long as you like.'

They danced on; later, they drank coffee and sat together in the bar without talking. As the last couple in the ball still playing the peculiar game of being part of each other, there was oddly little to say. It was an adventure of subtler feeling than either of them had imagined. Hours drifted. The crowds thinned as couples wilted and departed. In tiredness, the lights seemed brighter, the music louder. They wandered about the ball, hand in hand, watching, reeling, floating, imagining themselves mystically united. At last they found their way back to the window seat in the jazz room, where Harry enveloped Odette in his jacket, sweaty though it was, and began to kiss her again, feeling her lips soft and open and pleading for more. He didn't care if the whole ball saw them snogging. He'd scarcely glanced away from her. He'd scarcely looked at the clocks. He no longer believed in time.

A gong sounded and one of Harry's acting colleagues from the Shakespeare Players, dressed as a town crier, began to process from room to room, calling: 'My lords, ladies and gentlemen, breakfast is served.'

Odette extricated herself from his embrace. 'Morning?' she whispered.

'It'll be getting light soon.'

Her eyes turned to the great window behind them, patchwork sheets of small glass panes, beyond which the sky was already turning from black to grey.

'Come. We go, quickly.'

'Go? Where? Why?'

'Outside. The garden.'

'What? It's freezing out there! Come home with me.'

'*Outside.*' She pulled at his hand.

'Don't you want your coat? It's cold…' But she had already gone.

At the door to the gardens she rushed ahead, a lithe figure, white-clad, ghostlike in the approaching dawn. Befuddled, following her, chilled by the icy air on his neck after the overheated ball, Harry stumbled over a molehill in the grass. A thrumming filled his temples and inner ears and his calf muscles were seizing up as if he'd been running all night long. Her black hair blowing about in chilly gusts of wind, Odette turned on the frosty lawn and waited for him.

'Harry, game now finished. I must go!'

He caught her and reached for her hands. 'Game over? Really? No, please, just come home with me…'

'I see you soon,' she said, through her laughter. As she reached up to kiss him, a cloud blew away from the horizon and revealed, pale and clear, the first sunlight of a new winter's day. She turned towards it and it rebounded off her pale skin, her radiant features, her shining smile. Harry felt a current of air seize his limbs, making his hair stand on end. The light on the girl's face grew brighter and more intense, ultraviolet, until he couldn't look at her. The ground was rushing up sideways to meet him.

'*Odette!*'

Where she had stood a fraction of a second before, there was nothing. All he could see was a small footprint in the ice-dusted grass next to where he'd fallen. Beside it, he noticed the mark of a large, webbed foot of a waterbird. Harry stared upwards and saw, wheeling higher and higher into the morning sky, a white swan with a black and yellow bill. Its trumpeting call reached his ears, as if in farewell. They must have disturbed its rest on the Bardingley lake. He hauled himself upright, gazing after it as it made one last circle and vanished beyond the treetops.

'Odette?' he called. And then he saw her white cocktail dress, lying in a small heap a few feet away, together with her discarded shoes. Slowly, he bent to lift them out of the frost.

13

Mitzi was loading up her cafetière, barely awake, when she heard the soft tapping of feathers against the living room window. Soon Odette swung through the space and landed in her box, folding back the great arcs of her wings. Fresh morning sunlight streamed onto her. She turned herself round a couple of times, clattered her beak softly at Mitzi, then tucked her head beneath her feathers. In seconds she was asleep. This swan had had a heavy night out on the tiles. Mitzi wondered how long it would take Harry to arrive, and what frame of mind he'd be in when he did.

Sitting at her computer, drinking cup after cup of black coffee, her head was too full of Rob's amiable face and his warm hand around hers. He was natural, genuine, his own person. Mitzi considered, almost perplexed, the ambitious corporate men she used to date. If she were to see Pete for the first time now, would she give him a second glance? Something had shifted in her responses – perhaps something that involved the rustle of snowy plumage and the spreading of a wide wingspan.

A long ring at the doorbell – Harry – at noon. Early for a man who had been up all night dancing with a Russian princess, especially if that man was Mitzi's brother. He climbed the stairs two at a time, but beneath his cap indigo shadows were sketching themselves under his eyes. Over one arm he carried Mitzi's old red coat and in his other hand a Sainsbury's bag containing something white and beaded plus a pair of small white shoes.

'Is there coffee?' he grunted.

Mitzi fetched him some, then waited for him to start talking.

'Fuck,' said Harry, pulling off his cap and slamming it onto the table. 'Fucking *hell*! People just don't – they don't just… Mits, I'll tell you what happened as it happened, or as I think it did. So, we go to the fucking ball. We dance all fucking night. It's fucking incredible. And then, just as they're saying it's breakfast time, she runs out into the garden, I run after her and something happens to me – I dunno, maybe I blacked out. And no, I wasn't drunk. Not very. And when I come round, or whatever, she's fucking gone. There's only this. Her dress. Mits, she vanished *into thin air without her dress*. And her *shoes*. And I looked for her for *two hours* and then got her coat, or rather yours, from the cloakroom and left a message with the porter in case she turned up. Isn't she here? Is she outside, walking around without anything on?'

Before Mitzi could answer, Harry noticed, for the first time, the swan sleeping in the box. Mitzi had had no time to move her.

'What the hell is that?'

'My pet kangaroo.'

'Mitzi, what the *fuck* is going on?' He threw the carrier bag into a corner and grabbed the mug of coffee. 'First you let in some illegal sofa-surfing refugee you've taken your usual pity upon, and you pretend she's your lodger, and I bet your contract doesn't allow it, and then she disappears without her dress. Now you're keeping a swan. Are you mad, or am I?'

Mitzi tried to stay cool. 'Hal, can you just accept it if I say don't worry…'

At that moment, the swan peered out from under her wing. Her eye caught Harry's. Youth and swan stared at one another.

'That bird is freaking me out,' said Harry. 'What's it doing here?'

'It's the one that came through my window.'

'I thought you said—'

'It was hurt and I wanted to look after it. And, um, it keeps coming back.'

'Of course you did. You want to look after everyone and everything. I reckon it's a child substitute. Does that also account for Mademoiselle Dressless? Big sis getting broody?'

'I am not broody,' declared Mitzi through clenched teeth.

'Seriously, though, Mits, shouldn't we go to the police? I mean, I'm worried. Anything could have happened to Odette. And I've got auditions in London tomorrow and the next day – I *have* to go, I can't just drop everything and stay here hunting for her.'

'It's OK, Hal,' Mitzi said. 'Don't let's panic. If she hasn't shown up by this evening, then perhaps we could call the police, but I can promise you they wouldn't even think of doing anything about it before then. Let's give her a chance. There's probably a very simple explanation.'

Harry poured his coffee down the sink and walked out.

'Simple explanation means what?' Odette asked, through showers of laughter. She was wearing one of the t-shirts and the jeans that Mitzi had bought her, twirling a white feather between her fingers.

'It means,' said Mitzi, who had a splitting headache, 'just what it sounds like.'

'Is funny, no? I think is so funny.'

'I'm surprised he wasn't *more* worried. I mean, how weird is it when someone vanishes and leaves her clothes behind?'

'He cannot believe. He has not taken in that this is real. Simple explanation!'

Mitzi glanced at the phone. She'd been itching to pick it up and call Rob. She'd forcibly restrained herself.

'Mitzi! I telephone Harry? I never use telephone before.'

Mitzi guided the delighted girl through every step, hoping only that her brother might see fit to speak to her.

'It rings.' Odette pressed the phone to one ear, her eyes brilliant with delight.

'When someone answers, you say hello.'

'Hello? Hello, Harry! Oh – not Harry? Chris?'

'Tell him who you are,' Mitzi hissed. 'Say "It's Odette".'

The girl's smile widened. 'A wonderful night! Thank you for invitation. Yes, I love to sing, was very nice… Yes, I love to sing again.'

This was the first Mitzi had heard of it.

'I tell you later.' Odette said to her. She was listening intently. 'Please say to Harry I – I *telephone*!' And she dissolved into a gale of laughter, handing the phone back. 'Mitzi, I go to ball, I find piano! Harry has wonderful friend, Chris, who play piano and he lets me play and asks me to sing. I love so to sing, I love so to play music. Is so long… but I can still play – this I never dreamed! Soon I sing again.'

Mitzi gazed in some wonder at the light that seemed to suffuse her friend's face when she talked about music. Imagine having that gift – then being forced to turn into a bird for half of every day…

Meanwhile, she had a phone message for Odette from another source: 'Uma called from the shop and she says if you're free tonight you could go in for a few hours and help her. She'll pay you cash.'

Odette shook herself, bird-like, and clasped her hands together. 'I help Uma? I have work to help pay for things?'

'You're sure you want to try?'

'But of course.' Odette seemed never to have considered any alternative.

If this was the sole chance to help her guest achieve some measure of independence, Mitzi decided to give her the benefit of the doubt.

Uma welcomed the worried journalist and the eager, bright-eyed Russian girl with a big smile.

'We'll try it for a couple of hours, shall we?' she said to Odette. 'Then we'll see. Now, this is the till. You've used one before – no? I expect the system is rather different in Russia.'

Odette nodded, jumping slightly as the cash register rattled at her, and concentrating hard while Uma explained that they could take cash, debit cards, contactless payment and some credit cards, but not others because the charges were too high. Mitzi hovered, anxious, wondering how much Odette could really understand. 'Everything will be under control,' Uma assured her, 'and I'll send her home at closing time, OK?'

'Call me, I'll come and fetch her.' Mitzi couldn't decide which was worse: to leave, or to stay and watch.

At home, the time dragged. This must be how a parent feels when a child begins her first job, she reflected. Though she couldn't help hoping that, should she ever have a daughter who reached the age of nineteen and tried to find work, that daughter would know something about how shops functioned. Mitzi made some soothing herbal tea – ordinary compared to Rob's. The TV news flung images at her of migrants in dinghies, braving the wintery sea.

At ten thirty, her phone buzzed. 'Er, Mitzi,' came Uma's guarded tone, 'Please would you come over?'

Her usual Odette-related chill crossing her neck, Mitzi scrambled to her feet and into her coat.

At the store, the bell jangled as she pushed open the door. Everything looked much the same. The shelves were still standing, the freezer motor was humming and Uma was standing behind the till. Odette, though, was nowhere to be seen. Something moving on the floor in the breeze caught her eye: glancing down, she saw it was a ten-pound note. She picked it up and carried it to Uma, her heart sinking into the lino underfoot. 'What happened? Where is she?'

'In the back, having a nice cup of tea, Russian style.' Uma was smiling, her teeth set just a little too deliberately.

'I'm sorry,' Mitzi floundered. 'What happened…?'

'It's fine. Absolutely fine.' Presumably Uma wanted to keep her regular customer satisfied. 'I am sorry, I would like to help you and she is so nice, she's a sweet girl. But you see, she doesn't understand… well, *anything*. It has not been an easy evening.'

Mitzi's eye strayed to the till, which sported a new notice: OUT OF ORDER. A faint whiff of tomato sauce lingered in the air and now she noticed the light was catching on traces of red staining and a splinter of glass on the lino. There were no customers.

'I never knew things were *so* different in Russia.' Uma's bright expression did not change. 'You know, one of my customers who's a taxi driver was telling me the other day that he gave a ride to a Russian visitor who was completely *lashed* and said she'd never even been in a car…'

'Odette?' called Mitzi. 'Are you OK?'

There was a scuffling sound from the office and Odette emerged, head bowed. Her new t-shirt was splattered with red and the skin around her eyes had turned pink and puffy.

'Oh, God,' said Mitzi. 'Is that blood?'

'Tomato sauce,' Uma mouthed at her.

'I am sorry, Mitzi. I try, really I try. But I not know how this works—' Odette indicated the till – 'and I press wrong thing, so it break, and I not know which coin means what, so I give someone wrong coin, they shout at me and is not kind because I am new, I do not know things, so I shout *too* and this is wrong, I think – though it feel right to me – because people are angry and somebody throw something and it break and this is not good for Uma, who is so kind. It is all strange, strange, strange…'

Mitzi gave the tearful Odette a handkerchief and offered to pay Uma for the broken jar of tomato sauce. Uma refused, but said quietly, 'I think she must find something else to do, don't you?'

'Yes,' said Mitzi. 'Yes, of course.'

'Oh, Mitzi,' snuffled Odette, 'I want so much to find piano again.'

'I'm afraid,' Uma added, hesitating, 'that… then the police arrived.'

Mitzi turned cold. 'What happened?'

'It wasn't Odette who was responsible – they just gave the guy who threw the jar a warning and made him pay for it. But he blamed her for being foreign and clueless and then they started asking questions. They wanted to see ID, and of course she hasn't brought any…'

'Brought any? She hasn't *got* any.'

'She'd better get some, then,' said Uma. 'Because now my neck's on the line too.'

In the flat, Odette picked up her white dress, which was lying in its bag in the corner where Harry had dumped it. She stroked the beading with her fingertips.

'Is so difficult, seeing him,' she told Mitzi, who was making tea, 'and I can say nothing. And he not understand.'

'Call him again.' Mitzi dialled the number for Odette.

'I like telephone,' Odette beamed – and Mitzi, despite herself, realised she could, and would, probably forgive her anything and everything. 'Harry? It's Odette…'

Mitzi retreated to her computer to look up the Russian Embassy. She clicked on 'Russian Passport' – to find a sea of Cyrillic, and Cyrillic only, spreading over the screen. Across the room she could hear her brother letting out a distant diatribe, but Odette held the phone as if more interested in the phenomenon of listening than in what he was saying. Tussling with copying, pasting and Google

Translate, reading with one eye, listening with one ear, she managed to discover that Odette would need not only an international passport, but an 'internal' one as well – and that of course, to collect your passport, an identity document, you'd need... identity documents.

'Thank you for bringing my dress,' Odette was saying politely, in her best English. 'I know is strange. I know Franz Liszt sounds strange. I will explain – but please, for now, accept that it is strange, yes?'

Mitzi, despairing at the realisation Odette must have let slip her coaching sessions with Liszt, heard protests and swear words.

'But we meet very soon, *da*?' Odette maintained her steady voice. 'Sunday? Where is audition? For which role?... Yes, then Sunday.' She glanced at Mitzi and shrugged her shoulders.

Then Odette's eyes lit up. 'Chris! Is Odette! May I use piano? Please? I long so much for piano... no, day is bad. May I use in evening? Tomorrow?... Oh Chris, you are wonderful friend! Wonderful!! And I sing for you too? *Wonderful!*'

Mitzi looked on, bemused. Could it be that she had on her hands not just an illegal immigrant in search of work and legitimacy, not only a fairy tale character from some other dimension, but a full-blown and very frustrated musical artist? Watching Odette's face transforming from uncertainty and fear to joy and inspiration, she knew nothing she could say would change who Odette was or what she could do. If she were a musician, fine. As long as she did not tell too many people who her teacher had been.

14

The night was long; Odette needed to calm down, so excited was she at the idea of playing Chris's piano. After scant sleep, Mitzi felt drained – terrified by the labyrinthine processes of the Russian website, and all too aware that even if Odette had had a birth certificate, it would have carried the date 1833. If only she could talk to Rob and tell him everything, from the beginning – which under the circumstances was the very last thing she should do.

Once a phone interview with a local author was out of the way, she threw on a jacket and marched out into the morning, where a fierce north wind was making the prospect of walking a little more bearable than cycling. Book-buying would be her best cure for feeling supernaturally overwrought.

Plodding over Solstice Common, her head bowed against the onslaught, she began to feel dizzy. Was she going mad? Swans did not turn into girls, nor girls into swans, let alone spellbound girls who could be nineteen forever. Perhaps everything that had happened to her in the past week – from Odette to Rob himself – was a hallucination, induced by an otherwise undetectable tumour?

The gusting winds had scattered twigs across the grass and the tarmac paths. She picked one up and ran her fingers along the bark, felt the gumminess around where the bud should have been forming to produce an embryonic leaf. She could not be dreaming this wild winter – or the returning spring that must, somehow, follow it. The seasons would dance and the planets spin, whether or not Odette was a swan, whether or not she, Mitzi, was sane. As for her own future – there would have to be an alternative. Sometimes she was tempted by a vision of herself, cool and communicative outside the European parliament, declaring to the cameras, 'This is Mitzi Fairweather for BBC News, Brussels.' But Mitzi Fairweather, with her current attitude, delivering half-baked copy about front-page swan material, was unlikely to make it to the BBC even in Salford. Beside the universe turning and turning and beside the problem of Odette, and the chance that the police could turn up on her front step at any moment, it didn't seem to matter.

She made her way along Marian Lane, towards the town centre. There, beyond the marketplace, she made for the glinting windows of Cygnford's best bookshop, which was advertising its Christmas wares – cookery and craft books, plus a pile of volumes about how to create a cosy Nordic atmosphere in your home. Inside, she could find some escape in the smell of new paper and the sheen of the covers among dark shelves and quietness. She passed fiction and biography and headed towards a small section marked Folklore.

Moving round a bookcase, she glimpsed a familiar back ahead of her – a man wearing brown corduroy trousers and a familiar chunky sweater in earth tones. She stepped aside so that the Mindfulness shelves obscured her. It would be easiest to sneak out unseen. She had so wanted to talk to him – and there he was, as if on unspoken demand.

She forced herself into performance mode, sailed up and coughed.

'Mitzi! What are you doing here?'

'I could ask you the same thing.' At least if Rob were in a bookshop at half past eleven in the morning, talking to her, he had to be real.

'So, you haunt bookshops too? You're meant to be ferreting out stories and producing copious words per hour. I'm just meant to be bumming around.'

'Do you know, I nearly phoned you today and then didn't?'

'And I tried to phone you, but you were permanently engaged. How is everything?'

'Oh, fine. Never better.' Mitzi looked at the floor.

'How about a coffee, now that we've bumped into each other?'

Mitzi and Rob wandered down Duke's Parade and turned into the passage towards the health food café. Mitzi was beginning to feel that the white walls and paving stones were spinning around her. 'Come on, Mitzi,' Rob said. 'What's up?'

'This is going to sound idiotic.' She couldn't look him in the eye; instead, she busied herself with choosing a table well away from the other customers. 'But I'm so glad you're not a figment of my imagination.'

Rob's eyes sparkled.

'Please don't laugh. The trouble is, if you're not, that means a lot of other stuff isn't either.'

'Hang on. One thing at a time.' Rob, sitting down opposite, pressed her hand. The sensation, so warm and welcome, sent ocean waves up her arm. 'I'll get the coffee.' He went to the counter and she, alone for a moment, gathered up what shreds remained of any courage she'd once had. Perhaps she could explain the matter of lack of passport without the entire story?

When he was back with two steaming mugs, he took a breath and turned that now familiar hypnotising gaze towards her: 'Is it this strange Russian girl again?'

Mitzi sipped. This was the best coffee she had ever tasted. 'Kind of. The thing is, you're not going to believe it.'

'Yes, I am.'

'No matter how crazy it sounds? Because it is very, very crazy.' She bit her lip. Do not get into trouble here. Do not make things worse.

'I'll believe you. I promise,' said Rob.

Mitzi swallowed more coffee, then began to talk; now she could not stop herself. As the story progressed – carefully edited to avoid mentions of a broken window and someone else staying in the flat with her – she watched his expression evolve from amusement through dismay to speechlessness.

'You see? Who's going to believe that?' she finished. She felt swamped with relief at having unburdened herself. 'This girl really does turn into a swan at dawn every day. I promise I'm not making it up.'

'That is *so* bizarre that I shouldn't think anybody could make it up.'

'I swear it's true. And I don't know what to do, because now Uma is in trouble with the police, and Odette's having this thing with Harry and he doesn't know – and I just have no idea how to handle it.'

'Jeepers,' said Rob. 'I imagine you need sensible words, Mitzi, but I'm not sure I've got any. I'm doing my best to believe it, honestly, but...'

'I know,' Mitzi sighed.

'Look.' Rob seemed to be trying to turn practical. 'Let's get to the bottom of it. First of all, how come you're so involved?'

'I guess I didn't have any choice.'

'You always have a choice, though. There's a basic right to refuse to get involved with other people's problems, especially ones that put you out of your depth. She's evidently some kind of illegal migrant, whatever the truth about the swan business, and that's very dangerous. There can be gangs involved, international mafia, all sorts – not that it's my field, but we both see the news, we both know the score. What made you want to help her?'

'Well – she's not like anyone else. She's so *alive* that it's inspiring. She's so thrilled to be human that she does everything with three times anyone else's intensity. But she hasn't got the first clue about how we live or how people behave. It's like… an excess of innocence. And yet she's *right*. In some funny, nonsensical way, she's right and I'm wrong, Harry's wrong, we're all wrong. I can't explain it.'

'That's assuming there has to be a right and a wrong.'

'I don't know. I don't know anything any more. This whole thing is *actually impossible*! And yet, I promise, it *is* happening, and it's happening to me.'

'You didn't have to take her on, yet you did.'

Mitzi considered her response. 'She needed help. So I helped her.'

'Where's she staying? When she's human?'

'With a friend of mine,' Mitzi said, hoping her ears would not turn red with the lie.

Rob was silent for a minute, inscrutable, thinking. 'Impossible or not, if you want me to believe you, then I will,' he said finally. 'So here's what I think. First, the police. Two options: either you need to buy her some fake documents – yes, really – or you must lie low until the trouble passes. Chances are the police will be too overstretched to pursue it anyway, especially around Christmas. But also, you have to decide what to tell Harry. She's expecting something from him that, frankly, is going to scare him shitless.'

'How can she have given so much power to my dopey brother? He'll never believe it.'

'Exactly. Maybe it's best to keep it as quiet as humanly possible, for as long as you can…'

Mitzi nodded, in some surprise. 'I thought you'd say I should tell him everything,' she admitted.

'Er, maybe not yet.' He smiled. She pondered in silence, finishing the coffee, letting its warmth and strength revive her.

Outside, she tucked her arm around Rob's elbow. She could breathe again and the sight of the delicate stonework of Duke's Chapel and the cobbles underfoot struck chords of pleasure in her. She didn't feel alone. She felt safe, secure.

'How would you like, this Saturday,' Rob said, 'to come up to Branswell with me for the festival procession? It's going to be fun.'

'I'd love to,' Mitzi said without hesitation.

Next to his waiting bike, he bent to kiss her cheek. Mitzi tipped back her head and let him kiss her lips instead.

'I can go there alone.' Odette was determined.

'You'll get lost.'

'I will not. I can feel piano there, I will find my way to it. You tell me, I go.'

'OK, if you're sure. It's not far…' Odette had never been out alone in Cygnford in human form before. Mitzi pulled a blank page from her sketchpad and drew her a rough map. Odette glimpsed the dark pencil drawings on the pages flipping by and itched to look at them, but Mitzi, as usual, refused to show off her work.

The chilly air besieged Odette's ears as she walked. Not that it was bad compared to her Siberian forest, where she spent cold nights huddling under the bearskin in her log hut, her hands raw and blistered. At worst, she would have had to beg food from the nearest tavern – ten miles away – or from the Buryat Mongols, who might welcome her with warm fires and an occasional hot meal, but would never understand why she could not stay with them. Now she imagined she heard again the sound of Monsieur Liszt's voice encouraging her as she tackled her favourite of his latest pieces, 'Un Sospiro'. Over an accompaniment of rippling arpeggios, this 'sigh' was a melody that soared like a swan, its notes played alternately by each hand, crossing and uncrossing wave by wave.

'This is a good trick,' she twinkled at Liszt. A Russian and a Hungarian, they spoke French together.

'Perhaps.' The great pianist was nonchalant, gazing down into her face with heavy-lidded, sea-green eyes. He was six foot tall and thirty-six years old. The teenaged princess's innards turned cartwheels when she saw the light in those irises.

The harmonies chorused under her hands and her spirit flew with them, like a wild bird. When she had mastered a piece like this, playing it was like speaking with her body – the piano was just a tool to amplify all the poetry and vibrant life that filled her fourteen-year-old form.

She finished and turned to look for his approval, twisting her hands together. 'Odette, my little princess,' he mused, his smile always enigmatic. 'There is poetry in the core of your being. You must let it out – don't hide such beauty from the world. But you must not stop working. Yes, you are exquisitely beautiful. Yes, you can play your instrument.' He grasped her palms between his own, his huge green eyes almost too beautiful for her to look at. 'But don't think for a moment that this means you are entitled to anything. You have to work and you must not become swollen-headed. As beauty fades with age, so talent fades for lack of hard work. Don't let me down.' He stroked her cheek, and Odette closed her eyes, trying to preserve the sensation, like strawberries in sugar. 'Don't let me down,' Liszt repeated.

Wandering along the dark road, past little grey houses and traffic that threw spray at her legs from the puddle-ridden tarmac, Odette thought with longing of Liszt's voice, echoing around the music room in the Kiev mansion that belonged to her father's business contact; here Liszt had agreed to visit them. She had forgotten the brush of his index finger against her cheek. Yet now it came back to her, like a loyal homing pigeon. Liszt had had a great heart, generous enough to feed the entire world with his music.

'My dear maestro!' cried Odette aloud in Russian, stretching out her arms. A passing cyclist turned to stare at her and nearly collided with the kerb.

'Odette! Great to see you. Come on in.' Chris was in the doorway, nervous yet very pleased behind his red-framed glasses. She wondered why anyone would wear spectacles that colour. His face was everything she thought of as 'English': a thin-lipped mouth, small blue eyes, raw pink skin, fair hair and the reserved affability and awkwardness that went with it all. He reminded her of the English academics who had visited the castle to consult her father's famous library, the finest in the Irkutsk region.

He ushered her inside, away from the cold. 'Something to drink?'

'Oh no, Chris, please, I would like just to play piano. Is all right?'

'Are you sure? You must have been missing it. All right, this way.' He led her into a narrow corridor lined with thin brown carpet, then into the living room at the front of the house, where an upright piano stood in a corner against the wall. Odette went to it without looking left or right.

'Just yell if you need anything.' He must have sensed she wanted to be left alone. 'And when you'd like to start singing, yell again. I'll be upstairs, OK?'

'Thank you. Is strange, Chris, you know I never see piano this shape before.'

'Don't worry.' Chris winked at her. 'It works the same way as the others.'

Odette pulled up the chair by the piano, then grabbed two cushions from the sofa and sat on them. Now her hands were at a comfortable angle. She lifted them in readiness; then lowered them.

She had managed a slow Chopin prelude at the ball – she could hardly have played scales and exercises in public – but she knew that if now she tried to play the more demanding Liszt pieces straight away, she'd be so shocked by her diminished technique that she might never try again. She had to be sensible and start with the warm-up exercises she used to practise without fail. She began to play scales, instructing herself not to go too fast. She played B major, the scale always taught, she'd been told, by Monsieur Chopin as the easiest because it lay most naturally under the hands. Her fingers were working better than she had expected; she could play without breaking the flow. Encouraged, she speeded up.

Chris, marking an undergraduate's harmony exercises at his desk upstairs, supposed that he should not have been so astonished to hear classic Russian scales emanating from the living room. He'd imagined that Odette's impulsive personality would have had her playing straight away through Chopin and Liszt – of course – with wrong notes all over the place. Not so. He was impressed.

Odette worked her way through each key, remembering note combinations that were etched on her consciousness long ago. Movements of the wrist were coming back to her despite the intervening years, the right way to use the weight of the shoulder and lower back to produce a rich sound, working the sustaining pedal – not that this one worked very well, but what did that matter? All right. She took a deep breath, folded her hands in her lap, heard in her head the opening of 'Un Sospiro' – and sought out the first notes.

Chris dropped his pencil. Next he took off his glasses and sat with head in hands. Then he surrendered and slumped flat onto his bed. The sound of his beat-up little piano was unrecognisable – it was singing as it had never sung before. If Odette could play Liszt like that, he was never going to joke about anything she said, ever again.

She finished 'Un Sospiro' and he was about to clump downstairs to tell her how marvellous it was when she started on one of the Petrarch Sonnets, a piece he'd tussled with for two years. In her hands it sounded effortless – more than that, it sounded fun.

She carried on. She was playing, of all things, some of the *Transcendental Études*, 'Harmonies du Soir', then 'Chasse-neige' – admittedly with more wrong notes, but he had never before met anyone who *could* play 'Chasse-neige'. Finally the Liebestraum No.3. '*O lieb', o lieb', so lang du lieben kannst, so lang du lieben magst…*' it sang.

Oh love, oh love, love as long as you can, love as long as you may. Then: silence.

Chris tiptoed downstairs and peered in. She was sitting with arms folded on the keyboard, her head down, sobbing.

'Odette,' he soothed, 'don't cry. That sounded incredible. I've never heard anything like it. *Please* don't cry.'

Odette lifted her face, tears streaming from eyes that shone like a hundred candles.

'I cry for joy,' she said.

Chris hesitated, then sidled across and patted her shoulder. He was not good at expressing himself in anything but music, especially where girls were concerned, but there seemed little alternative. She turned and flung her arms round him. He had never seen anyone so consumed by emotion before.

'All right, all right.' He untwined her. 'It's OK. Do you want to try a bit of singing once you've mopped up? Here, have a tissue and I'll get you a glass of water.'

'I love to sing!' Odette patted the tears from her face and took a drink with gratitude when he brought it from the kitchen.

'Good. Shove over, then.' Chris took the chair at the piano and rummaged through the pile of music on top of the instrument. 'Cole Porter. How about it?'

'Cole Porter?' Odette sounded blank.

'You'll like him. Try this one – it's called "Night and Day". What key do you prefer?'

Odette tested her voice's range by humming up and down, looking at Chris for approval, much as she had looked at Monsieur Liszt all those years ago.

'Right. D flat.' Chris passed her the music. Odette began to sight-sing, discovering the chromatic side-steps and not just getting them right first time, but so obviously loving every moment that the song took on a new life even for Chris, who had played it more times than he cared to remember.

They read through all the songs in the book. Then they started on Gershwin and Irving Berlin. Hours flew by; it was only when distant chapel bells began to strike that they noticed it was midnight.

'Shit,' said Chris. 'We'll have to stop or the neighbours will go nuts. If a mouse ran through the room, they'd hear it. Cup of tea?'

Odette followed him into the kitchen, or what passed for one beneath precarious piles of crockery waiting to be washed and sundry heaps of discarded torn envelopes and adverts waiting for the recycling collection. Her arms, hands and throat were aching deliciously. 'Harry is not here?' she asked.

Chris cast her a shrewd look. 'He went to London – he had an audition for a show in the West End today and I think there's another one tomorrow, so he'll have stayed over somewhere.'

'Ah.' She did not ask anything else, and Chris, stirring sugar into black tea for her, said nothing. He hadn't told Harry that Odette was coming round – he'd hoped to have her to himself. Besides, Harry had been in too much of a tizz, gathering scripts, suitable clothing and a hat, to take much notice of anything beyond the task in hand. Clearly, Chris reflected, the girl was too far gone on Harry to look at an oaf like him, even though he understood the music that ran in her veins like blood, while Harry would scarcely notice it. Why did girls always make an unerring beeline for the biggest bastards in town?

Later, he walked Odette back to Mitzi's, pushing his bike. Most people he knew kept their heads down, especially in the cold, but Odette's was held high, her eyes were as bright as ever and she sang softly to herself as they went.

'Chris,' she said, by Mitzi's gate, 'you know why I love to play music and to sing? It is like flying. I am human being – yet there I can fly. You understand?'

Chris longed to stroke the soft hair that trailed over her shoulders. 'Yes,' he said. 'I understand perfectly.'

15

Mitzi, cycling through the first snowflakes of the winter, arrived at the *Cygnford Daily*'s front desk at 11am. She had sent John Wilkins her interview with Rob and the article about the local writer whose first Young Adult novel – a fairy tale updated for the present day – had just come out. John called her in by return email.

Upstairs, she found him perching on his threadbare black swivel chair at his computer, typing with his two forefingers.

'How are things?' Mitzi asked politely, pulling in a chair beside him.

The phone rang; John answered, uttered 'Yes,' followed by 'No,' then thumped down the receiver. 'Fairy tales... So, Mitzi. You'll have to be appointed folklore editor, I suppose. For a local newspaper, that's unusual. Did you spend time studying the occult at your nice college?'

Town and gown had never seen eye to eye and John liked to lend his weight to the former's war on the latter. Mitzi – though she had studied Beowulf, Shakespeare and Samuel Beckett, without a *Blue Fairy Book* in sight – had little recourse to self-defence.

'I don't know what you're up to, Mitzi. You were such a stalwart. Now you're on your little fairy tale ego trip, you miss the point of the big stories and you can't even get writers to talk about writing? What's going on?'

Mitzi had been up half the night with the ecstatic Odette, listening to her description of piano lessons with Franz Liszt and the songs she was going to sing in the pub with Chris on Saturday. The transformation between Odette at sea in modern life and Odette riding the waves of her music was almost as great as that between her swan self and her human incarnation. Now she had a calling, a vocation that compelled her and spurred her on – something Mitzi had never experienced to half that degree.

'I thought you were quite an ambitious lady,' said John.

'I am.'

'In which case, you should have been the first person I thought of to cover the big story that came in today.'

'Big story?' Mitzi's heart lurched.

'This.' John thumped the space bar on his computer keyboard. The screen brightened in front of Mitzi, showing a drafted headline: '*Dismembered corpse found in River Cygn.*'

'A bizarre case. Dismembered, mutilated, unidentifiable. May have been there for a week or longer. Found, in classic TV murder mystery style, by someone walking a dog. Nobody has any idea who it is – doesn't fit the profile of anyone reported missing, or any of the homeless ones around the town. And who do I call? I call the crime reporter, Mitzi. Not someone with her head in a cloud of fairy tales.'

'I see,' Mitzi said, miserable on several counts: not just that he was rubbing her nose in her unsuitability to report on a murder, but scared out of her wits that the body might belong to the homeless girl who had been trying to go home to Ripon.

'What is it you want, Mitzi? Where do you see yourself in ten years' time?'

'I don't know. Maybe a national. Maybe broadcasting.'

'My dear, let's face facts. You aren't going to get to the *Times* or the BBC unless you sharpen your act up a bit.'

'I'm not your dear – and nobody would ever make any progress if they never did anything but report on birds falling off roofs!' Mitzi declared – then remembered she couldn't take her words back.

'Oh yes?' said John.

Five years of frustration welled up in Mitzi's mind and then in her throat. 'There are thousands of refugees drowning in the Mediterranean, there's modern slavery right here in East Anglia, and our top story was a bird falling off a roof? How was that even news? And this murder story – of course you could have given it to me to report, but you chose someone else, and then you tell me I have to sharpen up my act. How can I do that if I never have the opportunity?'

John's glare made her imagine him as a frustrated army colonel without a war to fight. 'I guess we're not good enough for you any more.'

'I never said that. But while we're about it, I noticed the fees have been falling over a couple of years and nobody's ever told me why. You're paying me £120 instead of £200 for a piece of the same length.'

'It varies... it depends on the exclusivity of the story, and our ability to syndicate it,' John said. She wondered if he was improvising. 'Let's see.' He clicked on the email and scanned through Mitzi's copy, uttering a brief 'Hmm' now and then. 'Madeleine Philips wasn't very talkative, was she?'

Mitzi fought her own temper. 'You put my Romanian food-packers story on page ten. That should have been "front page stuff".'

John sat back in his chair, surveying her with his most enigmatic gaze – one she could fathom no better after five years than she had on the first day she came in to meet him. 'Young women who tell me how to run my paper have never been exactly welcome here,' he said. 'If I were you, I'd think very seriously about my options. As you're freelance, it might be a good thing for you to try lancing a little more freely. Try writing for someone you like, for instance. Think about it.'

Mitzi turned tail and strode out of the door. She knew she would never set foot through it again.

John might have enough chips on his shoulder to feed the whole of Cygnford University for the academic year, but he also had the power to remove her most regular source of income, diminished though it might be. Mitzi fought a rising inner tide of fury, fright and despair. What had gone wrong? Earlier she'd had no intention of arguing with him. A sea-monster seemed to have woken inside her and crashed up through the surf.

Outside a café in the next street, she paused, tempted by a whiff of chocolate. She tied up her bike and went in. Armed with a double espresso and a brownie, she sat at a table in the window, trying to close her ears to the soundtrack of American Christmas carols and watching the Cygnford street go about its business as if nothing had changed.

Licking chocolate crumbs from her teeth, she tried to calm herself and winnow out her different strands of response. First of all, she noted, she was madly happy at the idea of never having to speak to John again. Everything she'd said to him was true, which was why he didn't like it. Even he would never get beyond his current rut if he could put nothing more exciting in his headlines than 'Bird Falls Off Chapel Roof'. If the paper was struggling to stay afloat – as she often read elsewhere that it was – then should the editor not have to shoulder some of the blame? She was free to find better work. She could even pluck up courage to email *The Guardian* about her cheerful Romanians and the sleeping bags placed cheek by jowl on the floor of that village house. And yet...

Somehow she was feeling less enthusiastic about trying to get ahead in journalism. If it meant, as it seemed to, years of scribbling too fast about events that signified nothing, while stories of real interest were relegated behind clickbait and fear-mongering, while her pay was cut and cut again, and she could do nothing to stop that happening, and while quality coverage was being shredded in front of her eyes... There must be something else that would suit her better.

She couldn't sing, and God – plus the neighbours – knew how badly she'd played the piano as a child. But Odette was alight with love when she talked about music; once they'd set her free from her spell, assuming they could, she'd never turn back. Mitzi imagined her at the Proms, raising the roof. *She* wanted to switch on as powerfully as that. She wanted something that fed her with that same deluge of delight. She could string together a decent sentence. She had a degree. She could draw. That wasn't enough. Like Odette – like her own brother, on stage playing Shakespeare – she wanted to fly.

The trouble was that nothing she had ever done for herself alone had brought her such a degree of satisfaction. What was the greatest thrill she had found in anything recently? She took out her phone and began to make notes on it. Showing Odette Tolstoy on a tablet, and seeing the wonder in her face. Giving cash to a girl on the street to help her get back to Yorkshire. She thought of Harry, playing Romeo – of all things – last year at the Amateur Dramatic Club, and Juliet's line: 'My bounty is as boundless as the sea, my love as deep; the more I give to thee, the more I have, for both are endless.'

And there was that blasted conundrum again, threatening to drown her dream. She could volunteer for the Refugee Council, or go back to college and train as a teacher, but she still had to pay her rent. And what if she returned to Richardson Road to find the police waiting for her, asking questions about Odette? What in heaven's name would she do if Rob were to turn round, despite everything, and turf her out?

Twenty minutes later, at home – mercifully free of police – Mitzi dumped her coat on the sofa and plunged straight for her filing cabinet and a folder marked *FLAT*. There was her contract, with Rob's florid signature at the bottom beside her own. She ran one finger along the clauses on its three thin blue pages. '4.4 No subletting is permitted. The landlord's permission must be sought before admitting any other person(s) to stay overnight in the property.' And further down, '4.6 No pets or other animals permitted.'

Odette avoided the stretch of river where she had met the hostile swans. She flew for a long time, relishing the wind under her wings, sometimes letting the currents lift her, at other moments turning against them, using them to her advantage, testing her manipulation skills. Today, in the cold air with its whiff of incipient snow, she was in control and could do as she pleased. She followed the winding river until, a little way out of town, she noticed a widening of the channel and drifted down to land.

To one side lay an expanse of fields, brown, ochre and soft green; to the other, a towpath along a twiggy hedgerow still sporting its last scarlet berries. Small gaggles of walkers were braving the cold in laced-up boots, fleecy hats and gloves. In spring the dark tangle of overhanging hawthorn trees would brighten with a galaxy of star-shaped blossoms. The clouds reflected in silver ripples on the water and some ducks passed by, glancing nervously at the swan, but ignoring her when she ignored them. A pair of mute swans stared with more suspicion and Odette knew to give them a wide berth. She was a stranger to them and could be no different, just because her beak was a different shape and colour. A male on his own would avoid her at best, or more likely hiss to chase her away. Over the centuries she had met more avian suitors than human ones, at least when they first spotted her, but swans trusted their instincts more than human beings usually did. Male Bewick's swans sensed something wrong in her being, something peculiar in her behaviour, and if they didn't think better of involvement within a moment, they certainly would when she vanished at nightfall. They had no idea that the woman crouching on the threshold of her makeshift hut, watching them, held the soul they were seeking on the water. Swans were careful; they mated for life.

A flat wooden boat was drifting towards her. At one end, a young man stood on a platform, wielding a pole, dropping it so that its end pushed against the riverbed and propelled the boat forward. Reclining in the seats were two girls and another boy, wrapped in coats, hats and blankets, but sipping champagne from wineglasses; their breath rose in misty clouds while their laughter glittered through the hawthorn branches. Odette recognised them as two couples who had danced with her and Harry at the ball. She honked and flapped her wings.

'Look!' cried one of the girls. 'What a wonderful swan!' Her companions made exclamations of delight and the other girl produced a mobile telephone like Mitzi's, pointed it at her and pressed a button. 'Sorry, swannikins, we didn't bring any bread,' she called.

Swannikins? Bread? Odette watched the punt float on down the river, then turned her back and prepared for take-off.

She wanted to look at the town she was trying to make her home. High over the rooftops, she thought its scale mean and pokey. She was used to a different kind of beauty: endless, rolling, empty land; vast lakes and forests, realms where few people ventured even nowadays. This city was different. The outskirts were broad, new and lacking in any aesthetic dimension, with building sites and red bricks and cars on roads too choked to let them move. The centre was more concentrated, its streets haphazard curlicues when seen from above, yet everything was better ordered around the old market square and the spacious buildings near the river.

She let herself sink lower and idly watched two women pushing infants in buggies along the riverside path, talking hard and laughing; a man in blotched green and grey military trousers, alone on a bench despite the cold, drinking from a tall open can and staring into space; an elderly woman, alone too, making unsteady progress down the street with a three-legged frame in front of her and a patient terrier padding beside her on a lead. Students stood in groups, joking together over their bicycles. In several doorways lay piles of torn cardboard boxes and padded sleeping bags; in one, she spotted the long shape of a slumbering figure, ignoring and ignored by the people wandering past. A thread of music from a shop reached her: a child's voice singing about peace on earth, good will to men.

Someone was pointing up at her. Odette was enjoying herself so much that she looped the loop for them; she was just close enough to hear responding yells of surprise and joy. Beyond simple survival, she had not had much else to practise for the last century and a half. How was it possible that from where she was now, master of space that was barred to all these humans, the city could look so enticing? Yet when she was in the world, trying to be one of them, she was shouted at and censured just because she was a stranger and didn't know how things worked.

None of those people could fly, though they all wanted to. They'd envy her power. Still, they'd hate having to eat pondweed.

Tired but happy from her night of music and her day of flight, she turned homewards, her well-exercised wings aching. She followed the river until she could glimpse, tiny as a blade of grass, the chestnut tree and the bright new windowpane in Mitzi's flat. She felt uneasy for a second – but the owl was nowhere to be seen. Her new friends would help her; and as long as he didn't return, she was safe.

She swooped towards the window and tapped her wingtips on the glass. Mitzi was inside, tidying the kitchen; at the sight of the hovering swan, her eyes lit up and she stepped across to let her in. Odette noticed that her movements had changed: her steps were heavier and faster, her expression firm.

'Hello, Odette!' Mitzi pushed up the sash and Odette arrived in a whoosh of feathers by her box. Landing without water was getting easier, slowly but surely. Mitzi patted her on the head and filled up her bowl with water; Odette bent her long neck to drink. Mitzi was making coffee, as usual. Her eyes were too bright and her mouth was set. Odette lifted her head and watched her. She had never seen her so angry.

She waddled across the room to where Mitzi was settling on the sofa and rested her beak on her hand.

'Odette,' said Mitzi. 'Dear Odette. What's going on? You wouldn't believe it. I don't believe it either. First you come crashing in and now I've lost more than half my work, and there's a phone message from a terribly nice-sounding policeman who got our number from Uma. Any moment I'm going to wake up and find it's all a nightmare.'

Nightmare? Odette raised her head in protest and rustled her wings; she wanted to say that for her it was no nightmare, but a beautiful dream come true. All that emerged was a honk. She pumped her neck up and down.

'OK,' said Mitzi. 'You're having a good time. So am I, really. I wouldn't have missed this last week for the world. Do you know it's only a week since we went out for that Mexican meal, and you got plastered on chicken-tails?'

Odette as a swan was not blessed with the ability to laugh, so she squawked.

'So now I'm finished with the bloody newspaper – which everyone says is bound to shut down in any case. I just wish I had something like you have, something to love as much as you love playing the piano and flying. And there's you. And – oh God – there's Rob. I hate losing my temper, you know. I only lose it about once every four years. It's terrible, I start shaking all over and I run a fever.'

The swan rustled and pumped to show she understood. Mitzi held out a hand to her and Odette reached forwards and leaned her beak on Mitzi's lap, a human cry in her swan's throat. Her arms were fighting under her wings to embrace Mitzi, but her bones were the wrong shape. She clattered her bill in frustration, wishing that she could be saved, fast: if only she were human now, she could comfort her friend, make her see how little need there was to be angry, tell her how wrong anyone would be to cause her pain.

How much there was that human beings could do that she could not – little things, everyday things that existed as a matter of course in towns, cities and societies, yet went far beyond the basic survival tactics that were all she used at home in her forest. Resentment fluttered under her breast feathers that something so simple had been removed from her by force, and could only be restored if she found the right man to make the necessary vow – even though the growing friendship between her and Mitzi would have nothing to do with him or anybody else.

She had to bide her time. Soon she would see Harry again. Her hopes concentrated on him with all their might.

16

On Saturday morning Mitzi cycled out of town towards Rob's house in the woods, her hood raised against a dark pewter sky and the drizzle and bluster that appeared determined to stop her. She wouldn't be stopped. Pedalling along the country road, the wind slicing at her ears, she had to concentrate on every metre of progress, which had the side effect of removing her from the goings-on of her new life, at least for a while.

A note was pinned to Rob's cottage door: *STUDIO*. An arrow pointed towards the converted garage. She could hear a quiet, pulsing hum emanating from it, mingling with the soft tap of raindrops on the roof.

Rob was inside, in a spattered grey overall, his hands clamped around a lump of clay. The hum came from the potter's wheel, spinning hypnotically as his foot worked the pedal. A two-bar electric heater to one side warmed the studio, and a wet, earthy smell filled the air; Mitzi breathed in, liking it. Under Rob's fingers the clay became a smooth ball, then widened, and began to lengthen upwards. As he varied his touch, pressing into the hollow with his thumb or pinching and pulling the sides of the emerging pot, the shape became clearer. The vase, if vase it would be, began from a narrow base, then seemed to open up towards the light.

'That's amazing,' Mitzi exclaimed. Rob started; the pot on the wheel went instantly askew.

He scooped the collapsed object aside into a pile of discarded clay. 'Mitzi! I didn't hear you come in. How long have you been there?'

'I forgot to say hello, I was so busy watching you. I thought you'd be running around getting ready for this afternoon?'

'It's all done. The procession is all down to kids from the school, the classroom teachers have taken over sheepdog duties and I need only make a speech and take the credit. And we have to hope the rain stops.'

'Show me how this works?' Mitzi approached the wheel.

'Put this on first.' Rob fetched a spare overall from a hook behind the door. Mitzi pulled it over her head. 'Good, come and sit here. Now, take a lump, about this size, and the first thing you need to do is to centre it.'

At the wheel, Mitzi, awkward on the wooden seat, felt the pedal's resistance under her foot and the clamminess of the clay on her hands. The lump would not centre. The more she pulled and pushed at it, the more reluctant it was to cooperate. 'You made it look so easy.'

'You'll get it. Take your time.' He leaned over and clasped his hands over hers, warm above the cool clay. Mitzi's foot on the pedal accelerated and the wheel began to spin merrily.

'Slower,' suggested Rob. 'Then, like this... add a little water...'

Mitzi let Rob guide her hands and the clay until the lump sat plumb in the centre of the wheel, spinning like the world itself.

'Now make a hollow. Both thumbs, again not too hard.'

She pressed down, anxious, but the clay stayed on centre and, as she gained courage to mould it as Rob had, it began to move with her and shape into walls, albeit thick ones. She started to pull upwards; there in her hands she saw the embryo of a pot. Fired with enthusiasm, she pulled harder. The clay toppled.

'Never mind, you were doing fine. The thing is not to try too hard. Just let it happen.'

'Mm-hm.' Mitzi stood up. 'I'm not too good at that.'

'You did really well. Let's have a coffee and you can try again later.'

Mitzi, mystified by the whole process, scraped the clay from her hands over the sink. 'I don't know how you do it. It feels impossible.'

'Just lots of practice. Did you like it?'

'Yes... it's soothing.' The smell of the watered clay, its smooth, thick texture, the turning and turning of the wheel, had drawn her into a pleasant whirlpool.

'A lot of my Wednesday class say it's therapeutic. That's one thing that made me start in the first place.'

Mitzi couldn't imagine Rob needing anything therapeutic. If someone spent half his life creating wonderful shapes with part of the earth—

'How's Odette?' Rob asked. Mitzi's balance, like her pot, swung into ellipse.

While he made the coffee, she explained the latest developments, standing in the kitchen with her back to the plant-crammed windowsill. 'It's so good to have someone to talk to about it,' she added. 'I feel better just being here.'

'Good.' Rob smiled as much to himself as to her. 'I feel better having you here too. I got you some real coffee, by the way.' On the sink stood a large packet marked 'Extra dark roast'.

They drove up to Branswell in Rob's Mini. From a distance, parking on the street, the place seemed quiet enough; but in the drive three small electric trucks with tarpaulin-topped floats behind them were ready and waiting, and inside, the hall and entrance were teeming with dressed-up children and frantic adults.

'There you are!' A frazzled-looking dark-haired woman dived towards Rob. Three fairy tale characters were pulling at her coat from different sides. 'Rob, next time you have a "good idea", just remind me what this one was like…'

'I don't know what you were thinking,' grumbled a nearby grandmother, watching two small charges flinging themselves around in Spiderman costumes. 'It's Christmas. How is this the time for pagan myths and legends? How can you have Sleeping Beauty and a bunch of ancient Egyptian gods on show, at *Christmas*? What's happened to the nativity play?'

'It's the same thing, basically,' Rob said. 'If you think about it, "Sleeping Beauty" is a resurrection story.'

The grandmother froze in front of him, apparently lost for words.

'It's the perfect time,' Mitzi chipped in, to comfort her. '*Everything*'s magical at Christmas. And look, the sun's coming out.'

'Mr Winter! Mr Winter!' Small versions of Red Riding Hood and the Wolf rushed up to Rob, grabbing a hand each. 'Our mum made you some cake!'

'Hannah! Olly! Say hello to my friend, Mitzi.' Rob smiled as they pulled him along. Two huge pairs of ten-year-old eyes fixed on her. She smiled back, aware of school corridor smells around her of poster paint, paper and gym shoes, navigating her way between an Egyptian god with a blue face and golden cloak, a Native American chieftain wearing a substantial headdress of feathers, and a grumpy fairy in a tutu wielding a tinsel-tipped wand.

'Who are you being?' Mitzi asked the chieftain.

'I'm Hiawatha, *of course*,' he growled – as if astounded that she might not know.

For each of the three floats, the children had prepared a tableau showing a different story. Tarpaulins were poised above them in case of rain and on each float, near the children, sat an unobtrusive camping heater – but now the last clouds were drifting away, leaving a light blue sky to accompany the remaining scant hours of daylight. As 2pm approached, yells of 'Jack, come here!' and 'Grace, for the last time, stop that!' issued while the teachers tried to round up everybody to begin the procession.

The first float was unmistakeable: a long-haired little girl stretched out on a couch improvised from planks and a bedspread, with a reluctant boy kneeling beside her, while the still-scowling fairy held her wand over them, poised between potted plants representing the enchanted forest. Next came a scene that would show a group of ancient Egyptian animal-headed gods grouped around Ra, the Sun God – when Anubis and Osiris stopped fighting and got aboard, that is; as yet, only Bast, the cat goddess, was there, wearing a pair of furry ears on a headband and grumbling to her father that she wanted to go and play football. On the third truck, Hiawatha and his Minnehaha posed at the centre beside a sizeable dreamcatcher and assorted wild animals and birds; an eagle was protesting as his mother tried to clip on his beak. The sound of recorders and clarinets squealed through the mayhem as the school band assembled, alongside the rest of the children in their costumes.

'I wonder what Odette would make of it,' Mitzi reflected.

'I wonder.' Rob put a hand softly on her shoulder.

'The thing is, she'd adore it. She'd think it was all just wonderful. The kids, the stories, all these different places and traditions and everyone pulling together…'

Mitzi could see everything Odette would have loved. The excitement on the children's faces, the small drummer proud in his band uniform, the glee with which one Egyptian goddess was trailing a chiffon wrap in the air, the parents' delight when their charges were at last in place...

The church clock struck two. 'Everybody ready!' yelled the head teacher.

The convoy began to trundle towards the gates, pulled by the quiet electric vans. The marching band struck up 'Strawberry Fair' at a ponderous tempo, and the teachers, parents and Mitzi and Rob gathered to bring up the rear as the parade made its way down the road and into the town. Along the high street, people who had come out to watch soon darted over to join in. Linking arms with Rob, Mitzi moved in step with the crowd around them. To her own surprise, she couldn't stop smiling. Until recently, perhaps until Odette, she'd have run a mile rather than attend such a thing as a primary school festival.

Around forty minutes later the procession came to a halt by the stone arches beneath Branswell's Victorian town hall. Everyone filed inside; there, in the main reception room, a wooden platform and a microphone presided over tall windows and a tinsel-laden Christmas tree.

'Where's your speech?' Mitzi asked Rob.

'In here.' Rob tapped his left temple. He made his way forward through the crowd while the harried headmistress took charge.

'Thank you, everybody,' she was saying into the microphone, 'for making today such a triumph for St Thomas's School. This festival has brought out the best in everyone. Our classrooms have been buzzing with excitement ever since Rob Winter, our lovely pottery teacher who joined us just this year, first suggested a festival of international fairy tales, myths and legends. We therefore have Rob to thank for this happy day. So here he is to tell us about it.'

Rob bounded up to the microphone and gave the head teacher a kiss.

'Thank you.' He shifted from foot to foot. 'I'll be brief, as they say – yes, I really will,' he added as the crowd tittered. 'We grow up with fairy stories and they stay with us throughout our lives. I don't believe, though, that they're just escapism. I believe that fairy tales, folklore and the traditional mythology of any and every world religion enrich us, help us learn life lessons and allow us to see the magic in our world, all around us, every day. Some people would even say that everything in this world is based on legends and myths – essentially, magical stories.

'Our world is at a crossroads now – which means we can choose to make it the best it can be in the future. Last century was extreme, often horrific in its violence. Many of us dread that what lies ahead of us could be as bad, or worse. With such potential dangers to face, many of us easily mislay our sense of magic. We've lost our innocence. We're cynical, shocked, disillusioned. If we want to recapture our love for living, could it be that we need to recapture the innocence of childhood? It's difficult, but it's there for the taking, if only we know where to look…

'Anyway, I shall now shut up, but first I suggest simply that everyone looks for the wonderful tea that's waiting for us! Thank you.'

Mitzi clapped with the crowd until her hands tingled. As the parents and teachers streamed to the kitchen to fetch the sandwiches, cakes and urns, she navigated her way to the front to catch Rob. When he saw her, his eyes lit up and he held out both arms.

Standing in the thronging, echoing hall under garlands of Christmas paper chains, munching fruit cake that almost burned with brandy, Mitzi had little chance to talk to Rob; everyone was congratulating him on the afternoon's success. The headmistress, though, quickly identified Mitzi as the journalist whose preview had attracted an unexpected influx of visitors from Cygnford, and soon she too was being mobbed, questioned and thanked, while children bounded up to show her their costumes and offer her more cake and pieces of tinsel from the floats.

By the time the crowd began to disperse, it was pitch dark and well past six thirty. Rob caught Mitzi's eye across the room; she wandered over to him. Her feet were aching pleasantly and a piece of green tinsel was draped round her neck. Rob wore a paper rose from Sleeping Beauty's garden in his buttonhole. He extracted it and tucked it behind Mitzi's ear.

'I loved Hiawatha's feathers,' she remarked, strolling back towards the school where the Mini was parked.

'I liked the Sleeping Beauty's forest. Very exclusive, all that ficus...'

Talking about the afternoon kept them busy all the way back to Rob's cottage. There, Mitzi stood in the doorway, stretching her arms and taking deep lungfuls of the clear evening air.

'I think we've earned some wine,' Rob suggested. 'It's getting chilly now, too. I'll light the fire.'

'Why don't I open some wine while you get the fire going?'

Mitzi busied herself with the corkscrew and a bottle of purple Bordeaux; the debacle with John was long forgotten while she watched Rob's big-boned frame and craftsman's hands in the lamplight, building up logs, chippings and newspaper in the grate. One scrunched-up page was the front of the *Cygnford Daily*.

'So.' He sat back on his heels while the flame gradually engulfed the paper's logo and the story of the mysterious, unidentified corpse. 'The million-dollar question: what have you said to Harry about Odette?'

Mitzi described her brother the morning after the ball. 'It's impossible. He'll never believe it, not even when he's seen her change with his own eyes – though he only said he blacked out and she vanished without her dress. He can't even talk about it as if it's real. And now she's going off to sing in a pub.'

'You didn't want to go?'

'Somehow I get the feeling she's finding herself and she wants me out of the way. That's why it's so good she's found a place in the student hostel,' she added, rather too fast, remembering that Rob must not find out his 'study' was occupied.

'Relax, then. Cheers!'

They drank their wine, watching the flames rise and flicker in the grate. Rob sat on the floor and after a while Mitzi joined him, her back against the armchair. The room was silent but for the crackling of fresh fire; the aroma of red wine mingled with the woodsmoke as the warmth percolated through the cottage. Rob had lit several small lamps, which cast brief pools of brightness into his pitch-dark cavern of books and files. They both smiled at the silence after the rowdy afternoon. Mitzi stared into the blackening logs, the sputtering and dancing of the flames almost as hypnotic as the spinning potter's wheel.

'Will you teach me how to make pots properly?' she asked.

'Anytime.'

'Is that how you manage to be so calm and so kind of – well, you're so self-sufficient…'

'I grow my own spinach and milk the goat every morning,' he teased her.

'You know what I mean, though. You seem centred; you know who you are, on your own terms. All these weird things are going on around me, but there you are with this clear-sightedness and your pots.'

'I used to be the biggest worryguts in the world, and the pottery certainly helped.'

'Why were you such a worryguts?' Mitzi gave him a grin.

Rob smiled, more into his glass than at her. 'The City job was what so many people were thinking and doing – it was expected of you. But I couldn't stand it…'

He'd worked twelve- to fourteen-hour days, he said; saved money, met an equally ambitious woman, married her, grew more and more unhappy. Everything came to a head when, within six months, his wife left him, his father died and he considered swallowing a heap of sleeping pills. 'But I didn't – and that was the turnaround.'

She marvelled at his progress. He'd decided to change his life, rather than throw it away; to stop chasing after things he thought he should want rather than things he really did want. Then came the doctorate, the research post, the job and now the sabbatical.

'That's amazing,' she said. Along with the sympathy, though, went uncertainty; his inner self was settled, mature after the turmoil he'd described – but supposing he began to see how insecure she felt? Considering her bereavement and the shock of breaking up with Pete, what if he decided she was damaged goods and not for him? How could she protect herself against being shattered like her own window all over again?

Rob refilled her glass and lifted his own to clink. 'To Odette!'

'To Odette!' Mitzi tried to close the lid over her simmering anxieties. 'Rob, if you had Odette on your hands, what would you do?'

'Mitzi,' he said, 'I *have* got Odette on my hands. Because you have.'

Mitzi's solar plexus seemed to crumble: what extraordinary kindness, something she had always dreamed of and never found, and here he was, beside her, almost too good to be believed, simply waiting for her to give him the go-ahead to embrace her. What had she ever done to deserve such goodness, such caring? She turned to him, put down her glass, and reached out a hand.

17

'Um,' said Chris. 'Are you really going in that?'

Odette gazed up at him with pleading eyes. Her white dress's beaded fringes jangled a little as she moved. 'Is no good?'

'Well—' Chris felt his ears grow hot. He wasn't used to expressing views on women's clothing. Harry should have been there to help, but wasn't yet back from London. 'The thing is,' he improvised, 'you look sensational… it's just that we're, like, in the pub. It's like a normal evening in the pub, except you're singing – you see? Let's go back in and you can find something else. Is Mitzi here?'

'Mitzi went with Rob to festival.' Odette headed up the stairs; Chris found himself staring at her tiny feet. 'She is not back yet…'

'So, where do you keep your clothes?'

'I not have many clothes,' said Odette, pointing into Mitzi's room.

Swallowing nerves, Chris opened the cupboard and selected a black lace blouse of Mitzi's. 'With jeans,' he suggested. When Odette had put them on in the bathroom, he helped her to pin in the back of the blouse. Harry, who should have appeared ages ago, would have enjoyed this. Chris cursed his own ineptitude; watching a girl brush out a cascade of heavenly hair should have been a perfect opportunity. Couldn't he have stepped forward and offered to brush it for her? Yet all he did, in the accessible presence of overwhelming sensual gorgeousness, was look, drool, and freeze.

They set out ten minutes later, while the moon was rising over the river and the flat expanse of Solstice Common. As they walked, Chris, hoping he didn't sound too anxious, tried to explain how pubs work.

'… so you mustn't expect people to stop talking and listen, because most of them won't. Tonight we're entertainers, not *artistes*.'

'Yes.' Odette smiled. 'I never start expecting now. Whatever I expect, I find something else. You know, is strange: everything here is different from my old home. But people are same. They are kind or unkind, sometimes horrible or sometimes funny, and people that I remember from long ago are like this too.'

'Yeah, I guess so. I wonder what you'll make of the crowd tonight.'

The pub was still beyond what Odette had expected, even with her new principle of non-expectation. She'd thought the place would be bigger, with the audience seated in tidy, quiet rows. As she and Chris went in, past a gaggle of smokers outside, a wave of light and sound struck her with such unfamiliarity that she nearly turned back. The air was stuffy and stank of sweat and something damp and stale.

'Old beer,' Chris told her. 'All pubs smell of it.'

'But where is stage?' Odette was alarmed at the sight of a battered upright piano in the corner, a huge glass of frothing brown liquid perching precariously on top of it. Close by, Stuart was arranging a mass of wires and a set of drums.

'Don't worry, you'll be fine. You'll enjoy it once we get going.'

Odette glimpsed someone waving to her from just inside the door: Harry, back from his audition in the nick of time. When she caught his eye, he blew her a kiss. She felt blood rush, most unswanlike, to her cheeks and neck.

'How's my Russian girlfriend?' He shoved past a group of students and slung an arm round her shoulders.

'I sing here?' Odette wondered what Monsieur Liszt would say if he could see her now. Harry's arm was producing a sensation in her back that was part warmth, part ache, part comfort; she wanted it to melt around the rest of her.

'Yes indeedy,' he said, 'my lovely *ochi chornye*.'

'Have you used a microphone before?' asked Chris.

Odette shook her head. 'It makes voice louder?'

'I've an idea,' Harry said, before Chris could utter a word. 'Odette, everyone will want to know about you, so why don't you get used to the mic by talking into it? Say a few words about yourself and how you come from Russia and you love singing, yeah? You'll feel better and you'll adjust to the way your voice sounds. Let me get you a drink – what'll you have?'

Odette stood stock still in the middle of the pub. The regulars milled about, a few students here and there, but mainly townsfolk downing pints of lager. Some stared at her, sneering, she thought, because it was so clear she was a stranger out of her depth.

Chris lifted a tentative hand and touched her shoulder, as if afraid it might retaliate. 'I have to set up. Stay with Harry, or come over and lurk with us.'

Harry, who'd managed to sidle through to the bar, handed Odette a half-pint of lemonade shandy, then led her towards a corner table while Chris opened up the piano, Stuart plugged in and tested the microphones and a long-haired boy she'd never seen before, whose name was Paul, picked up a bizarre brass instrument with a turned-up bell at the end.

'How was the audition?' Chris asked Harry, over the piano.

'Useless,' Harry grunted.

'How many people?'

'About a thousand, give or take a couple of hundred. I wasn't counting. Another fortnight's preparation down the bloody drain...'

Odette's heart was accelerating, her throat parched. She escaped to the toilets, her skin prickling with fear, her nostrils full of the sour smells of too many people in too small a space. The crowd alarmed her: anyone could accidentally crash into her and crush her. Everybody in this modern world seemed taller and heavier than she was.

She locked herself in a cubicle and breathed. She couldn't cry if she had to sing. The insanity of it all struck her in the gullet: she'd accidentally flown all the way to England, she'd met Mitzi and fallen in love with Harry, and now it ended with her locking herself in a toilet in a Cygnford pub because it was too much to handle? Would she really prefer to be back in Siberia in her log hut, alone, with nothing to do except watch the constellations in the night sky and fend off the bears?

While Odette was gone, Chris rounded on Harry, who was leaning on the piano close to him.

'Where were you? I was waiting for you to come to Mitzi's.'

'I did try,' Harry protested. 'The trains are up the spout.'

'The trains are always up the spout. I thought she was *your* girlfriend. I had to help her choose what to wear and everything.'

'And you did well – she looks great.'

'Tell me about her. What's the story?'

'I get the impression she's from somewhere pretty remote, and Mitzi says she's arrived with, like, nothing – but I suspect chances are the family's filthy rich.'

'Hope so, for your sake. They're not dodgy, are they?'

'Mafia? Fucking hell, she wouldn't last two minutes in that kind of situation. She's a real…' He paused, trying to find the right words. 'I dunno. It's like she's from another world altogether.'

'She's really got to you, hasn't she?'

Harry drummed his fingers on the piano lid. 'You could say that.'

Chris noticed the dreamy, lost look in Harry's eyes as he spotted the tiny figure of Odette sliding back through the crowd like a bird on a rough sea. For his housemate, it was most uncharacteristic. Keeping his thoughts to himself, he turned back to the keyboard, beckoning her over: it was nearly time to begin.

Odette remembered asking Monsieur Liszt how he performed if he felt scared. He'd waved one beautiful hand and said, 'If you have to perform, you have to perform. You are not important. How you feel is not important. It is your duty and you must give everything, even if you are dying.' At least, she thought that was what he'd said. It was hard to think straight in the noise. Chris, sitting at the piano, was flipping over the pages of music in front of him.

'Let's do "The Man I Love" to get everyone drawn in,' he said, 'then "Night and Day" and then we'll see how you feel. I've written you out a crib sheet, but try not to look like you're reading from it? OK, let's go!'

From Stuart's corner came a clatter of drums and a crash on the cymbals. Chris took the microphone; people stepped back to make way. Odette hovered. She thought she could see some of the audience laughing at her.

'It's good to be back again, ladies and gentlemen,' Chris announced. 'We're the Cygnford Culture Vultures and tonight we have a very special guest singer – please meet, all the way from darkest Siberia, the lovely and talented *Ode-e-e-e-tte*!'

Stuart gave a drum roll; Odette cleared her throat and stepped forward. Never mind the strangeness, never mind the fright; it was time to perform. She positioned herself by the black bulb.

'Good evening, everybody,' she ventured, her amplified voice booming back at her. 'I am called Odette and—' She stared around the room, wondering how to continue. The sound wasn't so difficult to accommodate, though, and Harry winked at her, which helped. 'And – and – I come from deep forests of Russia. This is first time I have been in Cygnford. I love this city, I am very happy. And I love to sing. For me, to sing is like – to fly.'

Now everyone seemed to be listening, despite Chris's words earlier warning her that they might not.

'First song is "Man I Love" by Mister George Gershwin, very talented composer from United States of America.'

For some reason this drew a laugh, though a friendly one. Chris rang out the first notes; with the piano's ripple there came a slow, regular, gentle beat from the drums and, from Paul's brass instrument, an astonishing deep, dark, husky sound, like a voice, like chocolate. She was so taken by it that she nearly forgot to sing. But when she began, her voice was true-toned and pure, and her nerves began to dispel. Nobody talked; at the end, some of them cheered. They went straight on to 'Night and Day', which had seemed difficult when she first saw it, but was now easy, and this time the applause was almost louder than the music had been. She glanced at Chris; he stared back over the piano. 'What next?'

Odette had an idea that seemed crazy but wouldn't go away. She reached for the microphone. 'Thank you very much. *Spasiba bolshoy*! I would like to sing for you folk song from my homeland, which I will sing alone.'

Silence fell. The song was her favourite, about the gathered harvest, the end of summer and a dying love, the melody enshrining all her memories, the words part of her childhood. As she sang, the lake haunted her, the trees and forests she loved, their castle, now deserted; and, with intense clarity, the face of her father, so kind and wise, raddled with sorrow since her enchantment. She imagined him at the window, searching the skies for the swan that was his daughter. She never knew her mother, who died giving birth to her. Odette was all he had. His hair turned white overnight when she was bewitched. As the song ended, tears shone in her eyes. Soon the only sound was a church bell striking ten.

A bomb of noise by the door shattered the rapt atmosphere. A group of new pub-goers pushed their way in, joking together, jolting Odette out of her reverie. The group, three boys and two girls, pulled up short in the silence. Several pairs of curious eyes stared straight at her in astonishment. Then one of the girls let out a guffaw.

'Fuck!' shouted the tallest boy, 'More foreign crap. What's it this time? Immigrant shite? Fucking Poles? You're going home soon, just you wait.' He marched up to the bar. 'Pints for five, mate.'

Odette, crumbling, longed for her wings to grow back so that she could fly away. Chris reached out a hand to her, but she was staring at the floor, lost in humiliation, wondering what a 'Pole' might be and why it was bad and why she was thought to be one, when she was an enchanted Russian princess musician.

At the bar, the publican froze, glasses in hand.

'Nope,' he said. 'Find somewhere else.'

The entire pub seemed to have frozen with him. Seconds ticked by like hours, with icy gazes deepening the winter. And Odette knew she had seen the intruders before, over the centuries, from a distance: hunters with rifles, oblivious to the nature they would kill, or looters of villages, or the ones who set fire to the little towns where the Jews lived, or to the encampments of the Roma, or of the Buryat Mongols, who were always so kind when she asked them for food. The faces were always the same; eyes looking with no sight, hearts beating with no feeling, minds working with no thought. And they were here in Cygnford, too, celebrating Christmas along with everyone else?

'You're joking, mate,' said one of them.

'Hop it,' said the publican. 'You can't just come in here and wreck my jazz night. People have paid good money for good music, so go and find your fun somewhere else.'

Odette saw Harry's hands clenching around his glass – was he preparing to get up and fight them? Surely not? She couldn't breathe for fear. And then, in a swift rush of air and a stream of expletives, the intruders turned tail and vanished the way they'd come in. A shimmer of clapping and some quiet cheers went up around the pub.

It was Paul who finally moved. He waved a signal to Stuart on the drums and the two of them played something that sounded to Odette like a lurid fanfare, flourishing and then setting up a rhythm. Stuart kept the beat steady, and over the top Paul began to improvise.

Odette had watched Monsieur Liszt improvise in that music room in Kiev. Paul bizarrely reminded her of him – not Liszt's figure or his charisma, which were unmatchable, but his concentration. Chris joined in; they started a duet above the drums, throwing phrases between them, playing with the tune as if it were a ball, conversing with musical ideas as if they were words. They challenged each other to do better and better, faster and faster, until Stuart, who wanted more beer, signalled the end with a hiss of cymbals. A roar of approval went up around them.

'We'll take a break now,' Paul announced. 'Back soon.'

Harry bounded up to Odette and hugged her. 'You're a star! You were brilliant. Really fantastic, and I'm not just saying it.'

'And those?' Odette pointed at the door, after the intruders.

'Hey – you're not worried about that? It was all about them, not about you. These things always are. Let me get you a drink. You OK?' His blue eyes came up close to Odette's face, intense with concern. She flushed. She could smell sweat, beer and something behind it that unsettled her, yet made her lean closer for more of it.

'Come on, Odette, you're a big hit,' Chris said. 'These things happen in pubs. They didn't mean what they said – they're just wasted and they don't know anything about good music.'

'I understand.' She took a sip of the beer Harry had brought over; and soon, refreshed, was smiling up into his attentive gaze.

When their second set was done, the final applause had ended and last orders had been called, the band began to pack up. The wires coiled down and vanished into backpacks, the cymbals were zipped into heavy cloth bags and the microphones came apart in sections; Stuart was placing them in big black cases.

'Right, chaps, we're off,' Harry told the musicians, gallantly helping Odette into her outsized red coat. 'Laters.'

Stuart pulled a face at the envious Chris while Harry, arm clamped round Odette's waist, ushered her towards the door. 'Win some, lose some.'

'Shut it,' said Chris.

Odette, so elated that she felt she might fly without wings, was enjoying the feel of Harry's arm, pleasurable and troubling at the same time, like his scent. She wanted to savour her night of humanity and success, and was longing for it to progress – and as soon as possible, please – but now she knew enough to blame the beer, the excitement, the nerves, the music.

'So, gorgeous, we've got our date tomorrow,' Harry said. 'Shall we have dinner, just the two of us?'

'That will be very nice.' Odette smiled, trying to suppress a hiccup.

'Methinks the fair Odette hath drunk muchly of beer! Come here, you.' Harry stopped in his tracks and began to kiss her.

How soft his lips were, and how welcoming, how much a part of herself that she missed – but she couldn't dare to hope. Nothing had been said that could help her. Not yet.

Harry thought it restrained and worthy of him to leave Odette at Mitzi's gate, watching like a gentleman to make sure she had gone safely inside. There was no point taking her home – Chris, Stuart and Paul would be there, unwinding post-gig. They'd drink, talk and smoke all night. And he retained uncharacteristic scruples, which he couldn't quite explain, about trying to jump on Odette in his sister's flat. He'd bide his time – at least until tomorrow.

Odette hurried upstairs, let herself in and called out to Mitzi, 'Hello! It was good! It was wonderful! You were not there?'

No response: the flat was empty.

170

18

Mitzi, half asleep, was vaguely aware that a thudding sound had woken her. She opened her eyes and stared at the unfamiliar ceiling, the noise pounding in her eardrums. Beside her, Rob was asleep, one arm trailing across her body. The thumping was unbearable – surely a rarity here in the woods? As her consciousness strengthened, she identified it. It was her heart.

Oh no. Not again. I meet someone, Mitzi thought, I like him, we end up in bed and then I can see so well that I shouldn't have. We had a wonderful day together, and a marvellous dinner in front of the fire. Why couldn't I have had the good sense to go home?

It was her fault. She had definitely, without a doubt, wanted to sleep with him. And it had been better than she'd imagined; better than anything since Pete. Better than Pete.

Last night had been intense, full of expression, especially from him – but he was her landlord, for goodness' sake, and she couldn't have someone getting hung up on her, let alone him, however much she was falling under his spell. And if he felt something for her, she didn't deserve it… She turned and soaked in the sight of him sleeping, a pale, bulky curve of shoulder, a muscular arm across her waist, the gentle, regular rise and fall of breath. How could she ever be good enough for such a kind, thoughtful, wonderful, enchanting man? Perhaps she should be the one to leave, while she still could. Her bicycle was by the front door and it was, she realised, past ten o'clock. Admittedly they hadn't slept until nearly four.

She tried to slide out from under his protective arm. She didn't want to be protected. She stood, her head heavy with hangover, casting about for her clothes.

'Hmm?' Rob mumbled. Mitzi pulled on her knickers, which had fallen beside the bed, then found they were back to front and inside out.

'What're you doing?' He sat bolt upright. 'Mitzi? What's the time? You haven't got to work today?'

'Not exactly… ' She cursed her clumsiness.

'Come back?' He held out his arms, his face open and adoring. Nothing in him doubted her. Yet she stood paralysed.

'Whatever's wrong?'

'Rob, look, I – I should get going.'

'Was I that awful?' A mocking glint in his eyes – he knew how much she'd enjoyed their night. 'How about thirds?'

Before she knew it, she was back in the bed, she didn't know how. Pulled by that bizarre hypnosis that seemed to be Rob's speciality. Somehow she couldn't make herself stand up again even if she wanted to. At the side of the curtains she could see brilliant sunshine outside, decking the garden in diamonds of frost.

'Mitzi? You feel panicky.'

Mitzi stroked the hollow under his neck, fighting back the lump in her throat.

'Shh.' He pulled the blankets back over her and held her warm and still. She couldn't bear the tenderness; it made her want to cry. 'I thought you liked me.'

'Of course I like you… I just…'

'Mitzi, I don't like you. I love you.'

'Don't say that. Please don't.'

'I don't mind if you don't love me back.'

'It's not that I don't love you back. But I don't want to lose it all again… find out it's not true after all…'

She was back where she'd started, lying flat, with Rob's arm across her, holding her there.

'Why, Mitzi? Tell me. Tell me everything. From the beginning.'

'I don't know what the beginning was. I don't know if there was one.'

He seemed peaceful beside her. 'Then just tell me whatever comes into your mind.'

Slowly she began to explain. Her father's death. Pete. 'I went to bits.'

'That's natural.'

'Maybe I was asking too much of him. He dumped me for someone else a few weeks after Dad died. Actually,' she added with a nervous laugh, 'I was so upset I nearly went for him with a bread knife.

But… there'd been so much feeling and it was as if it just disappeared, overnight.'

'You must have been close to your father?' Rob fortunately ignored her remark about the bread knife.

Mitzi pictured their outings to the Dorset sand dunes. 'When we went for family walks there'd always be me and Dad ahead and then Harry and Mum behind. That was when we were very little. Later Harry decided he was too old to be a Momma's boy, and then there were fights… It's such a long time ago.'

'Pete's a bastard,' Rob remarked. 'Dumping you at a time like that. Was it really so great with him? It's easy to idealise. I did that when I was married… and then I found the house. A hidey-hole where no one would see this miserable git who couldn't hold on to the one person who meant something to him… Look, it's too easy just to stick to your notions of what should be happening and close yourself up to other possibilities. You could be fighting off something wonderful, just because you didn't expect it. Do you see?'

'I don't want to fight, but I can't help it.'

'But what is there to fight?'

Mitzi looked into his eyes, three inches from hers, and saw nothing that needed to be battled except her own reflected anxieties.

'Mitzi, give yourself a chance. Give me a chance. Let's try. If it doesn't work, it doesn't work, and you're free. But why throw away something this special because you're too scared to let yourself have what you just said you wanted? It's a leap of faith, but if you don't try, you'll never know. There's joy to find, not only sorrow. Happiness, Mitzi – real happiness.'

Shortly after midday, Mitzi took a shower, then dried her hair in front of the fire while Rob put on the radio and pottered about, tidying the kitchen. It seemed natural to be there, to know inwardly that she had taken the leap, but was still standing in a country cottage on a patchwork rug, listening to *Any Questions*. No thunderbolt had yet struck her down for daring to be happy.

'I should think about heading off – I've got a deadline,' she told him, unable to explain that she was concerned about what was happening to Odette in her absence.

'Let's put your bike on the car roof rack and I'll run you home,' he suggested.

In the Mini, Mitzi found she was twisting her hands together as Odette did when she was anxious. The traffic built up towards Cygnford. She tried not to tempt herself with visions of living with Rob in the peace of the cottage in the woods instead of the traffic-plagued flat. Summer would bring fragrance to the garden and the herbs in the window box. It was too idyllic; something had to be wrong.

In Richardson Road he pulled up opposite the flat and gave her a quick kiss. 'I've got some work to do too, so I should probably head back. Tomorrow evening I have to teach one class, but how about we meet after I've finished? Shall I come over and get you?'

Mitzi put her arms around him. Was he, too, over-idyllic?

'We'll never know if we don't try,' he reminded her, as if reading her thoughts.

The swan was fast asleep in its box, a white mound of wings, feathers and long neck. The flat was its usual self, letting in slanting rays of light upon the books, warming the radiators, admitting the sounds of passing traffic as if nothing had changed. Outside, Mitzi heard Rob's engine fade into the distance.

She checked the answering machine. Chris's voice asked for Odette, telling her she'd been brilliant. Then the pub manager wanted to talk to Odette about a regular booking. Next, Harry said, 'Mits? Me,' and demanded to speak to her flatmate. And there was a message from a studenty voice wanting to know if Odette could join a university jazz tour of the States.

She glanced at the swan. Supposing Odette had been the girl she met by the music shop? Or supposing she had been not a transforming creature under a 166-year-old spell, but a refugee from a war zone, Africa or the Middle East, and she had been exactly the same person, with the same love of life, the same warmth, wisdom and talent, but

Mitzi had never had a chance to find out and Odette had never been able to reveal her true self to anybody in this icy, insular town? She slipped off her shoes, made for the bedroom and sank into a deep sleep.

The swan stared at the pale December sun, remembering the music – Chris, his friends and her own voice rising above them. She'd heard the phone messages, but of course she couldn't pick up the handset and laugh with Chris over their success, or say 'See you this evening' to Harry, or even tell the touring group with regret that though she'd love to go with them to America, she couldn't. America! She wondered whether it was safe there. Last time she'd overheard talk of this country, a civil war had been in progress.

And she remembered Harry's kiss, and ached beyond aching for her human body so that she could experience it again. She wanted to ask questions. Where was Mitzi last night? What had taken place in that distant bedroom? Was this the fulfilment of love? As a young girl she had had the information drummed into her, by her father and her governesses alike, that such things must never be so much as contemplated without a marriage ceremony first. Today, in Cygnford, this did not appear to be true. Did that mean the mysterious process could itself amount to a real pledge, an everlasting commitment – just as it was for swans? And if so, was the breaking of her spell within her grasp after all?

The doorbell shattered Mitzi's dreams; in an instant she was on her feet, pulling on her jeans, her hands shaking with fright. She peered out of the living room window, from a safe distance. By the gate, a car had pulled up, with a flashing blue light on its roof. On the front step stood two people who could only be plain-clothed police offers, having a joke – of sorts – with Professor Maggie. 'She's there,' Mitzi heard her insistent voice, 'obviously.'

Mitzi scooped up the swan and the box, shoved them into the study and locked the door. Then she gave her hair a cursory brush and sauntered down, trying to look relaxed and weekendishly content.

'Here we are!' said Professor Maggie, triumphant. 'This is Mitzi Fairweather.'

'Miss Fairweather?' The young policewoman spoke first. 'DC Rayfield, from Cygnford Police Station. This is DC Wakeham. May we ask you a few questions?'

'Of course. What's it about? One of the newspaper reports?' Mitzi said.

'Er, not exactly... can we come in? Thank you, Professor,' she added to Maggie, who gave a cheery wave and vanished behind her own door.

Mitzi had no choice but to show them up the stairs. What was there in the lounge that might betray Odette? 'Would you like some tea?' she offered. 'I have some lovely lime-blossom stuff, quite unusual.'

A few minutes later, both police officers were equipped with mugs and were sniffing the tea's honeyed fragrance with interest.

'So,' said DC Rayfield, 'we understand you have a friend from Russia who was working in the corner shop on Garden Drive for Uma Verjee, is that right? We know her as Odette. We don't know her surname.'

'I think she only ever did a two-hour try-out, if that.' Mitzi gave her brightest smile. 'I heard it wasn't a success.'

'Do you know where we can find her? We believe she may need some help, you see.'

So Uma hadn't said she was living with Mitzi? Oh, thank goodness...

'I'm not sure. I haven't actually seen her since then...'

'Are you likely to see her?' said DC Wakeham.

'I've told her to keep in touch and let me know how she is,' Mitzi bluffed. 'But so far she hasn't.' A rustle in the locked study caught her ear and she held her breath, watching her visitors' faces for any sign that they'd heard it too. But sign came there none. DC Wakeham, sipping the tea, seemed more interested in its flavour than in any peculiar noises nearby.

'If she does, will you call us?' DC Rayfield, draining the mug, handed her a business card. 'The thing was, your neighbour thought she had heard someone else in here besides yourself. "Obviously", she said.'

'That must have been my boyfriend, Rob,' said Mitzi, for the first time ever, surprised at how good it sounded and felt. 'Odette isn't in trouble, is she?'

'Not exactly, but according to Mrs Verjee, she has no papers, not even a passport, and she's going to need some. She absolutely shouldn't be trying to work without them. There's a crackdown on the black economy at the moment. What *is* her surname?'

'Actually,' Mitzi said, smiling. 'I haven't the faintest idea. But I'll give you a call if I hear from her.'

After she'd watched the police car pull away, Mitzi let the swan out of the study, then quickly trawled the living room, too late, for giveaway signs. They could have spotted her sketchpad and picked it up; there they would find drawings of Odette, Rob, and the swan itself in all sorts of avian poses. They could have examined her tablet and the lighted screen would have shown them *War and Peace* in Russian. They could have looked at the draining board and seen that two of everything sat drying upon it. But as far as she could tell, they weren't looking at all. Or were they? How could she be sure?

19

At sundown, Odette shook out her feathers and made her way to the bathroom. Mitzi, who had retreated to the sofa, held Rob's book of fairy tales on her lap. Her blue eyes, deeply shadowed, turned towards the window.

'Mitzi, you love Rob?' Odette asked, the moment she was on her human feet and back in the living room.

'I hope so… I don't know yet. I'm so afraid, Odette – but I'm so happy! It's weird to be afraid to be happy, isn't it?'

'If you are happy, I am happy too,' Odette declared. Her words twisted Mitzi's heartstrings. Would any of her Cygnford friends ever express such a thing, with such innocent sincerity and, essentially, such truth? Had anybody she knew ever done so?

'Thank you, my dear,' she said softly.

'Those people. The police. They look for me?'

Mitzi nodded.

'But they did not find. So is all right?'

'I hope so, Odette,' Mitzi said, with a deep sigh. 'But you must be really careful…'

'Good.' Odette seemed to consider the matter closed. 'Mitzi? May I ask something?'

'Of course.' Mitzi was startled, half expecting Odette to demand whether after last night Mitzi must be pregnant, or if she could help her acquire a passport by some peculiar means, or…

'Please,' said Odette, 'may I have bath? I have never had bath in house as human, not since *before*.'

Odette poured out some exquisite-smelling potion that mingled with the water into milky foam. Cautiously she removed her white shift and lowered herself in. The heat diffused like oxygen into every bone. Bubbles tickled her skin. Her hair spread out around her while she closed her eyes and breathed in scented steam. Most of the time water was a necessity; this, though, was pure luxury. Baths in the castle had been functional, involving pitchers of water heated over giant fires in the kitchen, then hauled up through an elaborate pulley system, while icy draughts from the stone corridors blasted against one's bare skin. To the swan, water was home, unfelt and without a hint of sensual effect. As for Mitzi's power shower, she had found that excellent and cleansing, but nothing compared to this… She breathed and dreamed, willing the scent to encourage Harry. If he broke her spell, she could have a bath every day.

The buzz of the doorbell brought her back. Now she had to make it happen.

'Odette!' came Mitzi's voice. 'Harry's here. Do you want the red jersey?'

'Yes, please!' Odette wrapped herself in a towel, a treat in itself, and prepared to dress.

'So you're seeing him again tomorrow, eh?' Harry was asking Mitzi when Odette came in.

'Maybe,' said Mitzi.

Harry turned, saw Odette, sleek in jeans and red cashmere, and his mouth fell open. Strands of her hair, still slightly damp, curled in a frame around her face. '*Ochi chornye*! My Russian beauty, you are a vision to behold! Hungry?'

'*Da!*' Odette beamed, bounding across to him. 'Mitzi, please may I borrow coat again?'

Mitzi couldn't help grinning, so vivid and hopeful was the expression in her guest's dark eyes as Harry held the scarlet sleeves ready for her arms. Nor had she ever before seen Harry behave in such a gentlemanly manner.

'Now, let me get that door for you, madam.' He swung it open and Odette swept grandly forward and out.

From the window Mitzi watched them go. No police car lingered outside. Professor Maggie's light was off. And in the tree there was no—

Yes, there was. She couldn't see the owl, but its call came to her, low and unearthly. She heard the hoot of a night bird, but Odette would hear the same sound in quite another way. A bewitched and bewitching captor. A summons.

'I'd like to take you somewhere posh, but I can't afford it,' Harry admitted while they walked. He knew Odette would respond best to directness. 'You like pizza, don't you? Like Mitzi made for us?'

'I like everything.' Odette gave a giggle that she stifled at once.

Weird girl, thought Harry proudly, caught off guard yet again by her gleam. Since the ball, he'd somehow become used to thinking of her as some elusive part of himself. Her hand slid into his and stayed there all the way to town.

The pizza place seemed mundane as a destination for someone so exotic, but once they were installed at a small marble table in the window, lit by a candle in a blue glass lantern, her magic began to work on the surroundings. He watched her studying the menu. Around her there seemed to hover a slight but definite glow. She was changing the texture of his world. When he looked at her slender wrists, her small breasts, the swan-like curve of her neck beneath the cascading hair, his stomach began to churn. He'd never experienced any sensation as bewildering as being near her. Almost afraid – and he hadn't been afraid of a woman since his first girlfriend – he took her hand in both of his.

'You – are – incredible,' he said.

'Tell me things, Harry? We dance at ball, and we play pretending game, I sing in pub, but we never just talk.'

The restaurant was spinning around his head. He smiled, afraid she'd think him an idiot. 'You know I'm an actor. I don't know what else to tell you. It's always been my life.'

'Why?'

'Maybe it's like your music. It's the feeling of being up there on stage with an audience watching you and becoming someone and something else. The adrenaline takes you over, you become – you *are* – what you're doing. There's no character and no play and no you – you lose yourself in it. And when you have that feeling, you've done a good show. You know why you're alive and why you have to do this crazy thing.'

'Yes,' Odette breathed. 'I understand exactly.'

She stopped herself saying that this was how she felt when she flew. There is no me; no bird, no woman, nothing but flight itself. Her

181

music was the same. It was when the Baron heard her play the piano that he chose her fate: to fly.

A waitress came to take their order; Harry chose a vegetarian pizza for Odette, spicy beef for himself, and a bottle of house red.

'How *did* you end up living with my sister?' he asked when the wine arrived. 'No one's bothered to tell me.'

'It was accident,' Odette hedged. 'She find me. I was in... some trouble, and she help me, you not know how much. One day I tell you, perhaps.'

'So it's not Airbnb and it's not some funny arrangement that... sorry to keep asking, Odi, but it's so strange. Mitzi won't tell and neither will you? And what happened to you the other night? You left your dress and your shoes! What am I to think?'

'You may think anything,' Odette said, with a smile, 'and maybe you think right!'

'OK.' Harry sat back. 'I'll tell you what I think. My guess is: you're the daughter of some mega-rich Russian man. Am I right?'

'Perhaps.' Odette gave a wry grin. 'What else?'

'I think you're trying to escape something by setting up in Cygnford, apparently with nothing. Maybe it's so you can do your music, when possibly people didn't want you to. Right again?'

'Partly...'

He wondered why she was laughing. 'I think you've been a dancer. You're way too thin, but you've got fantastic muscles and your feet turn out like a duck's. And I think you don't eat enough. Do you mind me saying?'

'I am not dancer, but is true that I do not eat much for long time... And my feet are definitely not duck!'

'I think, also, that you've been on your own for a bit and you're looking for the right man.'

Odette dissolved into laughter so wild that it rendered her unable to speak. Harry poured the wine, puzzled by her hilarity, then stared into her eyes as they clinked glasses. 'Odi, Odi – come on, calm down... I'm sure you'll tell me the truth when you want to – yes?'

Odette curved her neck in graceful assent. Harry took her hand.

'Let's talk about now,' he said. 'I'm in *Twelfth Night* in the summer and we're taking it to the Edinburgh Festival Fringe. Edinburgh is a beautiful town in Scotland, a long way north of here. Each year there's a massive arts festival, the best in the country, and in the Fringe loads of young theatre groups go up with their shows and people come along from all over the world to see what's new and exciting. It's an incredible atmosphere and we're going for two weeks. Why don't you come with us?'

Odette's eyes widened.

'Don't look so shocked. I thought it might be nice for you: see the city, see the festival, be with friends, play music, have fun. It'd be cool.'

'Harry, you are so kind, but – I not think—'

'Don't worry.' Damn; he'd jumped the gun. 'I understand if you don't want to.'

'I *do* want to. But I cannot.' Odette lowered her gaze – beyond his reach, absorbed in an abrupt melancholy, a sphere where there was no place for him. When she swam back from that other world, her gaze made him feel transparent. 'I wish I could tell you…'

'Tell me anyway.'

She shook her head.

'Come home with me later and tell me then.'

Odette followed Harry into the house, where he rapidly steered her past the piano and towards the kitchen. He couldn't lose his Russian beauty to the lure of Chris's rickety upright.

'I like it here,' she remarked, placing her coat over the banister with all the others.

'You do? Sorry about the mess… You're not one of these obsessively tidy women, are you, the sort that goes berserk if there's a crumb on the tablecloth?' He watched her slight figure in her jeans and red jumper as she accepted a glass of orange juice, her face with its contrasts of jet-black against snow-white, her huge eyes that showed not a hint of tiredness.

'I like house because here I make music. But I do not know about crumbs.'

'I can't believe you.' He was grinning like one besotted.

'Oh, but you must believe me, I really not know!' she protested. 'I never have real house, you see.'

'So where did you live in Siberia?'

'In forest...'

Odette, flushing, hated giving half-truths. She longed to let go and confess everything. If he loved her, he would understand, wouldn't he? She took a deep breath and said his name. But before she could utter another word he had moved across the kitchen, tipped her face upwards and begun to kiss her.

Her knees buckled. She imagined her whole self might dissolve into him. Never had she felt so wholly, indubitably human.

'Odette,' he was mumbling between kisses, 'let's go upstairs.'

'What is upstairs?'

'More comfortable than the kitchen.'

Her hands were clasped behind his neck. He bent and in one smooth movement picked her up and started to carry her towards the stairs.

'No!' she laughed, 'you drop me!'

''Course I won't. You're light as a bird...'

In his bedroom, surrounded by posters from his past plays, Odette feared he might find a telltale feather in her hair or her jeans, which he was unfastening. He had already tugged off his own shirt and she wanted nothing more than his skin against hers. She marvelled at the sensations cascading through her own body.

Outside, some way off, an owl hooted. Odette tensed.

'What's up?' Harry protested.

'Harry, you do love me? You said at the ball...'

'You silly, daft bird! I'm *crazy* about you.'

'Will you love me always? Forever?'

'Forever and ever and *ever*,' Harry declared, his fingers busy with buttons and zips.

And Odette smiled, not her usual lightning flash, but long and slow. 'Kiss me again...'

Harry's jeans landed on the floor.

Much later, they lay still, his head on her shoulder, recovering breath, thrilled, exhausted.

'I thinking,' Odette whispered to him, 'now I am free.'

'Free? You're *incredible*.'

'Now I maybe tell you.'

'Tell me…' Harry slid down beside her and cradled her against him. Odette closed her eyes and fell asleep in his arms, without telling him anything at all.

20

The telephone shocked Mitzi awake. Her brother's voice was sharp and strained. 'Mitzi, where's Odette?'

'What?' Mitzi rubbed her eyes. It was 7.45am. She had been so tired that she hadn't listened out for Odette returning.

'Is she there?'

'I don't think so.' Even if she were, she wouldn't be able to speak.

'So where is she?'

Mitzi dashed into the hall. She'd shown Odette how to make up the bed herself, but the study was as she'd left it, the mattress and frame folded away, the sheets safely hidden in a filing cabinet. No one had been there all night.

'She's done it again,' said Harry. 'She's gone. She didn't even say goodbye. *But her clothes are still here.*'

'She's not been home,' Mitzi said, trying to be diplomatic and read the situation.

'So she walked out? Barefoot and coatless? Without so much as a thanks-for-the-pizza?'

'I'm sure she hasn't,' Mitzi ventured. 'Maybe she borrowed some jeans and a jumper when you were sleeping. I'll phone you as soon as she turns up, OK?'

'Shoes, Mitzi. Shoes…'

The line went dead.

Mitzi sat down on the floor beside Odette's empty box, head on her knees. She guessed at once what Odette had tried to do. She could assume, too, given her brother's track record with girlfriends, that it had failed.

What happens when a spell goes wrong? Mitzi picked herself up and went to search the book of fairy tales. Most of the love stories ended happily, with marriage, though if the narrative ran beyond that, sometimes things went terribly awry afterwards, especially between a mortal and a supernatural creature. But the boundaries were clear. There were no shortcuts to freedom.

She waited by the window for the familiar swish of wings and gentle honk of the arriving swan. Nothing. Chapel bells chimed the hour, then the quarter hour. If Odette had indeed fled Harry's house in avian form – where was she?

In the cloister court of St Barnabas College, Stuart, Chris and Harry were plugging in heaters with lengthy extension leads, setting out sugar-dusted mince pies on foil-coated platters and filling jugs with mulled wine, ready for the Shakespeare Players' Christmas meeting. This afternoon they were supposed to plan out *Twelfth Night* and the trip to Edinburgh. None of them had much to say about it yet, but it was a good excuse for a seasonal get-together.

'Outside?' came a familiar female voice behind them. Caroline had brought an extra armful of mugs borrowed from neighbours on her staircase.

'Cheaper than a meeting room at Christmas,' Stuart grunted. He was still in his gloves, which didn't make the refreshments any easier to set up.

'Let me give you a hand...' Caroline, her red hair catching a beam of sunlight, began to lay out the mugs and fill them. 'Hello, Hal – God, you look frightful.'

'All kind compliments gratefully received,' said Harry, under his cap.

'Rela-a-a-x.' Caroline rubbed his shoulders. 'What's eating you, anyway?'

'A big, fierce lion that escaped from the zoo.' Harry clawed the air.

The rest of the company, the designer and the stage crew were wandering through the college's arched doorway into the colonnade; Stuart was looking up notes on his iPad and Chris was whistling one of his own tunes to a sceptical-looking clarinettist. The designer remarked to Harry and Caroline that her job was to rustle up as many suitable outfits as possible from the actors' cupboards, conscript a few plants and, for anything else, become a smart bidder on eBay.

'I'm sure I've got something suitable for Olivia to wear,' Caroline remarked. 'Hal, come up sometime and help me choose?'

'Only Mum, Mitzi and Chris call me Hal.' The fresh, cold air, the steaming mulled wine, the company of friends, Caroline's green eyes sparkling at him – all this seemed delightfully normal, after such an intense night into which Odette seemed to have disappeared without so much as her socks. His obsession with her was easing at last; the full extent of her bizarre behaviour was beginning to strike home. Perhaps she'd come back to him, perhaps she wouldn't. She'd more or less told him her family was filthy rich. Oligarchs? Dirty money? She'd be fine. She must have been spoiled rotten and was used to doing what she wanted, or what Daddy wanted her to do, rather than taking anyone else's wishes into consideration. In which case, life would go on; there was acting to be done, friends to be made, and plenty of other girls.

'The trouble is, Olivia's got to be horribly pure,' he said to Caroline. 'You look good in those slinky little numbers and it's sadly, y'know, not quite in character.'

'Sadly?' She nudged him. He nudged back, then slid an arm around her.

At college, Caroline, who was on the performing arts course, had mixed with the theatrical set from the start. Every time Harry made his way back to his old group for a meeting, audition or impromptu session over a late-night bottle of wine, there she'd be, talking non-stop or being difficult for the heck of it. Fresh from a posh boarding school, she looked up to him; he assumed a brotherly role, being several years older, a graduate supposedly trying to make his way in the world, and busy, at first, with another girlfriend or several. In her third year, though, she grew her hair, updated her style and started flirting. He was impressed by the change in her and in her acting: she'd just taken the lead in the Amateur Dramatic Club's *Hedda Gabler*, for goodness' sake, and brought the house down. Then Odette appeared. Yet given her predilection for disappearing again… maybe it would be best to keep his options open. And Caroline was quite an option.

'Look, there's a swan flying.' She pointed. A huge white bird was winging over the college roof towards the river.

'Funny there's only one,' Chris said. 'My grandpa's a great twitcher – he always says swans fly in pairs or flocks.'

'*So* romantic… They mate for life, you know.' Caroline shuffled closer to Harry. Stuart clapped for attention and began to outline the plans, such as they were, for Edinburgh.

A shadow was moving across the cloister. From under an arch, Harry saw the swan passing over them a second time, in the other direction, a little lower than before, but he was more interested in Caroline's smooth, pale neck beside his arm. Although Odette could win any Oscar for fine necks, becoming obsessed with her was too much like falling in love. Scary. It was such a relief to be back in the real world: the sooner he escaped her, the better. He started to stroke, with one finger, an exposed area close to Caroline's jugular vein.

'What's that swan doing?' said Chris.

Stuart stopped speaking, annoyed by the interruption. The bird was circling above them, barely clearing the roof with its wingtips. 'I've heard of pigeons and starlings and even seagulls coming down and eating the sandwiches at garden parties, but not swans,' he said. 'Now, as I was saying, if we book train tickets three months ahead it'll cost—'

'This is like something out of Hitchcock,' Chris mumbled.

'Prince Hal will protect us,' Caroline laughed, while Harry, gazing up at the circling bird, twizzled with his left hand a long strand of her hair.

'Shit, this really is like Hitchcock!' Stuart broke off. The swan seemed to be trying to hover above the courtyard. Harry found himself wonderstruck: the great wings swishing back and forth, the pure whiteness of its feathers, and the extraordinary grace of its movements were uncanny, disturbing – nature meeting supernature…

'Come on, guys, have a refill,' Stuart offered, 'and let's get back to business.' But cast and staff ignored him, transfixed by the swan. It completed another circuit of the building, then manoeuvred itself into an angle facing the group.

'What's it doing?' Caroline clutched Harry's arm. The swan was pointing its head down and forward, straight at her. The massive wings beat once, twice, three times and then bent back, set behind the bird's body with the air-searing streamline of an Olympic diver.

There was a fierce gust of air under the arches, the hissing of wind in feathers and the crash of breaking china as the swan's headlong descent swept the mulled wine from the table. The actors, frantic, scrambled for the protective doorways, but Caroline, caught in the swan's path, appeared frozen with terror. A long, high scream flew from her throat. Harry flailed at the bird as it reared above her. Its wings lifted in a blazing arc over his head, its eyes fierce, the coldest gaze he had ever seen. It was overwhelming him like a tongue of flame that could swallow his vision and his mind.

'Help me, somebody!' Some of Caroline's red hairs were drooping from the swan's black and yellow beak. It reeled, gathering its energy, then redoubled the onslaught. Caroline, trying to strike at the creature with what remained of her mug, missed her footing and fell to the flagstones, beside the stone step to the dining room door. Feathers scattered, clinging to her black jersey. Harry felt a wing thud against his abdomen and found himself on his knees, winded. Caroline was rolling over, shielding her eyes with her arm. On the side of her head, where it had struck the step, was a large and bloody gash.

'Morons!' Harry yelled at his friends, who were cowering inside the nearest door. 'Call a fucking ambulance!' He glimpsed Chris pulling out his phone, before the swan turned on Harry, striking his shoulder with such force that he fell prostrate.

'It's going to kill me!' Caroline shrieked.

'It can't.' He was fighting for breath. 'It's not possible.'

He tried to clamber upright, but the colonnade looped vertiginously around him while the swan beat Caroline over the head with its wings until her screams stopped and she lay silent amid spilled purple wine that was streaked scarlet with her blood. The bird flapped out over the courtyard grass, as if surveying its handiwork; then it turned away and rose towards the gathering clouds.

Slowly the actors ventured out to gather around the unconscious girl. Harry, crouching beside her, tried to pick up her hand, but couldn't. His own was shaking too much.

21

'Is that Mitzi Fairweather?' The voice was unfamiliar, female, friendly. 'It's Joanna Hill here. I'm one of the home editors on the *National News*. I got your number from *Nature Now* and I wondered if you could help us out with a story in Cygnford.'

The *National News*? Mitzi's mind reeled. Half a million readers, maybe more? She held her breath.

'We had a call from a student at St Barnabas College who said a swan attacked a girl called Caroline Simpson at an actors' group meeting in the cloister and now she's in hospital, unconscious. And we heard there was an incident recently when a swan stole a dress from the market and then fell off the roof of Duke's College Chapel. We couldn't help wondering if there's a connection. Some sort of rogue waterbird... Have you heard anything? Could you find out what happened and write us the story?'

'A swan?' Mitzi turned numb. 'Someone's in hospital?'

'That's right. We'd need about three hundred words, depending on how much info you get, by tomorrow morning. It'd be great if you could do it, because I saw your piece in *Nature Now* and I really enjoyed it. Could you call the hospital, then speak to the girl's friends, and maybe the woman who kept the market stall...?'

Mitzi mobilised every shred of courage. 'Leave it with me and I'll get it to you first thing in the morning. What's your email?'

At least now she knew where Odette was. She remembered Caroline Simpson: the red-haired young actress, rather talented, whom Harry liked. She'd seen *Hedda Gabler*, and spotted them getting along quite well at the party on the last night. And Odette had so much to lose... Where was she, anyway? What had happened to her?

She opened the window wide, urging herself not to panic, but she needed to think fast and she couldn't. How to get her byline in a national paper while allowing the story to blow over and be soon forgotten? This was a national broadsheet; the all-important foot in the door. She knew full well, heart sinking, that any other journalist would have been capitalising, contacting the BBC and Channel Four and every radio station on the digital listings to offer to comment. John would jump on the story too, even though he normally took no interest in matters concerning students that didn't involve drugs or suicide. Cygnford wasn't accustomed to irrational, violent behaviour in its waterbirds.

A familiar shape blotted out the window and a second later Odette had come to rest on the living room floor. On the pure white feathers of her neck and wings lay russet streaks of drying blood. Mitzi slammed the window shut, in time to glimpse on the path below the gangly figure of Professor Maggie, returning with her shopping, gazing upwards in alarm.

'What have you done?' Mitzi demanded.

The swan stared at her, its eyes cold and angry. Mitzi shuddered. Imagine being attacked by a creature like this one, incandescent with rage and power.

'Now listen,' she said. 'Stay where you can't be seen from the street. You're in trouble.'

Odette had begun to preen her feathers, working at the traces of blood with her beak.

'Taking it out on her isn't going to help,' Mitzi said. 'Oh yes, I know all about it. A national newspaper has just called and asked me to write about an attack by a swan on a student actress during a meeting in a college cloister. You spent the night with my brother, he must have been at the do as well, no doubt turning on his legendary charm with Caroline, and I imagine you weren't too pleased. And here you are with blood on you that isn't yours. This isn't rocket science, so please go and hide.'

The hospital press office agreed to give her a statement. 'It's extraordinary,' the spokeswoman told Mitzi, sounding dazed. 'She was admitted with wounds to the head and arm, bruising and concussion. We can hardly believe it was really a swan.'

'Will she be all right?'

'Her condition is stable, but we're keeping her in overnight.'

'Thanks for your help,' said Mitzi.

Who had witnessed the incident? Harry, of course, her own brother. His mobile was off. Mitzi, who had never believed in any form of God, began to pray for guidance to whichever supreme power happened to be listening.

'Chris Lovell speaking,' came the polite voice of Harry's housemate.

'Chris, it's Mitzi. Look, I'm writing about the swan attack for the *National News*. Were you there? Can you talk?' She scribbled notes sideways against the lines of her notebook as Chris began to recount the day's events.

'You say it picked on Caroline. What about the others?'

'Well, Harry was trying to help and the rest of us took cover.' Chris sounded embarrassed. 'I called the ambulance,' he added. 'The thing is – I know it sounds crazy, but it made a beeline for her.'

'Where was Harry beforehand?'

'He was with her... He'd been kind of flirting with her.'

'Mm-hm,' said Mitzi. Just as she'd thought. 'Flirting how much?'

'Well, er...' Chris apparently couldn't get the words out. 'He had his arm round her. Does it matter?'

'Is he there? Can I talk to him? He's not answering his mobile.'

'He's at the hospital. I'll get him to ring you.'

'Thanks, Chris.' Mitzi put down the telephone and began to type.

'A 21-year-old student from St Barnabas College, Cygnford, was in hospital on Tuesday after being attacked by a swan,' she wrote. 'Caroline Simpson, who starred earlier this year in the Cygnford Amateur Dramatic Club's production of *Hedda Gabler*, was attending a courtyard meeting of the Shakespeare Players, a nationally celebrated, university-based theatrical group that makes regular appearances at the Edinburgh Festival Fringe. The swan, which seemed to have lost its companions, made a rapid descent and appears to have beaten the young woman unconscious before flying away. The hospital has described Simpson's condition as stable.'

She stared miserably at the words. She needed to write three times as much, making it exciting. Adventurous. Sexy. She added quotes from Chris and the press officer, then waffled a bit about the Shakespeare Players' recent tours and successes, Caroline's great promise as an actress, the scarcity of the Bewick's swan in Cygnford, and a quick mention, right at the end, of the incident with the dress and the chapel. She would send it to Joanna by email in the morning and not before. With luck, there'd be no time for anyone to expand the story, so, assuming nobody glanced at the paragraphs more than once, Odette should be safe.

The daylight was fading. Mitzi automatically began to think ahead to supper for two. Rob was teaching a pottery class that evening; they'd agreed he would come round afterwards. She was grateful for his absence in the meantime. She could do her best to calm Odette and learn a little more about the truth. Then she must think of a way to persuade Rob to take her back to the cottage with him, instead of coming up into the flat. She longed for comfort food – perhaps a vegetable stew, which could simmer slowly if she started making it now.

Chopping carrots with her largest kitchen knife, her hand slipped. Blood spouted across the gash in her left forefinger. She ran into the bathroom for a plaster and as she did so, it seemed to her that the darkened space filled with a strange luminescence, pale violet, a stirring of the air like the motion of many wings, as if space were rearranging itself around her to fill a vacuum. For a second the breath seemed to be sucked out of her. She felt for the edge of the bath, something solid – but a moment later the room was normal, the air still, and Odette was beside her, anxious, taking her arm to help her up.

'You blooding!' Odette cried.

Lost for words, Mitzi switched on the cold tap, held her finger under the flow and let the chill of it calm her mind as well as her wound.

'How is it,' she said to Odette, hunting in the medicine cupboard for a plaster, 'that you can be so sensible now and so totally insane earlier?'

Odette sat down on the bathroom floor; she was all eyes and hair above the white shift. 'Please, do not be angry.'

Mitzi had meant to sound firm and authoritative, but she couldn't. Instead she knelt down and hugged Odette, whose bony frame was cold, sinewy and shaking. 'I'm not angry, really I'm not.'

'I think I am free, but...' Odette pressed her bare toes into the pink bathmat.

'Then morning came.'

'Yes, and I am swan again! Mitzi, I not understand, I cannot see why, because I expect I am now free, after this night... then I see Harry and he is with girl with hair that is colour of carrot, she tries to kiss him. Oh Mitzi, you know what happen before, you know Baron and his daughter he makes to look like me, and this so horrible...'

'Shh... Caroline's not a magician's manifestation, she's just a girl. She fancies Harry and he probably fancies her too. That's all. Though the timing wasn't too sensitive.'

'For swan, there is no reason. And for swan, this action should be forever. You see?'

Mitzi did. There's no arguing with pure instinct, no hiding from an unspeaking creature behind a web of fabrication. Perhaps Odette as a swan had clearer vision than Mitzi, with her English degree and NUJ membership, could ever hope for.

'Listen,' she offered. 'I do know what must have happened with Harry.'

Odette reddened.

'You really, honestly thought that sleeping with him would be the same as a vow of everlasting love?'

Tears loomed in Odette's eyes. 'For me, is same thing. For swans, is same thing. And he says – before – that he will love me "forever and ever and *ever*"... He use these words!'

'But for Harry, that probably doesn't mean quite the same thing it means for you.'

Odette was silent.

'You've got to understand: he doesn't know. He doesn't realise you're not like everyone else. He doesn't know that swans mate for life, or if he does know, he's not aware that that might affect how *you* behave, because – as far as he's concerned – why would it? He has literally no idea what this means to you.'

'You think,' said Odette, after a long pause, 'for everyone else, *this* means *nothing?*'

Mitzi sensed her grip on the situation sliding away. 'I'm not saying it means nothing to Harry. I'm sure it means a lot to him. But it's not – necessarily – everlasting. It doesn't affect the shape of a spell. It's not a vow.'

'I want to tell him about spell,' Odette said flatly, 'but you say I must not.'

Even Rob had thought it was best not to tell Harry the truth. But supposing she *had* come clean with him from the beginning? Odette was suffering because of the deception; perhaps she, Mitzi, was to blame?

No, she told herself. She was responsible for Odette only because the swan happened to have picked her window to crash through. She couldn't take Odette's choices on her own shoulders. She fought the lingering sense of guilt. 'I think we'll have to tell him. He may come round later this evening.'

Odette wiped away a tear with one finger. 'What will I say?'

'You want me to do it?'

'I hate him.'

Odette trailed off to the study. Mitzi heard bumps and rattles as she unfolded the camp bed and set out the sheets.

'I'm making food,' Mitzi called. There was no response.

She switched on the local radio station, her hurt finger still throbbing under the plaster.

'*... was said to be recovering, but suffering from shock. The swan has been identified as a Bewick's, rare in Cygnford where mute swans inhabit the...*'

She turned it off again and picked up her knife to finish chopping the vegetables.

A long hour went by while the stew cooked. Mitzi tinkered with her words in the article; Odette, confined to the study, must have been resting, or stewing in her own way. Later, the two women ate together in silence; Mitzi could scarcely swallow. When they'd finished, Odette retreated to the armchair and declared that *War and Peace* would take her mind off things. Mitzi moved the swan's box to the study, hoovered up some stray feathers, then switched on the television and sat in front of it without watching or listening. She knew she needed to text Rob, to stop him coming over, or at least in. Whatever could she say? Her mind had frozen up with alarm and no excuse presented itself. The flat itself seemed to be waiting.

At last the ringing phone jolted them both back into the present.

'I hope you've got this business plastered on the front page.' Harry sounded tired and irritated.

'Is she OK?'

'Yes, but the wretched thing knocked her over and she hit her head on the side of a step.'

'Are you *sure* it was a Bewick's swan?'

'What's that when it's at home?'

'What colour was its beak? Hal, I'm serious, it's important. If it was black and yellow, then it's a Bewick's swan.'

Harry paused. 'I remember seeing a bit of her hair in it – she's got red hair, very long red hair... yes, I'm sure it was black with a bit of yellow... Mitzi? Are you there?'

Mitzi's heart was in her mouth. 'Listen, Harry. Supposing I were to tell you that that swan *is* Odette?'

'*What?*'

'And that's why she keeps disappearing.'

The line crackled. 'Earth to Mitzi? Earth to Mitzi? Come in, number 105?'

'Supposing I were to tell you that Odette is a swan by day and a woman by night.'

'Mits – what are you on about?' Harry groaned. 'You've been watching *Swan Lake* and it's turned your brain.'

'Harry, I know you won't believe it right away, but...'

'I'm coming round. There in five.'

He'd rung off. Mitzi poured herself a cognac. She reserved her VSOP for Very Special Occasional Panics.

While the warmth of it spread through her stomach, she noticed that Odette had wandered to the desk and picked up the sketchpad. As she leafed through the drawings, Mitzi saw her whole form cease natural movement, as if turned to stone.

'No,' Odette said. '*Nyet...*'

'They're that bad?' Mitzi swallowed brandy. 'I thought I'd improved recently.'

'Who this is? Where you see this face?'

'That's Rob,' Mitzi beamed. 'It's not very good, I know.'

'Is it *very* like him?'

'Not enough... it's just a first try, from memory... Why, what's the matter?'

'Mitzi, it is so much like...'

Odette's words vanished into the ring of the doorbell: Harry was already there, fastening his bike to the railings beside the river, opposite the house. Mitzi pressed the buzzer to let him in. Odette waited with her by the door, slight in her jeans and white jersey, hair loose and wild around her.

22

Harry stopped dead in the doorway. He was clutching a bulging plastic carrier bag in one hand, with the red coat over the other arm. He and Odette stared at one another, motionless. '*Spasiba bolshoy* to you too,' he grunted. 'What the heck happened? Why did you run off?'

Odette folded her arms in front of her heart. 'I cannot explain.'

'You'd better try. Cos people don't just disappear without their clothes and shoes. I nearly called the police.'

'Please forgive.' Odette's tone was businesslike. 'I know you not love me. So I leave.'

'*Love* you? But I hardly *know* you! It was our second date, for God's sake – you can't start talking about love!'

'You lie to me. You say you love me, you say you are crazy about me, forever and ever and ever, you say. Then you go with carrot-hair girl!'

'But Odette… look, if you hadn't run off, we'd have had breakfast and talked some more, and arranged to meet again, and – why can't you relax and let it happen, like a normal person?'

'I am not normal person.'

Harry dumped bag and coat on the floor. 'Mits, you got a beer? I'm in need.'

Mitzi glanced from the tearful Odette to the angry Harry. When her brother made no move other than towards the fridge, she crossed the room and embraced the swan girl. Odette hid her face on Mitzi's shoulder and burst into tears.

'All I want is for someone to please tell me what's going on.' Harry opened a can.

'I told you, but you wouldn't listen,' Mitzi said.

'You didn't tell me anything.'

'Harry! Sit down and *listen to me*. Put down that beer and don't say a *word* until I've finished!'

And Harry, who had never seen Mitzi white with fury before, sat and listened.

As the story progressed and Mitzi forced him to stop laughing, Odette slipped across to him and took his hand, which was icy.

'Prove it,' he muttered at last.

'It is proved,' Odette said. 'Twice we have been together at dawn. Twice I have gone away without clothes. Twice you could not understand. And once you saw it, yourself. You saw me change.'

'I did?'

'We go to ball, it is dawn, we go to garden, I disappear, you fall, you pick up my dress. And you see swan.'

'Oh, fuck… You mean… you really think you *did* have piano lessons with Franz Liszt…?'

'Of course. I do not think. It is true.'

'But what do you mean, a *spell*? Like – like that ballet? *Swan Lake*? The one all the girls blub over for their birthday treats?'

'Sort of,' said Mitzi.

'So you have to break the spell and then you're a normal person again?'

'Harry, please help me.'

'What do you want *me* to do about it?'

'Mitzi told you spell.' Odette maintained her princess-like dignity. 'When man swears to love me forever, and keeps his vow, I am free.'

'But that's crazy! I can't do that.'

'You say you cannot vow,' Odette stated, 'but there is no other way to break spell.'

Harry stared from one to the other. 'I'm sorry,' he said. 'I don't believe in magic, I don't believe in spells and I'm not going to play the game. This is Cygnford. This is the twenty-first century. So, Odi, I like you very, very much, I loved our night together and under normal circumstances I'd have liked to start having a relationship with you and see how we get along. Does that help, even a little bit?'

At that moment there came the sound of the front door opening and footsteps on the stairs. It must be Rob, finished with his evening class and letting himself in with his landlord set of keys. Strange that he hadn't even rung the bell. Mitzi just had time to mix her delight at seeing him with dismay that she had not managed to ward him off; Odette's camp bed was still open in the study and she had told him nothing of the past weeks' reality.

'Rob!' she said brightly as the door swung open.

Odette let out a cry. Her hands lifted and pressed to her mouth.

Rob seemed not to have seen Harry. He seemed not to have seen Mitzi. He took two steps towards Odette.

'Rob,' Mitzi improvised, 'I was going to tell you – Odette's been staying, just for a couple of days…'

'I know,' said Rob simply, without taking his eyes off the transfixed swan girl. 'Our downstairs neighbour, Professor Maggie, called and told me there's been someone else living up here. Mitzi, you're in breach of contract.'

Such calculation, such contempt, seemed to fill his face – was this a trick of the light? She found herself reaching for her brother's arm and holding on.

'Come, Odette.' Rob's tone was unlike any Mitzi had yet heard him use. 'It's over. Let's go home.'

Odette sank, silent, to her knees. Tears streamed from her eyes as she pressed her fists to her face, rocking herself back and forth. 'Mitzi – I tried to tell you – face in sketch,' she managed to say.

Rob glanced towards Mitzi and the flummoxed Harry. Mitzi tried to smile, reaching out a hand to him; he did not take it. 'Rob,' she said, 'what's going on? Please tell me? I don't understand. Something's wrong, so let's put it right? There must be some mistake, or misunderstanding… I promise you, Odette is only here very temporarily, I've been trying to help her find her feet and…'

'Indeed, you don't understand,' he said. 'You haven't even begun to get it, have you?'

'The contract – I can explain everything…'

'No need. I'm not here about that. Or not only that.'

'Mitzi – this person – is not who – you think – he is,' Odette said, struggling for breath between words.

'Do you not see? Do you seriously still not see?' Rob turned his gaze back towards her. Staring into its crimson depths, Mitzi, beginning to freeze on her feet, felt a dawning – or a setting – or a recognition

– the cracking of a shell within her – and from inside that, a gradual seeping of all she had failed to grasp before, befuddled as she was by her cobweb of hopes and dreams. A web within a web.

'Where's Rob?' She controlled the tremor in her voice as best she could. How far back did this go? How deep was her mistake?

'Nowhere you need worry about him,' said Rob, who was not Rob. 'Reported in the papers, naturally, but your editor won't call you. May I introduce myself? If you like, you may call me Baron von Rothbart. My specialities over the centuries have been mining, investment, herbalism, a little light murder, and, to use a common if vulgar term, shape-shifting, on behalf of myself and sometimes others. Harry, you'll appreciate the skill involved in turning yourself into someone else, won't you? In addition to being a fine actor, my friends, here in pretty little Cygnford I've been gaining some new skills: giving expert interviews to newspapers, making splendid pottery, teaching cute kiddies about fairy tales and enjoying fine vegetarian cuisine in a pathetic English backwater where people think themselves terrifically clever. Mitzi, my dear, why don't you sit down? You're very pale. You must have had a terrible shock.'

Mitzi found herself slumping on the green leather chair. Rob's green leather chair. That ability Rob had to snatch away her willpower – or was it ever Rob?... 'Then... when did you come in?' she asked. 'Did I actually meet Rob?'

She understood, even as she spoke, that she had not. What was in that 'lime blossom' tea? Whatever was the soothing substance she'd been feeding the policemen? No wonder they hadn't looked around her living room. A vortex of darkness was spiralling through her mind, beneath an avalanche of confusion. The night of passion in the cottage. The lure of happiness, 'real happiness'...

The pain of recognition, when it arrived, was so intense it was almost physical, stabbing her through and through until she doubled over, fists pressed to her mouth to stop herself from screaming aloud. The shards of glass from her broken window seemed to be slicing through her just as they had sliced at the swan's wing.

'The storm,' she gasped out. 'Did you arrange that as well?'

'I used that storm as I needed to,' came the reply. 'It was not ideal – but this is the art: to take nature and master it. When I knew the storm was coming and that my swan princess was likely to be blown far away from her winter hidey-hole, I decided to be the advance guard. The gale was already getting up, after all, and there's nothing to beat a good tail wind in such circumstances.'

'Mitzi.' Harry was beside her, arm clamped to her shoulder. 'It's OK. Breathe. Keep breathing…'

'And Rob – did I know the real Rob? I must have! I spoke to him before Odette came here.'

'Indeed. A good likeness in the voice, don't you think?'

So she'd spoken to Rob – been invited to lunch – and by the time she'd gone to visit him he had been… replaced. 'You knew I was going there. You knew why, and how, and what he was doing, and how to…'

'I make it my business to know such things.' Von Rothbart gave her an elegant bow.

The owl. The 'advance guard'. Mitzi clutched her head. She'd heard an owl the day before Odette arrived. Was that him too? How did he know? What powers did this demon in her living room really have? Another shell broke apart in her brain.

'It's logical,' he declared, apparently reading her mind. 'If you know the velocity of the wind, the mass and weight of a swan, its aerodynamic potential, its endurance limits and the likely path of travel, then even taking into account the vagaries of journeying through a strange land with unfamiliar air currents, it's possible to calculate quite quickly where it might come to earth. But as you told Odette, there are plenty of owls in this little country. Don't beat yourself up over that one.'

Harry, she realised, might be holding her arm, but had not uttered one word to either the cowering Odette or her enchanter. She had never seen a look like this on his face before: he was as pale as she must be, his eyes wide and watchful – observing, as he always did, but being careful not to show how afraid he felt.

'You think I'm one of you,' said Rob, who was not Rob, who had never been Rob. 'You sit there reading your fairy tales, writing articles to attract people to gatherings that make them think they understand "folklore" and "magic". You think magic belongs to children, because it's harmless. Can't you grasp the scale of our reality, Mitzi? You live in a little town among little people, and you think these streets, in this famous university, are old. You don't understand the first fraction of time, age and space. If you knew how vast and ancient our universe is, how immeasurable the might behind it, your brain would burn up like one of your nice home-made vegetarian pizzas.'

He crossed the room to her, brushing Harry aside, and took her face gently between his hands, as if it were a sheet of tissue paper that he could crumple at a touch. She stared back, paralysed, words deserting her as he spoke.

'You were so easy to see through, Mitzi. You're a good person. You lack any semblance of malice. It was so deliciously simple to find him, dispose of him and take his place – and delightfully easy to get into your heart, your head and your bed, or at least to get you into mine. You know, I think you'd have found the real Rob Winter a little less sympatico. No sense of humour, that one. You know these worthy, too-good-to-be-true types. Anyway, what was to stop me – when my swan princess had gone and I had to find her? And now this oafish creature, your brother, has violated her. You are so pathetic, so undeveloped, so numbed by your alcohol, your fashion and your technology, that you can't see truth when it's staring straight at you. You don't know the first thing about nature, or God, or power, or life, or death.

'Can you understand that the substance of your body and the substance of the stars are the same? That all your molecules are held together by the same force that created the earth billions of years ago? You see stars as pretty, twinkling points of light, when in reality, as you know, they are a seething, gaseous, magnificent cosmic fire. We *are* this substance, Mitzi, we ourselves. Can you conceive of what a human being can do and become, if other humans don't kill his brain power with too much comfort and too little questioning? Mitzi, Harry, all you have to do to understand is look at me. I have seen it and I have mastered it. What you call magic is nature, as I manipulate it. You call it supernatural. It is not. It is nature unlocked; and I have the keys. But I still need one thing. I need my swan princess back.'

'Like hell you do,' Harry growled. 'Just you try taking her away from me.'

But Odette was still on her knees in the centre of the room, staring askance at Harry, her eyes filled with tears.

'Why?' Mitzi demanded. 'You've been holding her since 1852! Why can't you let her go?'

'Because, my dear, I don't want to let her go. Therefore I will not. I love her, you see.'

Von Rothbart smiled, a smile nothing like Rob's. In slow motion he let one hand caress the length of Odette's hair, twisting the locks between his fingers, pulling ever so slightly. She flinched, but did not – perhaps could not – move. 'Odette is my all, my world, everything I want. Yes, I want her and I will keep her, because it's the longing for her, the wanting, the desire, that gives me my strength. Mitzi, Harry – do you know the energy of yearning? There's nothing like it. They say it's the vilest thing in the world, unrequited love, but my goodness, it gives you impetus. If I had her, if I just took her, and I could, I would stop wanting her – and that's no good at all. That's not what she's for. So here we are, living out our continual cycle of endless yearning. I keep you alive, my angel, and you give me my vital energy. Without each other, we'd be lost.'

Mitzi, the boundaries of her world splintering, saw Odette's downcast eyes, helpless, humiliated. She remembered Odette saying her situation was difficult to explain.

'Oh, and Mitzi.' Triumphant above the shivering Odette, von Rothbart's eyes blazed across the room. 'Here's something your late father should have taught you: never take in a stranger, and never violate the terms of a flat's lease by letting another person live there without permission. The same goes for "pets and other animals". Because you could find yourself turfed out. As I'm effectively your current landlord, I can reveal that your lease is terminated as of tonight. Meanwhile, your precious Robert Winter is in the morgue, waiting for those bumbling little policemen to identify him, limb by severed limb – except that they won't, because he's not technically missing.'

Odette rose from her knees and walked to the door without a word.

'Odette,' gasped Mitzi, with a strength she didn't know she had, 'you don't have to go. You don't have to believe him.' Harry plunged across the room to place his substantial frame between Odette and the escape route.

'Nor do you, Mitzi,' said von Rothbart, 'but you might have to believe Cygnford Estates when they call you, and Mrs Verjee, and the police, and the hospital that's tending poor little Caroline. Professor Maggie is an excellent lookout. Obviously. Nice new window there, though. Let's test it.'

He pushed up the sash and some whirl of rearrangement in the air flung the three of them to the floor; in place of him, nothing existed except the tawny owl, its feathers the colours of Rob's sweater, springing out into the night. Clambering to her feet, gasping for breath, Mitzi found herself making for the kitchen and lifting the knife from the chopping board where she had left it. She opened the window wider, hunting the darkened sky for any sign of the creature.

'What are you doing?' Harry demanded, helping Odette up with one hand, scrabbling for his mobile phone with the other.

'Looking for the owl. What he's done to us… I'll kill him with my own hands.' Mitzi knew, with the last shred of her mind that could remain detached from all this, that she'd felt such a degree of fury and despair once before. She remembered the cool silkiness of the stainless-steel bread knife handle in her fist. Pete had got it away from her, talked her down. Not this time.

'No, Mitzi!' Odette cried, from the depths of Harry's embrace. 'I become swan forever if he is killed.'

'I don't believe that! You think you're dependent on him, and he's as good as said he's dependent on you. So he's told you you'll be a swan forever because that's his way of stopping you having him killed, by your prince or Harry or me or anybody else. It's just that you believe it! It's rubbish. I'm calling his bluff. He's told me nothing but lies. He's…' An image of him in bed flashed through her mind – his eyes closed in ecstasy, shoulders curving above her – moving with him, thinking herself in an earthly heaven, she had given herself, body and soul, to a perverted captor who lived only for his unfulfilled longing for Odette? 'Oh God,' she said, her gorge rising, 'why should anyone believe him now?'

'But spell!' Odette's face betrayed exasperation as well as fright. She shook Harry aside – he'd got through and was bellowing into his phone, 'Chris, mate – come to Mitzi's *now*, we need help…' Darting to Mitzi, she grasped her arm and tried to prise the knife from her fingers. 'Mitzi, spell depends on man.'

Mitzi rounded on her, incandescent. 'Are you telling me,' she said, 'that just because I'm not a man, I can't help you? Are you saying that friendship isn't as strong as some idiotic infatuation? You're *my* friend, *I* look after you, you're my responsibility, which I've accepted since you crashed in here, and I love you simply as one human being caring about another. So I shall free you myself. Keep back!'

In the chestnut tree, the outline of something black and rotund was silhouetted against the bare branches. Its feathers were dappled in reflected light from the window. Its eyes shone straight towards her, deep red, bringing her out in a cold sweat, making her nauseous. She used to dismiss the uncanny as a figment of her imagination. No way, though, could she have imagined this. The creature carried with it an atmosphere she'd never encountered before – she could have described it as a chill from the grave, a glimpse from some distant, hellish realm, but she, Mitzi Fairweather from Dorset and Cygnford, had never before described anything in such terms. Odette stood beside her, transfixed, as if in silent communion with her enchanter. Mitzi's head was swimming. She breathed deeply, tried to focus, then leaned out of the window, the knife quaking in her fist.

The tree trunk partially concealed the owl. As she strained to see it, there was an upheaval among the twigs and, spreading its wings, it launched itself into the air. She mustered strength and flung the knife. It dropped into the front garden as the owl disappeared into the night.

Odette, in a white flash, bolted for the door. Mitzi heard her footsteps tearing down the stairs.

'Harry! Come on,' Mitzi said.

'What's she doing? Where are we going?'

'To help Odette, and if you don't come with me I shall never see you again!'

Odette was running along Richardson Road, a pale slip of a figure with her head back, scanning the sky. Mitzi searched the dark soil in front of the house for her knife; half concealed by a tree root, it caught the gleam of a streetlight. Her fingers closed around its handle. A hundred yards behind Odette, sprinting, she felt the wind catch in her throat. A wide-winged, soundless shape was circling above Solstice Green across the water. Odette, heading for the footbridge, cut into the road; a car hooted and braked as she darted in front of it. Its headlamps lit up her face – transfigured, desperate. Mitzi and Harry had been gaining ground, but a stream of oncoming traffic left them stranded while Odette ran on, over the bridge and onto the grass. Although Solstice Green would be lively with bicycles and joggers during the day, now there was not a soul to be seen. The owl, wheeling in the sky, seemed to have taken possession of it.

The traffic cleared and Mitzi shot ahead of her brother onto the bridge. Odette was standing still, the owl gliding lower and lower above her. She reached up towards it and Mitzi heard her voice, speaking in Russian, pleading – not tearful, but true and strong. Odette fell to her knees, her arms extended to the bird; it was teasing and worrying at her, retreating, approaching, attacking. Mitzi, powered by an anger and a love each more ferocious than the other, would not plead with the owl, or the man who had so used them; she gripped her knife and lunged, while Harry flung himself at the creature as it swooped, its outstretched talons aiming at Odette's head. He tried to separate them, but the owl and the girl were locked in struggle. One wing flailed into Mitzi's face, knocking her to the ground. Pain slammed through her left leg and a deep, cold darkness blotted out her vision. The creature turned on Harry, the wings struck his temples and as he fell its red eyes willed him to lose consciousness. Odette cried out in pain, the owl seizing her by the hair.

'Be strong, Odette!' Mitzi cried, hauling herself up. Her left ankle was badly twisted and her jeans soaked with blood from a cut acquired from the knife, she did not know when. And, hearing her, for a moment Odette seemed to be gaining the upper hand. She broke free. The owl soared towards the street. Mitzi took aim as it circled above her. She flung the knife in a strong, clean arc, glinting silver under the moonlight.

The blade caught the bird by one wing. A few feathers spiralled down through the air. The creature reeled, flapped, then tumbled, a mass of feathers, into the road. Odette let out a scream.

'He's not dead, Odette,' Harry gasped with what breath he had left. The owl was fluttering on the tarmac. Odette ran into the road towards it, straight into the path of an oncoming bicycle.

Mitzi just had time to recognise the rider as Chris, responding to Harry's summons, when he swerved to avoid the girl and his bicycle's front wheel instead struck the fallen, disoriented owl full on. The bike jolted. Chris tumbled over the handlebars, crashing down on top of the owl's body, his glasses slipping off to the side. Harry and Mitzi rushed to him. Odette stood white-faced and petrified. The owl was lying still in Richardson Road, squashed by a bicycle and its rider, nothing now but a heap of dark feathers matted with blood.

Chris staggered over to the kerb and slumped there, head down, trying to get his breath. *What the fuck was that?*

'Odette,' said Mitzi, her voice shaking, 'the owl's dead. However it happened, it can't follow you any more. You're safe.'

Odette took both Mitzi's hands in her own. The dark eyes met the blue in a profound contact – and then, as her friends watched, a violet radiance began to quiver in the air around them. Her fingers slipped away from Mitzi's. The vibrating air trembled, space rushing into a vacuum.

Helpless, Mitzi watched the swan take the sky towards the north-east – and now the full knowledge struck her, the understanding, the shattering, the loss. She thought she could hear somebody screaming. Harry was holding both her arms, pinning them to her sides. She struggled free, wondering where the noise was coming from, and struck him across the cheek.

'You!' She couldn't recognise her own voice amid its screams. 'It's your fault! What you did to her! What you did!'

'Hush!' Harry put his arms round his sister, trying to calm her down. 'How was I to know? I'm sorry, Mitzi – hush, now...'

Mitzi fell to the pavement, hammering it with her fists. Physical pain seemed all that could ease the agony as every hope, plan and dream lay in pieces in the road with the dead owl that had never been Rob Winter, or fled with the friend who had brought in the magic that gave life to those dreams. Chris, though bemused, terrified and nursing a damaged knee, managed to crouch beside her, coaxing her to get up and lean on him. His eyes, sharing her pain, followed the great white swan while it soared away from them forever.

And Harry walked aside, gazing into the night sky as the swan's shape diminished, and continued to stare long, long after she was gone.

23

The swan had never flown by moonlight before. Winging along the expanses of sky that encased the fenland, she found it hard to see her way. She made slow progress. Her heart, beating human, overflowed with despair. She could still hear Harry's voice calling out to her as her fingers began to dissolve into feathers, and Mitzi's cry of anguish as dark hair folded into white plumage. Her spell would commit her to life as a swan forever, but – like Mitzi and Harry, who couldn't be blamed for not understanding – she could scarcely take in the emotional impact, such was the scale of this recognition.

If only she could have kept her human voice long enough to explain: to tell them that the Baron would have come after her no matter what happened, determined to spirit her away home where he believed them safe from interference; to tell them that he would stop at nothing, that there was no subterfuge or crime or transformation he would not effect in order to recapture her. Now, if Chris's bicycle was to be believed, the Baron was no more – could it be true?

What now? Could she live a normal life as a swan? At one time this might have seemed a reasonably attractive prospect: an avian mate, cygnets and a natural death after a natural lifespan. But now she knew the mystery of human intimacy, the soft touch of a man's fingertips, the mingling of breath and being, and to go back from that to the lakeside seemed a cold, cruel prospect.

Travelling onward, the icy landscape reflecting back a shimmer of moonlight, she discovered she was beginning to feel sorry for Harry. This wasn't his fault; he hadn't known the truth. Should he have? She had been complicit in deceiving him. She could have told him. She hadn't. Her sorrow calmed her as she flew. The moon rose higher above her, huge and impersonal; closer to it than she had ever been, she remembered staring at it as a child from her castle casement. Perhaps she would soon see her home again.

Later, when the moon was turning from milk to copper against a veil of cirrus clouds, the swan began to feel tired. Nearby, she could glimpse the coastline and beyond it the sea she had crossed in the storm not quite two weeks before. The wisps of cloud heralded a great bank of darkness rolling across the sky from the north. Soon there would be snow – and a long journey lay ahead, this time with the wind against her. She must rest first; she couldn't attempt the crossing in a blizzard. She tilted towards the earth, scanning the ground for reflections of light that might indicate a lake or river. Close to the estuary that led into the northern sea, there lay a slice of mirrored sky. Some ducks were asleep on it.

She slid out of the air, extending her feet to skim the lake's surface. The water welcomed and rested her. A drake looked round, curious, but decided to ignore her. The swan dived for food, which was plentiful and good, then swam to the shore to find a place to shelter, disconcerted to experience night in her bird form. She clambered onto the bank, chose a shadowed spot in a hollow formed by the roots of a giant oak and settled there, cold and miserable, her head under her wing. Overhead, the gathering snow clouds blotted out the last of the stars.

Drifting towards sleep, she could see Mitzi again, the way she stood with her hand on her hip, head on one side, every passing thought and feeling visible on her face. Her long legs, her large hands and her fair hair, the way her nose tilted slightly down at the end, the gleam of her sudden smile. 'I shall never see her again,' she thought. Pain welled up in her and she found she was trying to cry.

Swans cannot cry. When she'd flown away, devastated, from the prince's ballroom, she couldn't cry. The release, when her humanity returned to her, had been an indescribable relief. Half asleep, she reflected that it wasn't the thought of Harry that made her want to weep, but the thought of his sister. Harry was the one who had let her down, yet all she felt for him was pity – and a new emotion, a big, benevolent kindness, involuntary but definite: forgiveness. Mitzi had tried to save her; she wanted to kill the owl, peaceful Mitzi who never hurt a fly, though she was so easily pained herself. Mitzi, who had taken care of her when she might have thrown her out, had taken her to the vet, bought her clothes, found her that incredible book to read, which now she would never finish. Mitzi had tried to help her, for no reason but that she was in trouble.

How tender her days in Cygnford seemed. She leafed through her human hours. She remembered her father, dead so long ago yet as vivid in her mind as if she'd only just left him. Her nurse and her governesses, their fondness and their strictness. Once she'd been sent to bed supperless with a dose of something ghastly for knocking over a pile of books in her father's library. She'd spotted a volume that she wanted to read high up on the shelves. If only she could remember what it was.

She recalled her first days as a swan, how frightened she was – and then how she had grown to love the power of flight that was suddenly hers. Flight was freedom: the air, the sky, the vast lake, the deep forest, all belonged to her. But if she were free now, she was also alone. It wasn't only the love of men she would miss, but companionship: a friend, someone to talk to, someone to trust. She wanted to finish *War and Peace*, to read as many books as she could lay her hands upon, to see plays like *Hamlet* and *Romeo and Juliet*, perhaps with Harry in the leading roles. She wanted her piano back so that she could learn to play all the music written in the century and a half since she met Franz Liszt. She wanted to master a computer like Mitzi's – she would write about her experiences and perhaps become as famous as Pushkin. She remembered how it felt to say, 'I feel so happy'. Swans were peaceful companions, as long as they didn't feel threatened. Yet to dance, to play music, to sing, to shout with joy, these were not within a swan's capability. And to cry—

She thought of her last glimpse of Mitzi and Harry, the way the brother had held the sister with such sorrow and let her sob on his shoulder as Odette rose into the sky. She thought of the devastation in Chris's light, short-sighted eyes – hadn't he loved her more than anybody, through their music? They would miss her as much as she missed them. She could see their closeness to each other and to her; and with that, she understood that she loved them all, Mitzi, Chris, her father, Franz Liszt and Harry, regardless of the spell, for no reason other than that she did. She loved them and their world, she loved to be one of them and to give her love and express the music that welled within her, and now she felt herself so filled with that love that she imagined the floods of it could spill out and drown the whole earth.

Her heart swelled and seemed to burst beneath her feathers. She had to weep for all she had learned and all she had lost, and her need to cry was so great that nothing, not even her physical form, could prevent it. A sob escaped her throat and then another, then an uncontrollable torrent took hold of her, and Odette, curled up in a space that was much too small for her, felt the tears springing in her eyes and sliding hot and fresh along her cold skin and plopping onto the old material of her white shift. She buried her head in her arms and wept and wept. A couple of ducks drifted past her to find somewhere quieter. She wept as the snowflakes began to fall from the yellowing night sky into the water and sprinkle their transformation upon the trees, she wept on as the first light of day brushed the lakewater with lilac. She wept without noticing that sunrise had begun, without feeling the winter wind and the crystals of snow on her bare arms, without even noticing that she had human arms and hands to feel the air and human eyes with which to weep. At last, exhausted with crying, she sank into her tree hollow, rested her head on a curving root and fell asleep, while the snowflakes fluttered down to lay a soft white blanket over her body.

'Hello? Can you hear me?'

Odette, drowsy and sluggish, sensed a touch on her shoulder and light in her eyes. The snow seemed to have seeped into her bones and she could scarcely move or speak for cold. Someone was shaking her.

'Are you all right? Give me a sign you can hear me.'

She tried to sit up and rub her eyes in the sunlight. The snow had passed. A middle-aged man in a flat cap and a green rain jacket was staring at her, speaking to her.

'*Da?*' said Odette.

'You're OK? Thank almighty God. I thought we'd lost you.'

'I'm sorry,' said Odette. 'Thank you for finding me.'

'Normally I'd have to ask you to move along now,' said the warden. 'Bird sanctuaries aren't a place for you people to sleep. But just last week we found a guy here who was sleeping rough too, and he wasn't as lucky as you. We got him to hospital, but he didn't make it. Come with me, let's get you into the warmth.'

Helping the befuddled girl to her bare feet – no shoes, in the snow? – the warden scrutinised her. She did not have the look of the vagrants who sometimes came into the wetlands trying either to reach London or to escape it. The softness and wonder in her face was disarming, though she was shivering from dark hair to blue-tinged toes. His van was nearby; he pulled a large sheet of something crinkly and silver from the back of it and wrapped it around Odette's shoulders before helping her into the passenger seat.

'Where are you trying to go, love?' he asked.

'I am trying to go home,' said Odette in her best English, pulling the foil blanket around her.

'That's good. Where's home?'

'I – I not know – you see – but I do not understand!' For it had dawned on Odette that she was speaking with a human voice to a human being, twisting together her human hands, and that it was broad, shining daylight.

The warden started his van, shaking his head. Something about the young girl reminded him oddly of his beloved waterbirds. She had the same poise, the same unaffected and unconscious perfection in her face. 'You're not from these parts, anyway. You haven't fallen off the back of a lorry, so to speak? You're not from Syria or Libya or been through those shitholes in Calais?'

'No, I come from Russia,' Odette told him, encouraged by the kindness in his voice. 'I stay in Cygnford with my friend, but because – I cannot explain, but I must try to go home. I arrive here last night, I fall asleep, now I not know what to do.'

Strange, thought the warden. In some ways so typical – a lost kid who thought it'd be easy to get home without taking even a cardigan. The bare feet were bizarre, for sure, but the weirdest thing was that she was grinning from ear to ear.

'Have you got any ID? A passport? Cash? A bag of some kind?'

Odette shrugged and opened her arms. 'I have nothing.'

'So how on earth do you think you're going to get home?'

'I think I fly,' Odette let slip, quickly adding, 'but now I not know.'

'This is a bird sanctuary, love. Not many planes here. Look, I'll give you a nice cup of tea and some breakfast in the hut, and then you can tell me what's going on.'

'Tea?' Odette's eyes lit up. 'So wonderful! I drink tea again!' He watched, astonished, as she threw back her head and gave a shower of laughter so joyous that he found himself joining in, despite having no idea why.

Soon she was sitting at his office table devouring a bowl of cornflakes and some steaming tea, black with a generous spoon of sugar, in his biggest mug. 'Good thing I found you,' he told her. 'Anything can happen to a kid out there alone – you could have frozen to death. I'm amazed at your friend letting you set off like that.'

Odette, her mouth full, did not reply.

'Didn't you tell him – or her – what you were doing?'

'I not have chance.' Odette thanked Mitzi silently for having taught her discretion.

'Now, you were hungry, and you were cold, but you're not ill, are you?'

'I very well, thank you. And you know, this is not really so cold.'

She looked him straight in the eye and her gaze, if a little brilliant, was steady and quite sane. What on earth had happened to her? Why wasn't she telling him the whole truth? Surely she was too young, certainly too innocent and forthright, to have escaped from a women's prison? In any case, no women's prison he knew of dressed its inmates in white shifts. Perhaps she had indeed escaped from a trafficker – but even then, wouldn't she at least have had shoes?

'You'd better put on a jumper or you'll freeze. And some socks.' He rummaged in a cupboard by the sink and produced an ex-army sweater with green pads at its shoulders. Odette put it on; it reached to her knees. She laughed again.

'So, no suitcase, no bag at all?'

'Nothing.'

'Money? Getting to Russia costs money, you know.'

'No money.'

'And seriously, no passport?'

'What is passport?'

'You're a rum case, for sure. Are you going to fill in the blanks for me?'

'Very complicated, you see,' said Odette.

'I bet. Look, have you got your friend's phone number? We can give them a call. Assuming you want to, that is.'

'I do want, but I not have her number,' said Odette.

The warden sat, counting to ten before he spoke. 'But she has a phone, *da*?'

'*Da, da*,' said Odette eagerly. 'She lives in Cygnford and her name is Mitzi.'

'Mitzi what? What's her surname?'

'Her surname... that I do not remember.'

'Oh jeez...'

He managed to extract the information from Odette that her friend was a journalist; then, astonished at his own generosity, he spent most of the morning looking up the phone numbers of all the newspapers and magazines in Cygnford, calling them one by one, asking whether they had a journalist named Mitzi on their staff, and explaining why he was looking. At least there shouldn't be too many people in Cygnford named Mitzi. Hours ticked by and he was neglecting his work.

Eventually the assistant editor of one magazine, who had never heard of any Mitzi, thought the situation sounded intriguing. She misunderstood the warden's enquiry after a writer, and rang Joanna Hill of the *National News* to alert her to the story of a young Russian girl who might have escaped from sex traffickers but insisted she hadn't, even though she'd been found without money, passport, luggage, clothes or shoes beside a lake in a Suffolk bird sanctuary.

'Mitzi?' Joanna's voice was friendly. But Mitzi was in her dressing gown, purple shadows under her eyes, with Harry and Chris, who had stayed awake with her, administering cups of tea and giving her Kleenex when she needed them. All night long, every tear she had never allowed herself to shed had flooded out of her. Harry wept with her a little, protesting that he'd never got as close to loving any girl as he had to Odette. Chris found himself speaking hopeless platitudes about how it was more important that Mitzi had let herself risk loving Rob than that she had lost him, and that she would be stronger for it; and that they would ask Stuart to offer her a room in the house with them all if the flat was hers no longer; and that she was a writer and an artist, and a keen observer, so she should try her hand at writing plays for them to stage; and that she mustn't feel guilty about what had happened, because von Rothbart was destroyed through all their joint efforts, together, while they'd done everything they could reasonably do to save Odette. Mitzi's tears, though, flowed free as the dawn broke beyond the empty chestnut tree and the snow, falling faster, began to coat the branches in a magical transformation of its own.

'Oh, Joanna,' Mitzi snuffled. 'Was the article all right?' Chris had pressed the 'send' button for her at nine on the dot.

'Yes, fine,' said the editor, 'and something else has come up that I thought might interest you, to do with a bird sanctuary not so far from Cygnford. It's almost like an extraterrestrial thing. I just had a call from *Anglia Life* saying that the park warden had rung up looking for a local journalist because he found a Russian teenager sleeping rough by the lake – she's got nothing, not even a passport, and she's trying to get home. She insists she wasn't being trafficked or seeking asylum; she has no explanation of how she got there, she just wants to go home and the one thing she knows is that she has a friend in Cygnford who's a journalist. Can you chase it?'

'*What* did you say?'

'A Russian girl wearing a sort of white shift, but no shoes...'

'Give me the number?' Mitzi dropped her tissue and grabbed a pen.

Odette, in huge, borrowed Wellington boots, was walking on the grass outside the warden's office, bending to run her fingers through the green spears and humming to herself. The sun was at its midwinter highest: she felt its light flood over her as it melted away the last of the morning snow. She could not remember, at all, feeling the warmth of the sun on her body. The bright joy of it made her want to sing. She longed to fling herself bare-skinned into the best patch of sunlight she could find. She drank it in with every pore of her human self.

Inside the office a telephone rang. After a moment the warden came out of the hut, smiling.

'It's for you,' he said.

Acknowledgements

I first drafted the novel that has become *Odette* back in 1992. The number of people I must thank for their assistance over the intervening decades could fill the book all over again, so I'll be brief, and plead forgiveness from anyone I may inadvertently have left out.

First, profound thanks to everyone who encouraged me to keep going with it: those close friends and family members who said to me from time to time, 'What happened to the one about the swan? That was always my favourite.' This book wouldn't be here now without you.

Special thanks to Tom for a valuable suggestion that helped to transform the novel into the shape you now see it, and for putting up so heroically with my Very Special Occasional Panics. Another massive thank you to Sara Menguc, my literary agent, for her encouragement, efforts and patience.

Immeasurable thanks to everyone at Unbound for your confidence in this book and all your devoted hard work, especially Xander Cansell and his fabulous editorial and design team. Last but by no means least, *Odette* would also not be here now without the kind and generous input of everyone who has contributed to the funding scheme. Thank you from the bottom of my heart.

Jessica Duchen, London 2018

www.jessicaduchen.co.uk

Patrons

Unbound is the world's first crowdfunding publisher, established in 2011.

We believe that wonderful things can happen when you clear a path for people who share a passion. That's why we've built a platform that brings together readers and authors to crowdfund books they believe in – and give fresh ideas that don't fit the traditional mould the chance they deserve.

This book is in your hands because readers made it possible. Everyone who pledged their support is listed below (or in the list at the front of this book). Join them by visiting unbound.com and supporting a book today.

Lucinda Bevis Starling

Stephanie Bretherton

Luis Dias

Helen Donlon

Harriet Eisner

Jennie Ensor

Alicja Fiderkiewicz

Yvonne Frindle

Michael Gieleta

Miranda Gold

Harryfiddler

Anthony Hewitt

Simon HJ

Abda Khan

Steven Ledbetter

Chris Limb

Maria Ljungdahl

Fiona Maddocks

Peter Marks

Hugh Mather

Erin McGann

Murray McLachlan
Madeleine Mitchell
Mishka Momen
Carlo Navato
Kris Needs
Ivy Ngeow
Clare Norburn
Camilla Panufnik
Melis Peykoğlu
Nazrin R
Tomoyuki Sawado
Yehuda Shapiro
Barnard Sherman
Tot Taylor
Jenny Tonge
Beverly Usher
Haig Utidjian
Sally Vince
Beverley Vong

By the same author

Fiction:
Ghost Variations
Songs of Triumphant Love
Hungarian Dances
Alicia's Gift
Rites of Spring

Biography:
Gabriel Fauré
Erich Wolfgang Korngold